Cornish Castle Mysteries

Rubies in the Roses

Death Plays a Part

Country Gift Shop Mysteries

Written into the Grave

Grand Prize: Murder!

Dead to Begin With

Lady Alkmene Callender Mysteries

Fatal Masquerade

Deadly Treasures

Diamonds of Death

A Proposal to Die For

Merriweather and Royston Mysteries

Death Comes to Dartmoor

The Butterfly Conspiracy

Murder Will Follow Mysteries

Honeymoon with Death

A Testament to Murder

Last Pen Standing

A Stationery Shop Mystery

VIVIAN CONROY

Poisoned Pen
PRESS

Cover design by Adrienne Krogh/Sourcebooks
Cover illustration by Anne Wertheim

Published by Poisoned Pen Press, an imprint of Sourcebooks
P.O. Box 4410, Naperville, Illinois 60567-4410
(630) 961-3900
sourcebooks.com

Printed and bound in Canada.
MBP 10 9 8 7 6 5 4 3 2 1

Chapter One

Even though the sign of her destination was already in sight, calling out a warm welcome to Tundish, Montana, "the town with a heart of gold," Delta Douglas couldn't resist the temptation to stop her car, reach for the sketchbook in the passenger seat, and draw the orange-and-gold trees covering a mountain flank all the way to where the snow-peaked top began. From this exact point, their autumnal glory was reflected in the water of a clear blue lake that stretched without a ripple. Delta could just see this image reproduced on wrapping paper, notebooks, or postcards.

Until today, all her ideas for her own line of stationery products had lived only in her sketchbook, hidden away in her bag while she worked hard at her regular job as a graphic designer for a large advertising agency. But on Delta's thirtieth birthday, Gran had handed her an envelope. The elderly lady had had a mysterious smile that had made Delta's heart race. Leaning over and pecking her on the cheek, Gran had whispered, "Why wait until I'm dead? You're my only granddaughter, and I'd rather have you spend it now, while I'm still here to see what you do with it."

Inside the envelope had been a check for an amount that to some people might have represented a trip around the world, a boat, or the down payment on an apartment. But for Delta, it had symbolized independence—a way to leave her steady but stressful job with too many tight deadlines and finally do what she had always dreamed of: start her own business.

During summer holidays at Gran's as a little girl, Delta had sat at the kitchen table for hours drawing her own postcards, experimenting with watercolors and crayons, charcoal and felt-tips. Gran had arranged for her to man her own stall at the church fair and sell off her creations. It had been amazing to see her work bring in actual money. Some locals had even placed orders with her for Christmas cards, which she made back home and sent out to Gran to distribute. That sense of accomplishment had always stayed with her, and in her free time, she had continued to draw, cut, and paste with purpose, creating a portfolio of fun ideas that brightened her days. And suddenly, with Gran's gift, her own stationery shop was finally within reach.

It hadn't taken Delta long to take the plunge: she handed in her resignation at the agency in downtown Cheyenne, Wyoming, and crossed off the days until she could clear her desk, clean out her apartment, and drive away from the city she had called home for more than seven years. With every mile of her two-day road trip to the Bitterroot Valley, she had felt more excitement rush through her veins. She was now officially her own woman, ready to take a leap of faith and dive into a brand-new adventure in the small community tucked away at the foot of these glorious mountains.

Delta breathed in the spicy air, which still carried the warmth of summer. The sun was high in the sky, and the wind that had been tugging at her car during the ride had finally died down. She felt almost hot in her thigh-length knit vest, black jeans, and boots. Sneakers would have been better, but they were safely packed up in the trunk with the rest of her limited luggage. Since she had rented a furnished apartment in Cheyenne and donated to a charity shop most of the small stuff she didn't want to lug around, she hadn't had to pack a lot of things for the move. Just clothes, her many sketchbooks, pencils and other drawing materials, and laptop. In Tundish, she'd move in with her best friend from college, Hazel, who ran the stationery shop where Delta was going to be co-owner. Her heart beat faster just thinking about it. Her own shop, and the freedom to design products for it. She couldn't wait to get started. Having put the sketchbook with her brand-new autumnal design back on the passenger seat, she hit the gas and zoomed into town.

Tundish had been developed when settlers migrated to Montana for gold and logging. Most houses were made of wood and built in a sturdy Western style, some with dates carved into the front, placing these builds firmly within the nineteenth century. The word *gold* appeared everywhere: in street names, on signs pointing in the direction of an old mine site or to the gold-mining museum. However, Delta wasn't looking for gold. She was on a hunt for something even more precious: the old sheriff's office that housed the shop of her dreams.

Painted powder blue with black trim, the building sat on Mattock Street like a dependable force. It still had the hitching post in front where riders had tied up their horses before storming in to bring word of a bank or train robbery. The faces of the culprits had soon appeared on wanted posters between the barred windows, and even today, such posters were on display, but they no longer advertised the faces of notorious bandits, instead sporting the latest offering in stationery supplies: collectible erasers, washi tape, notebooks, and planners. A chalkboard on the sidewalk invited everyone to a Glitter Galore workshop on Friday night at the Lodge Hotel with a note at the bottom stating: *All materials included and mocktails to celebrate the results*. Sounded like a ton of fun, and Delta would be there.

Her eagerness to take in everything as she drove past had reduced her speed to about zero, and behind her, a car horn honked impatiently. Waving apologetically at the driver, who probably couldn't even see it, Delta accelerated and passed the neighboring hardware store and grocery shop, spying a parking lot beside the town's whitewashed church. She left her car there, then walked back the short stretch to the stationery shop's invitingly open doors. Over them, a wooden plank carried the name *WANTED* in tall letters burned into the wood, underlining that Western vibe. Delta grinned to herself, anticipating Hazel's expression when she saw Delta amble in. She could have called when she was almost there but had decided a surprise was that much more fun.

When she was a few feet away from the doors, her friend darted out of the entrance with a bright-yellow paper arrow gingerly held between the fingers of her outstretched right hand. Whirling to a stop in front of the wanted poster advertising notebooks, Hazel tilted her head to eye the poster, her blond bob swinging around her ears. She positioned the arrow over the right edge of the paper, moving it up and down as if to determine the perfect spot to stick it on. It read *two for one.*

Delta said, "That probably means I'll buy four. Do co-owners get a discount?"

Hazel swung around and whooped, the arrow still dangling from her finger. "Delta! I hadn't expected you yet."

She rushed to Delta and hugged her, then stepped back and held her by the shoulders, looking her over. "It's been too long. I mean, we did chat and all that, but it's not the same as a real meeting in the flesh. I can't believe you'll be living here now! The guest room at my place isn't all that big, but you can find something for yourself soon enough, once leaf-peeping season is over, and the cottages aren't all rented out to tourists who want to snap pictures of the trees."

"I'm in no rush to find something," Delta assured her. "Rooming together will be just like college." She surveyed Hazel's deep-orange blouse, chocolate-brown pants, and green ankle boots. "Wow, your outfit is fall to the max! Are there boutiques in town with clothes like that?"

"Sure." Hazel pointed across the street. "Right beside Western World, with all those Stetsons and boots on display, we have Bessie's Boutique. I've got a closet full of their pants. They're the perfect fit, and that's so hard to find. Besides, the owner is a friend of mine, so I get first dibs on all the new stock."

"Sounds great. Can I meet this friend?"

"Soon enough. She'll be attending our first workshop together." Hazel gestured at the chalkboard.

"Glitter and mocktails. Sounds posh." Delta nodded at the cocktail glasses drawn beside the workshop title.

Hazel laughed. "On Friday nights, the Lodge Hotel offers live entertainment for the guests and the locals. A big band for dancing, that sort of thing. This Friday night it's their gold miners' annual party, a sophisticated affair that's a throwback to the hotel's heydays when tourism was just beginning to boom. It's really fun, and I thought we should have the workshop tie in to that. Of course, we'll be in our separate space, away from all the high-profile guests dancing the night away, but hey, at least we'll be able to breathe the glam atmosphere."

"Sounds fabulous. I'll snap some pictures for Gran to show her what I'm up to."

"Great. Now..." Hazel clapped her hands together and said, "Guided tour of my shop. *Our* shop, I should say. Come on in." She led the way through the entrance's double doors.

Delta followed with a pounding heart. She had seen photos of the shop, but she had never been to Tundish in person. This would be her first real-life view of her new enterprise.

Hazel gestured around her at all the warm woodwork and the authentic hearth where a pair of dusty cowboy boots stood ready, as if the sheriff would appear any moment to jump into them and set out with his posse. "This used to be where the sheriff sat to wait for news about a bank robbery or a gang of cattle thieves. You can see that I kept his desk and used it to display the newest notebooks."

Delta jumped toward the notebooks, eager to pick through the stacks and take Hazel up on the two-for-one offer. But Hazel laughed and pulled her away. "No, no browsing yet. First, you have to see the rest. There, along the wall, I have shelves for crafting packages. You can find anything, from designing your own planner to making a birthday calendar. Then in that old cell..."

Hazel walked through a barred door that led into a small space with a wooden cot pushed against the wall. Above the cot, replicas of original newspaper pages displayed the faces of the Old West's most notorious gang members, some of them smug, others defiant.

"A few of them spent time in here," Hazel explained, gesturing around her. "And I put up that bit of rope"—she gestured to a rope tied around one of the bars in the narrow window—"to refer to all the escape attempts made. They tied the other end of the rope to a horse and gave it a scare so it would gallop off and tear the bar right from the window. Crude and often not very effective."

"I love it." Delta fingered the rope.

"If you have ideas to give it even more atmosphere, just say so. I'm constantly switching it up to attract people who normally might not walk into a stationery shop but who do want to breathe everything Western. In my experience, once they are sold on the shop's atmosphere, they also buy a little something, if only to show their appreciation for the way in which I preserved it."

"You did a great job," Delta said. "And that's all the washi tape?" She pointed at countless glass jars filled with rolls of tape.

"Yup. I have unique offerings from Japan and Australia that you can't get anywhere else in the country. You should see me salivate when those parcels come in. I was tempted to keep all the ones with the pandas to myself. And in the other cell, I have all the collectible erasers."

Delta followed her into the second cell, which had a rough table against the wall where small glittery objects were lying beside old-fashioned scales and yellowing papers, folded and unfolded so many times that they were torn along the edges. A plasticized card with information warned visitors not to touch the objects because they were authentic and breakable, while also explaining that mining had often been the seed of crime as people sold fake claims or ended up in fights about gold found.

Hazel gestured across the papers. "Real stake claims donated to me by the gold-mining museum. They have a ton of those and didn't mind me having some. They get attention here instead of sitting in an archive."

"I love the fake gold clumps. At least I assume they are fake?"

"Created by a loving volunteer at the mining museum who also puts these into small wooden mining carts they sell as souvenirs." Hazel gestured to the bunk bed against the wall. "There's our offering of collectible erasers."

Delta wanted to sit on her haunches to study the products closer, especially the miniature makeup replicas, including a blusher box that could be opened to reveal two colors and a little brush inside. But Hazel tapped her on the shoulder and gestured to follow her out of the cell, back into the main space where the sunlight through the windows gave the wooden surfaces an extra-warm glow.

Hazel pointed. "Now, there in the back we have the old umbrella stands with all the wrapping paper. Above, an old clothes rack with gift bags."

Bags in several shapes and sizes were hung by their ribbon handles from the rack. They came in bright colors with glitter or in intricate geometric patterns that created visual depth. Delta closed in and spotted a few Christmassy ones among the offerings. Picking out one with a cute design of cocoa mugs and sweet treats, she held it up to Hazel. "Candy canes already?"

Hazel laughed. "Christmas themes sell well all year round. There's just something quintessentially cozy about them. I've already scheduled some early November workshops we can do to teach people how to make menus and name tags to use on the dinner table, or teach pro-wrapping skills where we turn simple presents into gifts *extraordinaire.* I'll show you my idea list later on. I'm sure you have lots you want to add."

Delta nodded eagerly.

"But first to wrap up our tour: here's the old weapon rack where the sheriff could grab his double-barreled shotgun, now used to hold all my wrapping ribbons, stickers, and tags. The puffy stickers are selling especially well with kids."

Hazel smiled widely as she encompassed the whole

shop with a wave of both her outstretched arms. "Now you're free to take a closer look at whatever you want to. And yes, co-owners do get a discount."

Delta made a beeline back to the old sheriff's desk and took the top notebook off a stack. "These dogs are adorable." Her finger traced the rows of small dachshunds, poodles, and Labs that marched across the hard cover. "In the city, I never got around to having a dog, you know. I was away most of the time, and it just seemed sad leaving him or her alone in the apartment all day long. I wonder if I could have a puppy here."

She opened the cover and leafed through the pages. "Wow, every page actually has a different dog. Aw, this border collie puppy is chasing a ball!"

"Remember that it's two for the price of one now! Speaking of, where did I put that arrow?" Hazel checked both hands and then began to look around her. "Maybe I dropped it outside?"

"Then it must be gone. There was a strong wind when I drove over here. Or someone stepped on it and it stuck to their shoe."

Ignoring Delta's predictions, Hazel ambled outside, scanning the pavement for the missing arrow.

Delta was completely engrossed in choosing the four notebooks she planned to purchase. Four initially seemed like a lot for someone who already had more notebooks than she knew what to do with, but in no time, she had selected six and was eyeing two more: one with dancing flamingos and one with letters that formed hidden words. Why not take them all?

Vaguely, she heard a footfall behind her, probably Hazel entering the store.

Suddenly, she felt a slight tug at her hair, and someone said, "Two for one. Yes, please."

Turning around, Delta found herself face-to-face with a grinning man with wild blond curls and brown eyes, a dimple in his cheek. He wore a crisp, white shirt, unbuttoned at the neck, and dark-blue jeans with a silver belt buckle of a running horse. He held up the bright-yellow arrow. "This was stuck to your back, half in your hair."

Delta flushed. "It must have gotten hung up there when Hazel said hello to me. She's looking for that arrow. I'll take it out to her." She reached out her hand, and the man put the arrow in it. His infuriating grin stayed in place. "I haven't seen you here before. New to town?"

"I'm coming to live here. To run Wanted, with Hazel."

"Really? She didn't mention that to me." The man looked puzzled. Delta couldn't figure out why this man would think Hazel should have told him that Delta was moving to Tundish. Could it be her friend was dating him? Hazel hadn't mentioned anything about it, but then again, over the past few weeks, their conversations had been focused on practical details for Delta's move and the financial arrangements for co-ownership of Wanted, so maybe Hazel had figured she could tell her once she was in town.

Hazel's most recent relationship had ended in heartbreak when she found out the guy had been cheating on her. Delta had assumed her friend wouldn't have been eager to dive into something new, especially not one with a man whose athletic physique and cute dimple probably got a lot of female attention.

"Oh, there it is." Hazel buzzed up to Delta and reached out for the arrow with a smile. "I had no idea where it had disappeared to." Ignoring the man completely, she hurried outside again to put it in place.

To make up for her friend's rather brusque behavior, Delta asked quickly, "Is there anything you need from the shop?"

The man picked up a notebook with peacocks, their large purple-and-turquoise feathers adorned with little sparkly gold foil elements in them. It was the first on top of the stack, and he didn't look inside or check the price, just handed it to Delta as if he couldn't wait to get this chore over with. "Can I have this?"

"Of course, but"—Delta knew men often didn't like shopping, but still, he was entitled to a second notebook, under the deal advertised outside—"it's two for the price of one, so you can pick another for free. I can find you one that matches what you already have. Blue and gold..." She wanted to dig into the stacks, to extract those spines that looked like they might offer a color match, but he waved her off. "I only need one. Can you gift wrap it for me?"

"Certainly." Telling herself that the customer was always right, no matter how illogical their decisions might be, Delta took the notebook from his hand and walked to the cash register, feeling a little giddy at making her first sale. This was awesome, even better than she had imagined. She detected several rolls of wrapping paper stacked under the counter. "Blue and gold would be a perfect match." Delta tore off a piece the right size for the notebook. "Now, where's the tape dispenser?" She glanced across the length of the counter, then knelt down to look for it below.

Tilting forward to peer behind a stack of paper bags imprinted with the Wanted logo, she pushed herself up a little. The top of her head made contact with the counter's edge, and she winced.

"Are you OK?" the customer asked, leaning his hands on the counter.

"Yes." Delta rubbed the sore spot. "But a tape dispenser is nowhere in sight. Maybe I can dig out scissors somewhere. And a loose role of tape. Ah, here. No, this roll is empty. Let's see what's in here."

She pulled a plastic basket toward her that was brimming with elastic bands, pens, pencils, and scraps of paper with illegible notes written on them. This space needed to get more organized. She dug through the items in a rush. "Sorry about the delay."

"No problem." The customer rocked back on his heels, a surreptitious glance at his watch belying his casual reply.

Hazel came back in, and he immediately turned to her and lowered his voice in a tone of confidentiality. "I'm not eager to get back to the Lodge. Rosalyn is having a fit over the gold miners' party. The photographer she managed to get after lots of calls to friends in the right places decided to drop her like a brick for a chance to shoot some pop group in Vegas. I told her I could take a decent shot, but she just glared at me like I was suggesting she hire the seven dwarves. But she'll come around. She can't get anybody professional on such short notice."

"Why doesn't she ask Jonas?" Hazel said. "He's a professional, even if he usually has deer in front of his lens and not people."

"Now, there's an idea." The man smiled at Hazel, who kept her aloof expression in place and started to reorganize the gift bags, which were already perfectly aligned.

Delta finally found tape and wrapped the peacock

notebook, putting a gold ribbon around the parcel. "There you go."

He put a ten-dollar bill on the counter. "Never mind the change. See you Friday, then." Picking up the parcel, he walked out with an easy, athletic stride.

"Never mind the change?" Delta hitched an eyebrow at Hazel. "I thought people only tipped waiters."

"Oh, that's Ray Taylor. The Taylor family used to own half of the town. People worked at their Lodge Hotel or delivered goods to it or organized trips for guests staying at it. They're a household name in the region. You just work with them, not against them."

"The Lodge Hotel is where we're doing the workshop Friday night, right?" Delta wasn't sure if she was pleased or annoyed at the idea that she might run into Mr. Taylor again.

Hazel nodded. "Ray never wanted any part of the hotel business and left town to play football. He did very well for a couple of seasons, had a string of high-class girlfriends and was even set to be drafted into the NFL. But he was injured last spring, and there are rumors his career is over. Ray is the last person to say a word about it, but the fact that he's back in town and suddenly snuggling up to his father suggests he's looking for a way back into the family fold. Needless to say, the other Taylors are not pleased."

Delta frowned. "Let me guess. He has an older brother who worked his butt off for the hotel and now sees charming Ray sailing back into town and into his father's good graces."

"*Her* father's good graces. The eldest Taylor is a daughter. Rosalyn runs the hotel like a pro. Made a lot of changes, pulled in new guests. Saved it from mediocrity, really. I mean, there are so many places to stay now. They can't depend on their former monopoly in the region anymore. Mr. Taylor Sr. doesn't seem to see that clearly, but Rosalyn does. She's invested everything in the hotel's survival. It's still a family business; her younger sister, Isabel, is working at the hotel as hostess, welcoming the guests and arranging for all the entertainment. She got Finn a job there."

Delta stared at Hazel. "Your brother Finn?" She had had no idea that Hazel's brother had moved to Montana. Hazel hadn't mentioned him in ages, suggesting they were barely in touch. Last thing Delta knew about him was that he had graduated college with flying colors and started a job with a top-notch insurance agency in Los Angeles. And now all of a sudden he was living in Tundish?

Hazel grimaced, as if the subject were painful to her. "Yes, he came here last summer for the boating and mountaineering. Then he met Isabel, and they fell in love. She got him a job as wildlife guide at the hotel."

"Wildlife guide?" Delta echoed. "I thought Finn was in finance. Insurance and that sort of thing. Or am I confusing him with someone else you told me about?"

"No, he was in insurance, but it just made him unhappy." Hazel made a wide hand gesture. "He was always sporty and loved water, the great outdoors, a sense of freedom. He hated city life with all the concrete and the never-ending hum of the traffic. He's much more at ease here, bunking with another guide who has a cabin in the middle of nowhere. The deer are at his window in the mornings, he says. It would all be perfect, if Isabel would just stop pestering him about getting engaged at Christmas this year."

Delta tried to gauge her friend's feelings on the subject. Did Hazel not like Isabel as a person, or was she uneasy about the idea that her brother would become a part of an influential family whose lifestyle might be miles away from her own? Did she think that Finn, who hadn't liked high-pressure city life, wouldn't cope well with the demands his new family might make on him?

She tried to sound casual as she probed, "And you're not a fan of the match?"

Hazel sighed. "I'm not sure if they're really a fit. They're like day and night, you know, Isabel always in high heels, Finn in a fleece jacket and shoes full of mud. He still has this college student attitude, showing up for work when he wants to and calling off when he has suddenly thought up something else to do."

Delta wondered for a moment if Finn had also had this attitude during his work in LA. His bosses wouldn't have liked it. Had Finn really given up on his insurance job because he didn't like the city, or had he been fired?

Hazel continued, "On the other hand, Finn did think up some clever ideas to entertain the hotel guests, and Isabel incorporated them into their activity calendar. She claims they're a golden duo. That is, they used to be until Ray showed up, disturbing the balance."

Yes, Ray Taylor was someone who could disturb things, Delta readily accepted. He had a self-confidence that was hard to overlook. Maybe his siblings were afraid that, even after many years away, Ray had the power to convince his father he was the best person to run the Lodge Hotel.

"Why were you so rude when he came into the store?" Delta asked.

Hazel shrugged. "There have been rumors I'm after Ray because I'm doing my workshops at the hotel. People whisper that I just want to see him. But I don't have the space needed for the workshops here at Wanted. I guess it's because Finn is with Isabel now, and people are sure I want a part of the Taylor pie as well."

Hazel shook her head impatiently. "I know trouble when I see it. Ray isn't the type to stick around. He'll just stir things up all over town and then run off again, leaving others with the mess. When he does leave, I don't want to be caught in the middle. Same goes for Finn."

Delta studied her friend more closely. Hazel sounded a little too protective, given the fact that her brother was a grown-up who had to make his own choices and even his own mistakes if need be. There had to be more to Finn and his job at the Lodge Hotel that Hazel wasn't telling her right now, but she figured her friend would confide in her later when she was settled in.

Hazel smiled again. "I'm so glad you're here now and we can do things together, starting with the workshop on Friday night. It's fully booked, with twenty participants. Some of them are regulars. They call themselves the Paper Posse."

"Posse?" Delta repeated, not sure she had heard right.

"Yes, that was Mrs. Cassidy's idea. She has a slight outlaw obsession. You know these genealogy sites where you can build your family tree, dating back centuries, to see whether you happen to be related to royalty or to a famous inventor?"

Delta nodded. "I've thought about giving it a try, but it's a lot of work, I heard. Especially if you want to go back farther than just a few generations."

"Right. Mrs. Cassidy has been searching for years now, not for a link to the British Crown, but to find an outlaw in her family tree. To quote her, 'Those who stray outside the law are often more interesting than those who adhere to it.'"

"That's an original opinion. Well, as long as she

doesn't bring any outlaws to our workshops, I guess it can't do any harm."

Delta looked around her and breathed the scent of paper. The sun slanting in through the windows made all the colors come even more alive. Outside, traffic hummed, and a pigeon cooed as he strode by the open shop doors, pecking the pavement in search of food scraps.

Everything was just that little bit more leisurely here, laid-back, at ease. Finally, a break from hectic city life, late-night hours, and deadlines. And all because of Gran. The love of crafting that had been born at her kitchen table all those years ago would now provide Delta's bread and butter. Play with paper and make money off it too.

Delta smiled and vowed to herself that she was about to make her grandmother very proud.

Chapter Two

Hazel cleared her throat. "Ready to leave?"

Delta spun around, feeling kind of caught red-handed, standing in front of the long mirror in Hazel's narrow hallway. She smoothed down the sleek, ankle-length dress she had worn before to office parties. "I'm just worried about the color. Is the red too vibrant? Maybe as workshop host I should blend in with the wallpaper? Like a good butler: there when you need him and otherwise invisible."

"Not at all. They have to get to know you tonight and the outfit is their first clue to your personality. Without frills, energetic, and bright." Hazel winked at her. "Fits you to a tee. What do you think of my pantsuit?" Spreading her arms, Hazel turned in a circle so Delta could admire the black, velvet suit from all sides. She knew her friend hated dresses and hardly ever wore them. "Perfect," she assured her. "That gold blouse underneath adds a festive touch. Just right for a Glitter Galore theme. But what's that green stuff in your hand?"

"Oh..." Hazel glanced at the leaves. "Fresh mint I just cut for the mocktails. I'll put it in this bag with the other ingredients. Sparkling water, juices, fresh raspberries. The Lodge will provide the glasses, shaker, and strainer. And Rosalyn assured me a waiter would take in the ice we need around the time we're done with the crafting and ready to create our own mocktails. You carry this bag, I'll take the box with paper goodies." Hazel grabbed the big cardboard box from the side table at the front door and gestured for Delta to follow her.

Outside, they got into Hazel's Mini Cooper and turned left onto the road that led to the Lodge. Like the rest of the town, it was built on the edge of the lake, but higher up into the foothills, so it offered a gorgeous view of the water and the snow-capped mountains behind it.

Delta drank in the scene, half-twisted backward in her seat, while Hazel steered the car up the drive leading to the hotel's large parking lot. It was so full they had to drive around a couple of times to find an empty space.

"Glad I didn't come in something like that." Hazel nodded at a large, dark-gray SUV parked a few spaces away from them. "It would have been hard to fit into this narrow space. Can you squeeze out?"

Delta opened her door carefully and managed to wring herself through the opening with the bag full of fresh ingredients. The invigorating scent of the mint wafted at her.

A horse neighed in the distance. Delta turned her head around to locate the sound.

Hazel laughed. "Welcome to Tundish. That's not just any horse, but a Taylor horse. The stables are down that road there. They have a couple of horses of their own and stable some for friends. Both Isabel and Rosalyn did show jumping when they were teens, but I suppose they don't have time for extensive training anymore."

Voices resounded from the hotel entrance where people were gathering, exchanging greetings and interested questions about how they had been since last year.

"You said the party was an annual thing, so for how many years has the hotel been organizing it?" Delta asked.

"About a hundred, I guess."

Delta glanced at her friend. "You're kidding me, right?"

"Absolutely not." Hazel grinned at Delta's astonishment.

Balancing the cardboard box with crafting materials in her arms, she fell into step beside her. "Gold miners' parties are a really old tradition in the area. They started in the twenties when tourism around the lake began to develop. People wanted to get out and explore the great outdoors, but they also wanted to enjoy the comfort and luxury they had at home. The hotel offered just that. Entertainment was part of the experience. They hired singers, dancers, pantomimists. And they also had the guests perform little plays and sketches. They've held on to that tradition ever since. The guests' contributions are a major part of the show tonight."

They were at the entrance now, and a tall woman with straight, dark hair, dressed in a purple gown with silver embroidery on the bodice, came over to them. Elbow-length gloves emphasized the twenties vibe of her outfit. "Hazel! Everything is ready for the workshop in the boardroom. I hope you emailed your participants to turn right immediately after entering the hotel? We don't want them mixed up with our party guests." There was a slight hint of disapproval in the woman's voice.

Hazel said quickly, "Of course. Delta, this is Rosalyn Taylor. She manages the hotel."

"Pleased to meet you." Delta shook the woman's hand. She tried to find a resemblance to Ray in Rosalyn's features, but the guarded eyes and polite but chilly smile formed a stark contrast to the golden-boy joviality Ray exuded. Here was a woman who took life seriously. Someone who probably made a lot of demands on herself and others.

Delta said, "The hotel is in a stunning location. The view of the lake is breathtaking."

"Thank you." Rosalyn's gaze fell over Delta's shoulder. "Jonas! You're late."

A tall man with dark hair came over, looking slightly uncomfortable in his tuxedo. He had a professional-looking camera with a long lens around his neck and a dog leash in his right hand. A large German shepherd bounded beside him, sniffing the air and wagging his big, bushy tail.

Rosalyn Taylor frowned down on the dog. "I'd hoped you'd have the sense to leave the dog at home. You're here to work."

"I always bring Spud when I come to work. He'll stay wherever I put him and wait until I'm done." Jonas spoke without raising his voice.

"I can take Spud into our workshop," Hazel offered. "Hey, boy." She seemed to want to free a hand to pat the dog, but the big box in her arms wouldn't let her. "How does the theme Glitter Galore grab you?"

The German shepherd barked enthusiastically, as if he couldn't wait to get started.

Hazel laughed and said to Delta, "He's hardly a puppy, but I'm sure you'll love him anyway. Can you take the leash?"

Rosalyn Taylor turned impatiently to Jonas. "We want to do the family photo at the fireplace before the party starts. I'll tell everyone to assemble." She marched into the hotel on her high heels, Jonas following her after he had pressed the dog lead into Delta's hand. "Introductions will have to wait till later," he called to her as he left.

Spud watched his boss go without pulling to go after him. His tail was low and his eyes alert.

Hazel whispered, "That's Jonas Nord. He's a wildlife photographer working in the area. He also helps Finn with guided tours when it's a busy season, like with the leaf peeping tours now. Apparently, Ray listened to me and told Rosalyn to hire Jonas for the photos tonight."

Hazel sounded as if she was slightly surprised at her own success. With a grin, she added, "I bet Jonas had to borrow that tux. He's not the type to have a closet full of suits."

"It does look good on him."

Hazel looked at Delta curiously. "Oh?"

Recognizing the implications of that *oh* from prior occasions where Hazel had tried to pair her off with friends she considered totally right for Delta, Delta added quickly, "Just a factual observation. I'm here to settle in and work, not…get entangled in anything, you know." At least for the first few weeks she could do without matchmaking attempts.

"Sure." Hazel didn't sound convinced, but as people came up behind them, they moved on inside.

The hotel lobby had its reception desk on the right and a seating arrangement of cozy leather sofas on the left. Decked out with sheepskins, the sofas were grouped around a low, wooden coffee table holding a silver tray with burning candles. A big fireplace, in which a log fire crackled, spread the scent of pine. The marble mantelpiece was full of silver-framed photographs. Rosalyn stood a few feet away from the fireplace, explaining something to Jonas, who nodded repeatedly. A woman who looked like a younger version of Rosalyn came up to them with a tall, broad-shouldered man with blond hair, who had his arm around her waist. An elderly man with stooping shoulders and a sharply etched face followed the couple. They were all in evening wear.

Hazel whispered to Delta, "There you have Isabel, Finn, and Mr. Taylor."

Delta had never met Hazel's brother before, but right now seemed like a bad time to go over for introductions. Rosalyn looked flurried as she directed everyone to a spot for the photograph. Stepping back to take his place, Finn collided with Mr. Taylor and excused himself profusely. Rosalyn gestured at him, her hand up to her throat, making a folding gesture, and Finn, even redder in the face now, reached up to check his collar and bow tie. A smug smile flashed across Rosalyn's features, vanishing as she gave new orders to get everyone where she wanted them.

Jonas was waiting patiently, holding the camera in his palm. His gaze swept the room, and his eyes met Delta's briefly. Delta looked away to avoid the suggestion she was staring at him. She was only interested in the Taylors' family dynamics. Hazel had seemed anxious about the prospect of Finn getting into this family to stay, and she wanted to find out why.

Hazel jabbed her with an elbow. "This way to the boardroom where we're setting up shop tonight." They passed the reception desk, which held several brass, horse-shaped stands with information leaflets, to reach one of several oak-paneled doors leading off the lobby.

Through the first of these doors, Delta and Hazel entered a large room with an oval table in the center surrounded by comfortable velvet pile chairs. A smaller table against the wall held cocktail glasses, a shaker, strainer, and several plastic bowls for leftovers. Delta put the bag with fresh ingredients for the mocktails on the table, leaning it against the wall. On this wall hung a gorgeous oil painting of a running horse, while the wall opposite had a watercolor of the lake with boats bobbing on it.

"There we are." At the head of the oval table, Hazel put the cardboard box down and opened the flaps. "I'll put everything the participants can choose from here. You'd better return to the lobby and make sure the participants don't go the wrong way. Rosalyn seemed a bit tense about them getting mixed up with her guests. You can easily recognize our arrivals as they won't be in evening dress but in their normal clothes. Mrs. Cassidy will also have her dog with her. Nugget is a Yorkie."

Delta nodded and left again, positioning herself close to the entry doors without being in anybody's way. A swinging sax coming from open doors beside the elevators on the far end of the lobby suggested the party would be held there, and Delta would have loved a peek at the way the room was decorated for the big event. But thinking of Rosalyn's insistence that they keep to their own territory, she controlled herself, focusing her attention on the fireplace where the photo session was now in full swing.

Jonas went over to Isabel and touched her elbow, directing her to hold her arm differently. Apparently, it had been just outside the frame. On that arm Isabel wore a rather impressive gold bracelet with precious stones. Delta wondered if it was fake or real. Real probably, considering the Taylors' wealth.

Isabel spoke up, "Shouldn't Ray be in the picture as well? I could go get him. I think I just saw him walk down..."

"No, he doesn't have to be in our pictures," Rosalyn snapped.

Delta held her breath, waiting to see if another member of the Taylor family wanted to object, but the father's face was inscrutable, Isabel kept smiling, and Finn even looked slightly smug, as if he were happy that his future brother-in-law was being excluded from the annual family portrait.

Jonas took a few shots and walked forward to show them to Rosalyn, but Rosalyn muttered something, waving her hand, and rushed off. Jonas stared after her as if he wanted to call her back, then shrugged and hurried to the open doors beside the elevators. The sax was now joined by a strumming double bass, and Delta couldn't help tapping her foot to the rhythm.

A few ladies in their fifties entered the lobby, chatting busily. They were all casually dressed in jeans or corduroy pants, with long woolen sweaters or cardigans on top. One of them, sporting a knee-length woolen coat and big scarf printed with red-and-gold fall leaves, carried a Yorkie on her arm, the dog's fluffy head moving in the direction of the music as if she wanted to explore where it was coming from.

Recalling that Hazel had mentioned something about Mrs. Cassidy's dog, Delta went up to them. "Mrs. Cassidy? You're here for the Glitter Galore workshop, right? That way please."

"I've been before," Mrs. Cassidy assured her and directed the other women to the first oak-paneled door beyond the reception desk. Lingering to unbutton her woolen coat with one hand while holding her furry companion with the other, she said to Delta, "You must be Delta Douglas. Hazel mentioned to me over the phone that you would be here tonight." She reached out her free hand. "Orpa Cassidy. I'm so excited that you're joining Wanted and the Paper Posse."

Delta shook her hand. "Pleased to meet you. I still feel like it's a bit unreal. But this morning I had some business cards printed, proclaiming myself co-owner, and now it is starting to sink in." Delta grinned as the exhilaration of holding her very own glossy business cards washed over her again. She had had just fifty printed at the local printing shop, but it felt like another step into her new life.

She gestured over her shoulder at the boardroom door. "They are in there, with the paper crafting material, so you can take one along if you want to. Then you have my cell phone number and email, should you want to get in touch with me."

"Perfect, I'll do that. Oh, before you go in, you should have a look at the photographs over there." Mrs. Cassidy waved to encompass the right-hand wall, which was lined with framed photographs, some black-and-white, others in color. "They're fascinating. The Lodge Hotel was much smaller in the past, with more trees around it. Unfortunately, they had to make way for a parking lot. You can just see the vehicles change over time from the Ford Model T of the roaring twenties to the Porsches and SUVs of the present-day visitors. The clothes are fascinating as well, showing how people originally went hiking and boating in the same clothes they wore when they went dining, and only over time, outdoor clothing and plastic raincoats came along."

"I love knowing a bit more about the history of places." Delta smiled at Mrs. Cassidy. "Hazel told me you're into genealogy, but it's local history as well?"

Mrs. Cassidy shrugged it off as if it were but a small matter. "I work at the gold-mining museum, so I'm afraid sometimes I get carried away by my love of the past." She leaned over and explained in a confidential tone, "I've studied outlaws as much as I can. Did you know they actually had group portraits made of their gangs? Like they weren't afraid of the law at all. And there were also female gang members. Seamstress by day, bank robber by night."

She lowered her voice to a whisper. "Some of their loot was never recovered. I strongly believe there's gold hidden around Tundish. And someday we'll find it. Won't we, Nugget?" Mrs. Cassidy cuddled the Yorkie in her arms.

Before Delta could respond, Mrs. Cassidy said, "Oh, Hazel is waving at us from the boardroom door. I guess she wants to get started on the workshop." She waved back at Hazel, crying, "Coming!" and rushed over, her red-and-gold scarf flapping behind her.

Delta stared after her, almost forgetting she had to follow suit. Of course, gold had a mythical ring to it, but to believe you could still uncover an old stash... Seemed like with Mrs. Cassidy around, there would never be a dull moment.

When all twenty participants were inside the boardroom, the last one rushing in with red cheeks and hurried apologies about her babysitter being late, Delta closed the door and Hazel welcomed everyone and explained the theme for the night. "Glitter Galore means we're going to make something extravagant to treat ourselves or somebody else. I bet you all know some kind of inspirational quote containing a word like 'shining,' 'diamond,' 'gold,' 'priceless,' etc. We're first going to hand letter that quote onto a piece of cardboard. Hand lettering means that you vary the letters in size and font, completely by your own design. You can make them nice and sleek or big and broad, filling them in with colors or glitter or even small, sticky gemstones. You can then decorate the background, going as extravagant and over the top as you like. Remember, this is really meant to convey luxury and shine."

Hazel pointed to all the material laid out at the head of the table: glitter paper, feathers, glitter paint and spray, sequins, ribbons, and other small bits and bobs to use for decoration. "Feel free to choose anything you want. If you need help with attaching materials or deciding on colors, ask us. We're here to ensure you end up with something you really love. Oh, and to reward ourselves when we're done, I've brought everything to make mocktails." She gestured at the table along the wall with the glasses and shaker. "There's no alcohol involved, so we can all drive home safely."

The ladies gave her a spontaneous round of applause, the one closest to Delta remarking to their neighbor that she had never had mocktails before and couldn't wait to try one.

Spud was walking about the room, sniffing here and there. He halted at a purse someone had deposited in a chair and began to bark.

"No, Spud," Hazel said. "No."

The dog looked at her expectantly.

Hazel shook her head. "No."

She explained to the women who studied the dog with interest, "He's a retired K-9 officer. He was never used to find drugs or cell phones, but money. Is there a lot of cash in your purse?"

All the participants laughed. "Caught red-handed," someone commented to the owner of the purse.

"Is he yours?" a woman asked Hazel.

Hazel shook her head. "His owner is doing photography at the gold miners' party tonight. I'm just babysitting him."

"I think he's babysitting us," the woman said, nodding in Spud's direction.

Disappointed that no search of the purse would be allowed, Spud lay down with his bushy head on his front paws. He never stopped scanning the room with his amber eyes, keeping an eye on everyone present.

Nugget came over to him to make friends, but Spud ignored the energetic fur ball shooting around him.

Delta sat down beside one of the ladies, who wanted to make a sequined mask with feathers on the side for her granddaughter. It didn't really involve an inspirational quote like Hazel had mentioned, but it was very glam, and Delta was sure the girl would love it. "If you leave room here to insert two little holes for an elastic band, she can really wear it."

"What a great idea, thank you."

Delta smiled and picked up her own piece of cardboard to decorate. She knew exactly what phrase to write to celebrate her first workshop as co-owner of Wanted. It could go on her mood board, or maybe she'd send it to Gran.

"*Living the dream*," she wrote on the paper, the word "*living*" flowing in elegant curly letters, with *the* in bold, square print and *dream* in thinner strokes, which she wanted to fill up with glittery gemstones. Several women watched over her shoulder to see how they could apply the techniques to their own creations.

Mrs. Cassidy, who had obviously done hand lettering before, was working on a long quote, using several styles and sizes of letters while still maintaining perfect balance and symmetry on the page.

Soon, everyone was spraying and cutting and gluing to their hearts' delight. To drive the sharp chemical scents of paint and glue out of the room, Delta opened the french doors that led outside. She stood for a few moments, looking at the stunning view toward the lake and the mountains. With the sun down, the sky was showing small specks of stars and a sliver of silvery moon.

The main door opened, and a woman came in, her blond hair piled high on her head, her sparkly, blue-tasseled dress moving above her knees as she walked. She halted abruptly, glancing around with a slightly confused look.

Delta went over at once. "I think you have the wrong

room. You're a guest at the gold miners' party, right? We're doing a paper craft workshop here. Separate events."

"Oh! But I love stationery," the woman said, clasping her hands in front of her. "Can I have a look at what you're making?"

Without waiting for confirmation, the woman walked around the table and looked at what the participants were creating. "Very posh," she cried, spotting the sequined mask with feathers. She picked up a purple feather and blew it away from her hand so it fluttered slowly to the floor. She burst into a fit of laughter.

Delta cringed. The too-loud laughter and the woman's slightly tottering steps on her high heels suggested she had drunk a little too much.

And it was only nine in the evening.

But as the woman was probably a wealthy acquaintance of the Taylors, or maybe even a hotel guest, Delta didn't dare send her away. She just hoped the participants were so wrapped up in their creations that they didn't mind this odd intrusion too much.

The woman stopped at the table against the wall where, beside the cocktail glasses, Hazel had laid out some paper goodies for the women to browse over during the promised after-workshop mocktails. She grabbed a notebook with gold foil on the front and cooed, "How lovely. Can I buy this? I really need this. Yes, and this one…"

She chose a silver one with robins. "I'll put them in a bag myself."

She grabbed a Wanted paper bag and fumbled to slip the notebooks inside. She folded the bag closed and put it aside. "I'll come get them later. And then I'll pay you. OK? OK!"

Delta exchanged a quick look with Hazel.

Hazel shrugged. She said to the woman, "Thank you for your interest. We have a much larger offering at the shop in town. If you're coming that way, please feel free to drop by. Wanted, in the old sheriff's office on Mattock Street. You can't miss it."

"Thank you," the woman slurred, smiling at Hazel. She walked back to the door, again with those slightly faltering steps. She waved a hand in the air by way of a general good-bye and left, banging the door shut.

"How odd," one of the participants said, her red felt-tip hovering over the paper where she was decorating an *L* with tiny roses.

The woman next to her was carefully attaching sequins into a difficult symmetrical pattern. "I wonder if she'll remember anything about this tomorrow morning."

Mrs. Cassidy smiled indulgently. "I suppose she isn't having a very good time. Vera White is visiting from Miami. She's married to one of those two brothers who organize dolphin-spotting trips in the Florida Keys. Ralph and Herb White. You must have seen them around town. They're leaving their business cards *everywhere*. 'Your day isn't right without a trip with White' and 'With White there's always a dolphin in sight,' that sort of tacky thing."

She grimaced, and the other ladies laughed as she continued. "I even found one pinned to the bulletin board in the church hallway. Needless to say, I took it down. Advertising is fine with me, but not in church."

"Why do you think she isn't having a good time?" Hazel asked, breaking open a fresh pack of rhinestones for the participant beside her. "Doesn't she like mountains and the lake? If the Whites are into boat trips, you'd expect they can appreciate all the outdoor activities offered around Tundish."

"Well, it's a case of non-aligned interests, I'd say," Mrs. Cassidy responded. "The brothers are both middle-aged men, a bit addicted to their work, I suppose. Rumor has it they are here to find new business opportunities. They've been here for three weeks already and show no intention of leaving."

Mrs. Cassidy reached for the glue gun, continuing pensively, "On top of this business trip thinly veiled as a vacation, Vera White has to spend it with her sister-in-law, Amanda, who is at least twenty years older than her and the polar opposite personality-wise. While Vera is outgoing and bubbly, Amanda is quiet, someone you barely notice. They were at the museum the other day, you know. I showed them around. I think you can always deduce a lot from the way in which people interact with each other. Or do not interact."

Delta was amazed at the knowledge Mrs. Cassidy had about people who were apparently from out of town, but her Paper Posse friends seemed to think this perfectly normal and eagerly awaited more gossip.

Hazel spoke quickly, refocusing the group. "Yes, well, I'm glad she liked the notebooks. I'm sure she'll be back later to get them like she said. How's everyone doing? Need any advice? Oh, that looks very nice."

Delta assisted someone who needed a ton of small, sticky gemstones for her quote, tearing them off the sheet with tweezers and then carefully pasting them in place. It was a very delicate job, and she found herself at it with a frown and the tip of her tongue between her lips. A headache was forming behind her eyes because of the exertion and the heat in the room. The breeze from the open french doors barely reached her, and she longed to feel its cool touch on her cheeks.

As if Hazel had read her thoughts, she came over to her. "Spud wants a walk, I think. If you take him and Nugget, I'll stay here and finish up with the ladies. Then we can mix some mocktails. I brought raspberries because I know you love them."

"Great idea." Delta smiled at her. "Thanks." She took the dogs' leashes, and Spud immediately jumped up and came with her.

Nugget circled Mrs. Cassidy's legs, as if to ask for permission, and then ran out of the french doors after Delta and Spud. They emerged onto a terrace decorated with pots full of what had been plants in full bloom during the summer. Now, as fall reigned, they were just green stalks, looking rather sad.

But Delta breathed the crisp, fresh air and, detecting a path lit with electric lanterns leading a vantage point, followed it quickly. Spud stayed beside her, taking in his surroundings with his ears up, while Nugget tripped ahead, every inch the little diva who had a bodyguard following her discreetly.

The highest point, a narrow, wooden plateau with a railing, offered a full view of the expanse of water, this time not mirroring the snow-capped mountains, but the bright stars above. The crescent moon's reflection rippled in silver to Delta's right, while to the left, a dark shadow moved across the water.

"Fishermen, probably," Delta said to Spud. "I'm a little jealous of them." There was a breathtaking quality to these tranquil surroundings. It was good to be away from the heat inside the Lodge and just stand here and experience the charm of the view.

The only downside was the cold wind that breathed

through the trees and put goose flesh on her arms and legs. Nugget was also shivering. They shouldn't stay here for long.

Turning around, Delta thought she saw a path leading up on the other side of the plateau, a perfect shortcut back to the Lodge entrance. But a few steps onto the trodden earth, with tall trees towering over her, she began to doubt it was going in the right direction. Then she froze.

Angry voices resounded nearby. Instinctively, Delta stayed where she was. Spud pressed himself against her, not making a sound. Nugget stood between the bigger dog's legs, as if hiding there.

Voice high-pitched and brittle as if she were about to cry, a woman said, "You don't have to make such a spectacle of it."

"It's not my problem you can't move." The second voice was female as well, but not emotional, rather dismissive and callous.

"I'll tell Ralph to quit the dancing lessons." The words rushed out in a breathless hurry.

A scoffing sound before the second voice spoke with determination, "He won't listen to you. He loves dancing. Especially with me."

The silence stretched a moment as if the first woman fought for control, before she spoke again. "He won't love it anymore if I tell him the truth."

"But you won't." There was emotion in the second voice now, a menacing undertone. "Because it would hurt you just as much, and you know that."

A sound rang out, as of a hand striking flesh. High heels clattered, as if the woman on the receiving end had staggered back.

Delta raised a hand to her mouth, covering her lips to

prevent herself from making a sound. She hadn't expected the altercation to turn physically violent. Should she intervene to prevent the situation from getting further out of hand?

Spud lowered his head but stayed perfectly quiet.

In the sudden silence, the whisper sounded even more menacing. "You'll be sorry for this. Very sorry." Footfalls rushed away.

A voice said, "Wait. Wait up now." It sounded pleading, almost desperate. More footfalls resounded, and a rustle of fabric.

Then the quiet hung over the lake again, hovering around them almost like a presence.

Delta moved her head slightly to determine if the women were really gone. She was suddenly even colder and couldn't wait to get back to the boardroom, the crafting Paper Posse, pleasant company. She picked up Nugget and held the shivering dog against her as she pulled Spud along to get back to the hotel.

In her hurry, she took a wrong turn and found herself facing a low, natural stone wall. Uncertain whether she could just clamber over it—she might end up in flower beds and trample something—she decided to follow the wall and came to the front entrance of the hotel.

Seeing the friendly light streaming from the doors, she exhaled in relief and whispered to Nugget, "Almost there. That wasn't fun, right? But it's OK now." As she stepped into the lobby, Delta almost bumped into Rosalyn, whose face was mottled. "Where's Jonas?" she hissed. "The guests want pictures of them dancing."

Her gaze glued to the rash in Rosalyn's face, Delta had difficulty focusing on the question. Had Rosalyn been out just now, and had she been slapped by another woman? But the mention of someone called Ralph had prompted a connection with the Whites in her mind. Mrs. Cassidy had just told them Ralph White was married to Amanda, who was the polar opposite of outgoing Vera. That the sisters-in-law couldn't stand each other. And Vera had also been drinking. That could cause tensions to boil over.

Delta realized Rosalyn was waiting for an answer to her question about Jonas. "I, uh...don't know," she faltered. "I haven't seen him. I just took the dogs out for a few minutes."

Rosalyn nodded curtly and vanished into the restrooms.

Delta leaned down to put Nugget on the floor. The Yorkie had managed to entangle her legs in the leash, and Delta knelt to get the leather strap unwound from her front paws. "Stand still, girl, let me get that. That's right. Good girl."

As the lobby was practically empty, and the party music just at a soft piano intro to a big band hit, Delta could hear the voices of the hotel clerk and Finn, who was standing at the desk. He asked, "Mrs. White just wants to make sure her things are properly stored away. That box contains valuables. Are you sure it's in the safe?"

"Yes, Mr. Taylor put it there himself."

A clatter resounded, and Delta looked up, seeing Finn ducking to the floor to retrieve one of the brass, horse-shaped stands with information he had apparently knocked over. Straightening up with a red face, he asked, "Ray?"

"No, Mr. Taylor Sr.," the clerk corrected. "He and Miss Rosalyn are the only ones who have the combination."

Delta had disentangled the dog leash and rose to her feet. Rosalyn stormed from the restrooms, saw Finn, and sailed down on him. She whispered something in his ear, and Finn looked at her with an appalled expression. "How can you think that? I'd never do that!" He seemed to want to say more, then reconsidered. He rushed off, back into the ballroom, where the full orchestra was playing now, creating that twenties roar.

Rosalyn looked after Finn with a satisfied little smile. Her gaze drifted away to find Delta looking at her. "Is anything wrong?" she snapped.

Delta shook her head. "The ice for the mocktails..." She just mentioned the first thing that came to mind.

Rosalyn glanced at the grandfather clock on the lobby wall. "One of the waiters should bring it any moment now."

"Great. Thank you." Delta retreated to the boardroom, pulling the dogs along. There seemed to be quite a bit of tension in the air for such a happy party night. Still, it was none of her business. She couldn't wait to have Hazel mix her a raspberry mint mocktail so they could toast their joint venture's success.

Chapter Three

"THANKS SO MUCH, AND I'LL BE SURE TO DROP BY THE boutique sometime soon," Delta called after Bessie Rider, the last workshop participant to leave. Bessie had told her about the new pants, scarves, and accessories that would soon be arriving in her shop, and Delta couldn't wait to go there and add to her wardrobe. She also wanted to buy a present for Hazel to celebrate the start of their partnership. The beaded charm bracelets Bessie had described sounded perfect.

With a satisfied smile, Delta turned back into the boardroom, where Hazel had cleaned up the last paper snippets, errant sticky stones, and feathers off the floor and chairs. Putting the empty water bottles in the cardboard box, Hazel blew a lock of hair out of her face. "Done. I know Rosalyn will go over this room with a fine-tooth comb to see if we cleaned up properly. There could be some bigwig meeting here tomorrow, and she doesn't want the room to look like a kindergarten class was here. Her words, not mine."

Delta grimaced. "She doesn't seem to rate our workshops very highly."

"Well, Rosalyn doesn't want the CEOs sitting down and getting rhinestones stuck to their expensive designer suits. She does have a point, of course. We should leave it as we found it." Hazel scanned the room critically. "Looks OK to me. The used glasses, shaker, and restrainer can stay here, as a waiter will pick them up later. Time to find Jonas and ask if he's done with his assignment so he can have Spud back."

Spud looked up at the mention of his name and wagged his tail.

"If not, we could take him home for the night," Hazel said. "He's a cutie."

"What's that?" Delta pointed at the last item left on the now-empty oval table.

"Oh, yes, good of you to notice. It's the two notebooks that our workshop-crashing lady wanted to buy. She hasn't been back, so I think I'll leave them at the hotel desk for her. Mrs. White will have to come to the shop to pay for the notebooks she picked, and who knows, she might see other things she likes."

Delta laughed at her friend's trusting attitude and savvy business approach. "Good idea."

Hazel carried out the box, and Delta turned off the lights and closed the door. The clock in the lobby struck eleven, though it was partially drowned out by blasting trombones, indicating the party was in full swing. Delta threw a longing gaze at the doors, behind which the high-profile guests were dancing the night away, while Hazel gave the paper bag with the notebooks to the clerk at the desk. The clerk promised to give the notebooks to Mrs. White the first chance he got.

Just as Delta and Hazel were about to leave, Finn popped up behind them. Delta hadn't noticed him coming and started when she saw his appearance. His face was ashen and his tie askew. He said to Hazel, "You have to help me." His voice was breathless, pleading.

Hazel asked in a whisper, "What's wrong?"

"In the hotel bar. Someone had an accident. Please go get help. I can't do it." Finn looked around, ducked his shoulders as if he wanted to make himself smaller, almost invisible, and ran off, up the broad, carpeted stairs leading to the second floor.

"Accident?" Hazel echoed. "What does he mean?"

"I have no idea. Maybe we should just have a quick look in the bar to see what's up? If it's really an accident, we should call for help." Delta looked around. "Do you know where the bar is?"

"Yes, through there." Hazel nodded in the direction of a door with a tinted glass mosaic depicting a gold miner's equipment of mattock and sieve. Gold flecks shimmered yellow in the light that fell through the door from inside the bar.

They walked up to the door.

"Hey! Wait a minute." The clerk came over to them. "The hotel bar is closed tonight."

"We don't want a drink," Hazel said. "Uh, I think some-one had an accident in there."

"An accident?" The clerk gave them a dubious look. "I'll go and see. You stay here."

Hazel and Delta waited as he slipped inside, the door falling to a soft close behind his back. "If Finn is pulling my leg," Hazel whispered to Delta, "I'll have his hide for it."

Delta didn't think Finn's looks had suggested he was joking. On the contrary, he had looked positively spooked and ready to run.

Hazel groused, "That man is probably coming back to tell us there's no one there. He'll think it some tasteless joke and tell Rosalyn about it. We can then forget about ever doing a workshop here again."

But seconds later, the door of the bar was flung open so wildly that it hit the wall and the glass pane rattled as if about to shatter.

The clerk rushed out, deathly pale. "She's dead. She's dead. There's blood."

"Who's what?" Hazel asked, glancing at Delta in bewilderment.

Delta's heart skipped a beat. *Dead? Blood?*

The clerk's eye focused on her. "Mrs. Vera White. You just asked about her. Someone hurt her. She's lying there. She bled..." He swallowed hard. "We have to call the police. How did you know she was in there?"

"I didn't know anything." The color had vanished from Hazel's face. She clutched the box with leftover materials from the workshop. "I think I need to sit down."

"This way." With an arm around her shoulder, Delta led her friend to a nearby leather sofa and pushed her onto it. "Take a deep breath."

The shaken clerk hurried off to call the police.

Delta leaned over Hazel. Her mind raced to make sense of the situation. "Finn told you to go look in the bar. He called it an accident, but... If that woman is really dead..."

"He'll be a suspect." Hazel gripped the box as if it were a lifeline. "We can't let the police be suspicious of him. He's just rebuilding his life. Please, Delta, you've got to help me. We can't tell them what Finn told us."

"But we have to." Delta was perplexed that her friend would even suggest such a thing. "The police will want to know how we knew something was wrong in the bar."

"We can lie that we heard a sound, a scuffle...something suspicious. We were here all night, right?"

"But the boardroom is on the other side of the lobby. How could we have heard anything happening in the bar with all the noise coming from the party? That's not logical at all."

Delta's heart beat even faster at the prospect of making up some story for the police, who would see right through it and then suspect her and Hazel of being involved. "We have to tell the truth and let the police sort it out."

"No." Hazel grabbed Delta's hand, squeezing her fingers hard. "They can't start looking at Finn. Just help me, OK? I can't explain now, but it's really important. Please!"

Delta took a deep breath. She didn't want to lie to the police, but she also didn't understand what Hazel meant by saying Finn had just been rebuilding his life.

But before she could ask, Ray Taylor rushed over to them. "What did I hear? Is there a death? Have you seen it? Are you all right?"

Delta glanced at the desk where the clerk was standing with the phone pressed to his ear. Had he notified Ray? How else would Ray know about the death in the bar?

Ray sat down beside Hazel and touched her arm. "Are you OK? Say something."

Delta took the lead. "The clerk came out saying someone is in there. That she's dead. We didn't see the body. We don't know anything about it, really."

With a visible effort, Hazel added, "We heard something in the bar while it was supposed to be closed during the party. So the clerk went in to have a look, and he found the body."

"OK." Ray exhaled as if relieved. "Wait until Rosalyn hears this. A dead body at the gold miners' party! The newspapers will eat it up."

Delta couldn't quite determine if Ray was anxious at the prospect of the hotel being associated with the death of one of its guests. As an ex-football star, he had probably had his fair share of media exposure, which might not always have been a pleasant experience. Perhaps he was already thinking up the headlines, suggesting the hotel was somehow responsible? A lack of security, an intruder getting in?

Or would they assume it hadn't been an outsider? Her throat constricted. Could they keep Finn out of this? The clerk might have seen him speak to her and Hazel before he rushed off.

Desperate to understand how a woman could suddenly have been murdered, she asked Ray, "How well did you know the dead woman? Mrs. Vera White?"

"It's Vera White? She's the one that's dead?" Something flashed across Ray's face, some brief emotion that Delta couldn't quite define. Surprise? Disbelief?

"Yes. How well did you know her?" she pressed.

"Not at all. Apart from her staying here at the hotel, of course. We exchanged a few words about trivial things. What to see around here, what to do." He shrugged. "The kind of tips you give tourists eager for a slice of western life."

"Had the Whites stayed here before?"

"Not that I know, but then I haven't been here in years." Ray got to his feet. "I'd better go tell the others and prepare them for the arrival of the police. You stay with Hazel. She looks like she's in shock."

Delta watched his broad back and athletic stride as he made his way to the room where the double bass was thrumming.

Hazel whispered, "Yes, that's it. I can pretend I'm in shock and can't remember anything. Do you think they will buy that?"

She pinched Delta's arm. "I won't say anything to incriminate Finn. You understand? They can't make me, either. He's my own brother!"

"Do you know the sheriff? Could you explain that Finn asked you for help, but it doesn't mean he has anything to do with what happened?"

As she said it, Delta realized she wasn't even sure Finn had nothing to do with the woman lying dead in the bar. But of course, Hazel wanted to believe that.

Hazel shrugged. "I've hardly ever seen Sheriff West. His deputies are on Mattock Street every now and then handing out parking tickets, but I never thought the law had much to do around here. Game wardens have more of a job, making sure tourists aren't doing dangerous things or disturbing the wildlife."

Delta nodded. She was still clutching the quote she had made during the workshop tonight. She glanced down at it. *Living the dream...*

Right now, it felt more like a nightmare.

Upon arriving at the hotel, Sheriff West turned the boardroom into his headquarters. He was a tall, trim man in his fifties with a commanding air about him. Not in an unpleasant way, he simply took charge and people listened. Rosalyn went up to him first thing, telling him something that he seemed to take seriously as he pulled out a notebook and took it all down.

Hazel went in for questioning first, as she was supposed to be the one who had first noted something was wrong in the bar. The hotel clerk followed her in to give his statement, and shortly after, a deputy came out to ask for Finn. He stood with the Taylors, and only reluctantly left their side, looking back at Isabel as he went along with the deputy.

Shortly after Finn had gone in, Hazel came out of the boardroom and had to wait in the hotel manager's office. A deputy stayed with her.

What's happening? What does it mean?

Delta rubbed her sweaty palms, still seated on the sofa with Spud by her side. The sheriff's arrival had cut short the party, and without the big band music, it was suddenly eerily quiet, as if something menacing hung in the air. Behind the now-closed doors of the ballroom, the guests were waiting for their turn to give their contact information and make a brief statement about anything they might have heard or seen during the night.

Rosalyn Taylor gave whispered instructions to the others, but no one seemed to be listening to her. Their eyes were fixed on the boardroom door as if they wanted to see right through it and find out what was happening inside.

Without warning, the door opened in a jerk, and the sheriff appeared, holding Finn by the arm.

In the gleam of the lights from above, Delta caught the glitter of handcuffs on Finn's wrists. Her throat constricted. Her best friend's brother was being arrested!

With a cry, Isabel ran up to West. "What are you doing? Are you arresting Finn? What for?"

"Don't worry about it, Belle," Finn said in a strangled voice. "It's all a misunderstanding."

Isabel turned to Ray, who had come up behind her. He took her arm as if to pull her away from Finn and lead her back to the family.

Isabel squeaked, "Finn needs a lawyer."

Ray waved her off. "Rosalyn will take care of it."

But Rosalyn stayed in her place, giving Finn an angry, indignant stare.

The sheriff handed Finn over to a deputy, who led him outside to pack him into the police Jeep. West himself went to the hotel manager's office and said something to the people inside. Delta couldn't imagine how Hazel would feel once she heard the news that Finn had been arrested. This had to be the worst-case scenario for her.

Spud whined and leaned his head on Delta's knee. She brushed his fur absentmindedly, keeping her eyes on the half-open door that was blocked by the sheriff's broad back. It seemed to take forever until West stepped away and Hazel appeared on the threshold. She was still clutching the cardboard box with the surplus crafting materials, as if it were her hold on reality. A reality in which no dead body had been found and her brother wasn't involved in something as life-threatening as a murder investigation.

"You're coming as well," West ordered Hazel, gesturing to the deputy who had stayed with her to usher her outside where the police cars were waiting.

Delta's heart skipped a beat. Hazel wasn't in handcuffs, but why did she have to go to the station as well? And why had West kept her in a separate room? So she couldn't talk to anyone?

Learn things that had happened?

Or rehearse her own story?

Had West already concluded that Hazel was somehow covering for Finn?

"Is this really necessary?" Ray asked West with a worried frown. "It's close to midnight, and Hazel looks ready to collapse."

"I'll determine what's necessary," West barked. "I'm leaving a few men here to make sure nothing is touched or changed. All the party guests will be questioned before they can go. No matter how long it takes. Their testimonies could prove to be vital later on. Everyone follows orders, you understand?"

"Sure. Whatever you say." Ray sounded distracted as his worried gaze remained on Hazel, who walked out with her head down, ahead of the sheriff.

Delta wanted to follow and argue with West, but someone caught her arm and stopped her.

Jonas stood by her side. He had taken off the tie that came with his tuxedo and unbuttoned the top of his shirt. "Don't interfere," he said in a low voice. "West isn't in the mood for discussions. This is a huge job with so many people present near the scene when the murder was committed. He'll soon be swimming in statements that might not say much. At a party everybody is having a good time, so people were probably not looking at their watches. Everybody was walking here, there, and everywhere. The music in the ballroom would have drowned out any sounds from outside."

Delta studied him. "You sound like a professional. You have a retired K-9 dog, so...does that mean you're a former handler?"

Jonas shrugged as if it hardly mattered. "I handed in my badge when I left the force. I'm just a wildlife guide now."

"But you know how investigations work, what to expect in the next few hours and beyond." Relief flooded her as a solution unfolded right in front of her. "You can help Hazel and Finn."

Her mind raced. "Hazel told me you work with Finn, on the wildlife excursions. Does that mean you know the hotel guests? Did you meet up with the two dolphin-spotting brothers from Miami and their wives? The Whites?"

Jonas nodded. "I took them birding one time."

There was something in that curt sentence that struck Delta. She watched him with a frown. "And?"

"And nothing, that was it. During birding trips you're supposed to be quiet so as not to disturb the wildlife around you. We didn't talk much."

A high-pitched voice drew their attention to their right. Isabel was arguing with Rosalyn, saying she had to call a lawyer for Finn right away. "The lawyer has to go to the station so he can support Finn during questioning."

Rosalyn shook her head. "Why would I call anyone? Finn is not a member of the family yet. Luckily, I should say."

"You have to help him. He didn't do anything wrong."

"He didn't do anything wrong? When will you open your eyes, Belle? Finn had an affair with the dead woman, I knew that. Earlier tonight, when I was in the restrooms, she was there, restoring her makeup. She tried not to show anything to me, but I'm not a fool. There was a red print on her face, a spot where someone had hit her."

"You think *Finn* hit her?" Isabel asked incredulously.

"Yes, and I even told him I thought he had. He panicked and ran away from me. Clear sign of a guilty conscience. I told the sheriff as soon as he arrived. The affair and Finn's violence toward her prove he's the killer."

Delta's heart skipped a beat. Her mind whirred with images of earlier that night. She had seen the moment when Rosalyn had come from the restrooms and had immediately pounced on Finn. He had responded with indignation, but he had indeed also walked away fast. That had probably convinced Rosalyn she was on the right track. All the more as she *wanted* to be on the right track and think the worst of her sister's boyfriend. What better to do when confronted with the shocking news of a murder at her beloved hotel than point the finger at a convenient suspect whose arrest was very welcome to Rosalyn?

However, Delta was pretty sure it hadn't been Finn who had hit the victim, but another woman. Could her testimony help to clear him of suspicion?

But why was Rosalyn so sure that Finn had been having an affair with the dead woman? What else did she know?

"Finn would never do anything like that," Isabel insisted. Her fidgeting with her hair had ruined her hairdo and created loose strands that hung to her shoulders, giving her the appearance of a lost little girl.

Rosalyn scoffed. "Think again. We all know he has a terrible temper. He must have gone after her again later in the evening, probably after he had too much to drink, and he killed her."

"But..." Isabel's lips trembled. She glanced at Ray, who was standing a few feet away, swiping through screens on his phone.

Rosalyn straightened up, her expression cold and unyielding. "Finn brought all of this on his own head. And on the hotel. What do you think will happen when the newspapers start writing about this? Guests will cancel their bookings."

"The hotel, bookings, money! That's all you ever care about." Isabel burst into tears and ran off, brushing past Ray with a fierce "You're no help either."

Ray looked confused and went after her, calling to her to wait up and be reasonable.

Rosalyn looked after the two of them with a pinched mouth, then seemed to notice she had an audience. She barked at Delta and Jonas, "What are you gawking at?" and marched off into her office, slamming the door shut.

Jonas said to Delta, "She seems to think Finn is guilty."

Delta chewed on her lower lip. "It sounds like she saw a mark on the dead woman's face and assumed Finn had hit her. But I know for a fact that it wasn't Finn."

Jonas gave her a surprised look. "You do? How?"

"I was there when she was hit. That is, I overheard it. She was arguing with and was hit by another woman. I think by her sister-in-law. They were arguing about the sister-in-law's husband, Ralph. Apparently, the victim danced with him and..."

Jonas nodded. "Yes, the two of them did a demonstration dance. A piece of flashy footwork, I have to say."

Delta nodded. "That fits. I overheard the two women arguing about it. The wife wanted the victim to stop taking dancing lessons with her husband, and someone got hit. I heard it clearly, even though I didn't see who hit whom. But with Rosalyn's observations in the restroom, it must have been Vera White who was struck in the face."

"So, you think her sister-in-law killed her?" Jonas asked in a doubtful tone. "Amanda White is a very quiet type, lets others take the initiative. I can't see her lashing out at someone. Especially not her own sister-in-law."

Delta remembered Mrs. Cassidy's description of Amanda White as quiet, "someone you barely notice."

Was it likely that a personality like that would suddenly, in a fit of anger, kill someone?

She pursed her lips. "Well, all I know for sure is that Finn didn't hit her, so if that's the reason for the police to have arrested him, they're going down the wrong track. My statement can clear up things, I hope. Let's go to the station."

Chapter Four

In the Jeep, with Jonas driving, Delta stared through the windshield into the night. The dark surroundings that had earlier struck her as tranquil and beautiful now seemed menacing, closing around her like a tight grip. She couldn't make out where she was headed, and likewise, she had no idea what was suddenly happening to her. All she did understand was that Hazel had been keeping quiet about something having to do with Finn. Something serious.

And although she didn't blame her best friend for a little reluctance about what was probably a painful topic to her, Delta also realized that Finn's past would become an issue now and make everything even harder. And she didn't even know what Finn's past amounted to!

She glanced at Jonas. He leaned back in the driver's seat with a relaxed expression, his hands resting loosely on the wheel. In his tux without a tie and with the top buttons of his shirt undone, he presented the perfect image of a man who has escaped an occasion he wasn't too keen on and is now driving home, satisfied that it's over and done with. If he felt tension, heading for the police station where a murder case was unfolding, there was no trace of it in his demeanor. His presence eased some of the nerves curling in Delta's stomach. Jonas would know how to handle this.

And Jonas might also be able to tell her more about Finn.

"You see a lot of Finn, I suppose, through the work you do together?" she asked.

"I wouldn't call it together," Jonas said. "With leaf-peeping season, there's a lot of interest in the guided tours, the excursions to the birding hut and all. Finn and I divide the work between us. It's not like we work side by side on a daily basis."

To Delta, it sounded like Jonas was intentionally distancing himself from Finn, but she could be mistaken, reading too much in it, under the current strain.

And she didn't want to say anything that might sound accusatory. She needed Jonas's help. "So when you met Finn, for example, to discuss what tours each of you was going to do, did you notice anything strange? I mean, tension or him not feeling at ease with the work he had to do at the hotel?" During the photo session, Delta had observed how Rosalyn was critical of Finn, making him feel inadequate. Even unwanted?

And Hazel had said Isabel and Finn had been like day and night, so maybe Finn had been talked into working at the hotel, not really wanting to do that himself?

Jonas shrugged. "I think Finn loves being out of doors, just hiding in the forest. He doesn't like the planning part as much. That's where he and Rosalyn clashed, as he would book a group and then forget about it, or double book. Paperwork doesn't seem to be his strong suit."

That was odd, as Hazel had told her Finn worked in insurance. Didn't employees have to be very precise there?

She almost shook her head in irritation. She didn't know anything about Finn's previous job or why he had transferred to the Lodge. She didn't have facts, so she shouldn't speculate. She had to keep an open mind and learn more about all the people involved. "Do you know why Rosalyn suggested Finn was having an affair with the victim? She said she knew about that, as if it were common knowledge."

Jonas pursed his lips. "Who knows. Maybe Rosalyn saw them together some time and drew a wrong conclusion? She seems ready to assume the worst about Finn. After all, she said he might have killed the victim because he has a terrible temper and might have been drinking. Like I said, I didn't work with Finn on a daily basis, but I did meet up with him regularly, also for nighttime excursions, and I never found him to be either aggressive or intoxicated."

Delta felt a rush of relief. "Rosalyn might just not like him, think he's not right for her sister, and therefore accuse him of being involved in the murder?"

"Could be. Rosalyn usually thinks she knows what is best for everybody, so that could very well include her sister's relationships." Jonas glanced at her. "But back to this statement you want to make to the sheriff. You said you didn't see the women arguing? I mean, you heard a smack and you caught snippets of their conversation?"

"Exactly. But by deduction, it seems pretty clear the other woman was the victim's sister-in-law."

"Deduction won't be enough for West."

"Then what will? If *you* were leading this investigation, how could I convince you to look into the argument?"

Jonas frowned. That he took his time to answer the question unsettled Delta a bit. She had expected him to have a ready-made idea, some instinctive hunch about what had really happened in the bar.

Jonas said slowly, "You probably wouldn't need to convince me to let Finn go, as I wouldn't have arrested him. Not so quickly after the murder, anyway. People will assume he has something to do with it, and even if West lets him go again, those rumors will linger and make Finn's life here in Tundish very hard."

Delta's heart sank. She clenched her hands together in her lap. "Then why did the sheriff do it?"

"I have no idea. He might have believed Finn was lying. He might have heard a witness statement that put him on Finn's trail. Or he might have secured evidence at the scene of the crime. An object that belongs to Finn, maybe."

"Left beside the dead body?" Delta grimaced. "That sounds like a poor clue. Anybody could have left it there."

Jonas nodded. "He'd have to base his accusation on something stronger, like fingerprints on the murder weapon. But I assume that he can't have established anything like that in so short a time. When the crime has just happened, you bag all you can find on the scene and take it along for analysis. And I doubt West can even have done much bagging before he made his arrest. His men must still be busy on the scene, securing all traces."

They took a sharp turn to the right, and Delta saw light streaming from the windows of a square building. As they closed in, she could make out more details. Like most houses around Tundish, it was made mostly of wood, but the lower four feet were brick, the mortar between the stones standing out because it was lighter in color. A plaque inserted in the wall carried a gold star in the middle. It seemed luminous, lighting up as the glow from the headlights brushed over it.

Jonas parked the Jeep and slipped off his seatbelt. "You be careful what you tell West. He doesn't tolerate changes in your story later. He might think you're involved as well, covering for your friend."

"Hazel didn't even tell me..." Delta fell silent and bit her lip.

Jonas surveyed her with a frown. "You feel obliged to help her of course. But this isn't a small matter. It's an official investigation, and every move you make can have repercussions later on."

"You think I would lie for her?" Delta pulled back her shoulders.

Jonas shrugged. "I'm just giving you some friendly advice. Now let's go in. I want to talk to West myself and offer him the photographs I took tonight. There might be something relevant to see in those shots."

Delta hadn't even thought of that possibility yet. "Great thinking. Thanks." She waited a moment, struggling with herself, then added, "Also for your advice. You mean well. But I don't have to lie. I can tell the absolute truth. I know the victim fought with another woman shortly before she died. It can solve everything."

Jonas exhaled slowly. "I hope you're right. But West won't just drop Finn because you hand him another suspect. What reason could the sister-in-law have had for killing Vera White?"

"The argument provides that reason. Amanda was angry that Vera was dancing with her husband. She might have assumed the two were getting a little too close for her liking. In any case, she knew some secret about Vera, because she said she might tell Ralph 'the truth.' I don't know what she alluded to, but Vera said that in that case it would hurt Amanda just as well. Then, provoked and frustrated, Amanda hit Vera, something out of character for a normally quiet person. So we can safely conclude that these two women were tied up in some kind of potentially explosive secret. Now if you believe someone might tell on you, and you don't want that truth to get out, that's a motive for murder."

"Undoubtedly, but you don't know what 'the truth' is, what the secret could be, and if it is so big that it would be worth killing for. That's a bit thin. West might even believe you made up this entire argument to divert suspicion from Finn."

"No, no, no." Delta shook her head emphatically. "West knows for a fact that the victim had been struck in the face. Rosalyn told him so. She saw the victim in the restroom restoring her makeup."

"So Vera White was struck. That doesn't prove by whom. Rosalyn has been on top of things, making her statement while West was barely on the premises. She directed his judgment of the situation, and I can tell you from experience, it can be hard to keep an open mind once a theory is unfolding and looking so promising."

"Spud heard the argument too." Delta reached into the back of the car to pat the dog. "Too bad you can't testify, boy."

The German shepherd pressed his head against her hand, then suddenly leaned forward and licked her face.

Jonas hitched a brow. "He isn't very keen on new people, normally. Friendly, yes, but familiar, no. He must sense you're upset."

"I'm not upset," Delta said, reaching to open the car door. "Just worried for Hazel's sake." She looked at the police station. "This is not where we planned to end up after our first workshop together."

Despite the late hour, there was plenty of activity inside the station. A phone rang, a printer spat out a stack of papers, and a deputy behind a counter marked *Reception* was explaining something to two men. Both were dressed in evening wear, and as one of the men raised his arm to gesture, Delta detected an expensive watch on his wrist. But the impression of sophistication was shattered by the crude tone he took with the deputy. "If you just let me near him, I'll get him to confess. It's really easy. Just put a baseball bat on his Adam's apple and push."

The other man took his arm and said, "Really, Herb..."

But Herb didn't seem to hear him. His face crimson, he hissed, "The more time you give him to rehearse his story, the more likely he will come up with some cock-and-bull story about what happened where he goes scot-free. I want him prosecuted! I want him on the electric chair!"

The deputy stepped back. "Sir, you have been drinking."

"Yes, I was at a party. My wife died at a party! An innocent party, and she gets killed. And you people are doing nothing."

"I wouldn't call an impromptu arrest of the first suspect available nothing," Delta whispered sarcastically to Jonas.

She was sorry for it the moment it was out, because the foaming man spun around and pointed a finger straight at her. "What's that? Are you the no-good bastard's sister? I heard she was at the party too." Herb bent his finger as if squeezing the trigger of a gun.

Delta shrank back under the violence in his expression.

"I think this gentleman could use a cup of strong coffee to sober up," Jonas said to the deputy.

Herb turned his bloodshot eyes on Jonas. "I'm not drunk. Who are you anyway? The sister's fiancé? I knew it. In a small town like this, the entire family is coming over to bribe the sheriff into letting the killer go free. But I won't have it. I'm right here to prevent it. If he walks out, I'm waiting for him."

Spud stared up at Herb and growled.

Herb didn't seem to hear. He kept his eyes on Delta.

The other man put an arm around him. Judging by the similarities in their features—deep-set eyes under bushy brows, long nose, and broad chin with a dent in the center—they were related, so this had to be Ralph, Amanda's husband and Vera's dance partner.

Delta looked around for a woman in evening dress to complete the party. She was curious to see with her own eyes what kind of woman Amanda White was and how she carried herself now that her sister-in-law was dead. But there was no one around except officers going about their business.

Ralph ushered his brother away from the desk. "Come, Herb. A cup of coffee would be a good idea. Let's just sit over there, okay?"

Herb seemed to want to struggle, then suddenly he became pale. He hung his head and walked with Ralph to a group of chairs. He sat down and hid his face in his hands. His shoulders started shaking.

Jonas kept his eyes on him a moment, then turned to Delta, shaking his head. "Alcohol and a lot of emotions rarely mix well. Good thing he's not alone here."

The deputy, visibly relieved that someone had managed to deescalate the situation, came from behind the counter with a mug of coffee, which he handed to Herb's companion. Ralph tapped Herb on the shoulder and pushed the coffee mug into his hands, then came over to Jonas and Delta. "I want to apologize for what just happened." He extended his hand. "Ralph White."

Jonas shook his hand. "Jonas Nord. We met before when I took your group birding."

Ralph stared at him. "Of course." His gaze traveled the full length of Jonas's appearance. "You don't say. You look very different in a tux."

Jonas had to laugh. "Just the party's dress code, not my personal choice."

"I see." With a frown, Ralph continued, "I saw you taking snapshots at the party. But I didn't look twice at you, just thought you were hired for the occasion. I had no idea that you were the birder who took us out earlier."

"I was hired when the photographer who was coming in had to cancel at the last moment," Jonas hurried to explain. "I usually take pictures of deer and birds, but if necessary, I can also do people. Since I captured the entire night, I'm here to turn all of my material over to the police. Maybe it can help with the murder. My sincere condolences on the death of your sister-in-law."

"That's very kind of you. Thank you. I don't think anyone has offered condolences yet. I can understand they are busy with a lot of things but… It feels so distant and cold. They're treating Vera like a…thing." He reached up and rubbed his forehead, then looked at Delta. "Sorry, you are?"

"Delta Douglas. I run a stationery shop in town. I wasn't at the party really, just at the hotel. We conducted a paper crafting workshop in a separate room, off the lobby. The…"

She felt like it was wrong using the word "victim" to this man who had been related to her, so she continued quickly, "Mrs. Vera White happened to come into our workshop. I think she mistook the room, but she was very kind, showing an interest in what we were doing. She also wanted to buy two notebooks."

A smile lifted the weariness off Ralph White's face. "Vera loves notebooks. She has a ton of them, but she keeps buying more. Everywhere we go, she…"

The smile vanished, and he looked down abruptly. "I shouldn't talk about her like…she can still walk through the door and…" He stared at the entrance as if he expected his sister-in-law to appear and assure him it had all been a misunderstanding and she hadn't been murdered at all. "I can't believe she's really dead," he muttered.

"We're very sorry." Jonas glanced at Delta as if he wanted to know her opinion about something. Then he said, "Did you notice anything odd tonight?"

Ralph looked up. His vacant eyes focused. "Odd?"

"Anything that in hindsight might be related to what happened. Tension between someone at the party and your sister-in-law. Her being dejected. Afraid, even?"

Ralph shook his head. "On the contrary, she was very cheerful and laughing the entire time."

Delta wondered if Ralph hadn't noticed the tension between Vera and Amanda. Didn't he know Amanda resented him dancing with Vera? Or didn't he care? Hadn't he taken it seriously? She could hardly ask.

Ralph continued, staring ahead, "She had been looking forward to this party. To the demonstration dance. She's the better dancer of the both of us, you know. She puts such zeal into it. I can never quite keep up with her."

"I wouldn't say that," Jonas responded. "I saw you dancing, and you were both quite good."

Ralph made a weary gesture. "We had talked about doing more of it. Maybe participating in competitions and all. She was so excited about the idea."

"And how did her husband feel about that?" Jonas asked.

Ralph seemed surprised by the question. "Herb's fine with it. He's not much of a dancer himself, so he was glad I went to the dance course with Vera. So she'd stop bugging him about it, you know."

He glanced at his brother for a moment. Herb sat with the coffee mug in his hands, rigid like a statue.

Ralph said, "Vera could be persuasive when she wanted something."

He didn't speak loudly, but because the printer had just stopped churning out paper and the deputy wasn't typing or answering the phone, the quiet in the room seemed to amplify his words.

Herb broke to life, raising his head and looking at the three of them. His eyes went wide, and he rose to his feet. "Don't you slander her," he yelled. "She was a good woman. Nothing but a good woman."

"I'm not saying—" Ralph protested, but Herb didn't give him a chance to finish his sentence. Coffee sloshed over the rim of the mug as he waved his hand in Ralph's direction. "I see what you're all trying to do. Make her look like a bad person, who deserved to be killed. But she was a darling. She didn't do no one no harm. She didn't have to die."

His voice broke into a sob. "She didn't have to die."

The mug fell from his hand, shattering on the floor at his feet, coffee splashing over the pants of his tuxedo.

The deputy jumped to his feet at the crash of china, his hand flying to the holster on his hip.

Ralph rushed to his brother, reaching for him, but Herb pushed him away. "I need air," he muttered. "Air." Across the broken china, the pieces crunching under the soles of his feet, he walked to the door and out of the station.

Ralph stared after him. "I didn't mean to..." He looked at Jonas and Delta. "I just wanted..." His voice faltered, and he rubbed his forehead again. "Vera wanted to have a good time tonight. Just that. It was unfortunate, of course, that *he* was there. I guess that also unsettled Herb. You must forgive him for it. He's not normally like that."

"What unsettled him?" Delta asked, not quite following.

"The presence of that ex-football player. The one who had an affair with Vera last summer."

Delta's heart skipped a beat.

Jonas asked, "Do you mean Ray Taylor?" His tone was tense.

"Yes. Had we known he was related to the people owning the hotel, we would not have come there. But Taylor is a common name, and the place had been recommended to us. Herb got quite a shock when he recognized him shortly after our arrival."

"And how did Mrs. White take it?" Jonas asked, glancing at Delta as though checking to see if she realized how important this might turn out to be.

He need not have signaled her, as she was already straining her ears to catch every word Ralph might say, even the nuance in the tone. Ray Taylor having known Vera White, even having had an affair with her. And when she had asked him if he knew the victim, he had denied it flatly.

He had lied.

Ralph seemed taken aback by this question. "How did Vera take it?" he repeated as if he didn't understand what Jonas was saying. "Uh, how would she be taking it?"

Jonas narrowed his eyes. "Your sister-in-law has had an affair. I infer from your words about your brother Herb recognizing the man in question that he knew about this affair. Then they visit a hotel for an innocent vacation, and the very man she'd had the affair with is there, part of the family that owns the hotel. Painful to say the least."

He waited a moment before adding, "Potentially dangerous, wouldn't you agree?"

Ralph blinked hard. "I don't understand."

Jonas said in a low voice, "There would be tension between the former lovers, right? Someone might notice and start whispering about it."

"But Vera had nothing to do with him, really. She was with us. Most of the time."

The latter words were added in a doubtful tone, like he was suddenly not too sure anymore. He wrung his hands, glancing at the outer door. He lowered his voice. "Do you think that…that man killed her?"

"You have been here for several weeks now, I understood," Delta said. "Did you see anything pass between them that made you feel there was something going on? Did you see them together, for instance? Talking, looking like they didn't want to be seen together?"

She recalled Ray buying the peacock notebook at Wanted. He had obviously not been interested in stationery himself. He had bought it as a present. For Vera? After all, Ralph had just mentioned she was collecting notebooks wherever she went.

Delta pressed, "How about tonight at the party? What was the atmosphere then?"

Ralph shuffled his feet. "I'm not sure. I can't say I've really seen them together. They didn't even dance together tonight. Maybe he was avoiding her? Vera had given him money in the past, and he never paid her back."

"Money?" Delta echoed.

"Yes. I guess if things had been different, she would never have told me, but she was in a tight spot and had to ask me to chip in. I told her not to go shopping so often, half-tongue in cheek, half-serious, you know, and then she said it was all Ray Taylor's fault. He had asked her for money for some business investment he wanted to make. It had gone wrong, and she would never get her money back. She felt rather silly for having believed him, so she begged me to keep it a secret from Herb. I did."

At that moment a door burst open, and Sheriff West came in. He spotted Jonas, and at once his expression changed from half-satisfied to disbelieving, then annoyed.

He marched up to them but slipped in the spilled coffee on the floor and had to flail his arms to remain upright. "What's this mess?" he barked to the deputy. "Clean it up right this minute."

To Jonas, he said, "If I had wanted to talk to you, Nord, I would have asked for you to come in." He checked his watch ostentatiously. "Shouldn't you be in bed by now?"

Before Jonas could reply, West focused on Delta. "And you?"

"I'm a friend of Hazel. I own half of her shop now. The stationery shop on Mattock Street, Wanted."

The sheriff frowned. "I never liked a decent sheriff's office being turned into some frivolous little shop where you can buy pink pens. It's part of our town's heritage. It should have been preserved with dignity."

"But Hazel preserved the sheriff's desk and the cells. She's showcasing town history there, with replicas of newspaper pages and information about fake gold-mining claims—"

Before Delta could explain further, West cut her off. "Your friend is staying here for the time being, with her dear little brother."

Jonas said, "Excuse me, Sheriff, but where you might have a reason to hold Finn, I doubt you have anything to justify holding Hazel. Just let her go home."

West glared at him. "I didn't ask for your opinion, Nord."

Jonas exhaled in a huff. "It's not my opinion that matters, Sheriff, but the rules. You do have to stick to those, just like any other officer of the law. You need a reason to hold someone overnight."

"The little lady lied," West said between gritted teeth. "She didn't hear anything in the bar. The clerk told me that her brother told her something before he ran upstairs, and then she came over to the clerk to send him into the bar so he would stumble on the dead body."

"The clerk came over to us," Delta corrected.

West ignored her and continued speaking to Jonas. "It's clear that she knew something was wrong in that bar but didn't want to discover the dead body herself. She's covering for her brother. I intend to let her realize just what a big mistake that was. Nothing like a night in the cell to come to one's senses."

"And then what do you expect?" Jonas asked. "A full confession? Hazel should have told you everything she knew, but under pressure, people make mistakes of judgment. I think she realizes that now. She doesn't know anything about the murder."

"And neither does Finn?" West held his gaze, jutting his chin up as a challenge. "Is that what you were going to say next?"

Jonas didn't respond.

West grunted. "At least you have the decency to admit you don't know."

He leaned over to Jonas and added in a low voice, "You don't know anything about that, Nord. You've worked with him, so maybe you can tell me he comes in on time and he knows his swans from his geese. Or whatever you look at on the lake."

Delta bristled at the disparaging tone.

West continued with a smug smile. "You can't vouch for him. And if I were you, I wouldn't even bother. You might just hurt your reputation."

"I'm here," Jonas said in a neutral tone, "to offer you the photos I took at the gold miners' party tonight. You might be able to find something revealing in those shots."

West shook his head slowly, as if he felt sorry for Jonas. "I don't want anything from you. I already have a revealing shot, Nord, telling me everything I need to know. Want to see it? Why not? Then you'll realize the trouble the young man is really in."

He elbowed a deputy out of the way to reach a desk cluttered with paperwork, and dropped into the swivel chair behind it, his fingers working the keyboard with energy.

Jonas and Delta came to stand in front of the desk, waiting for the big reveal. Blood pounded in Delta's ears. How could a single photo have told the sheriff all he needed to know?

West clicked through a few screens in quick succession, and then turned the monitor toward them. The entire screen was filled with a photo of guests in evening wear talking animatedly.

It took Delta a few moments to understand the relevance of the shot. She didn't know any of…

Oh, wait.

She detected a couple in the back of the photo. In the left-hand corner, behind the lively group, she could just see two faces of people talking, a blond woman looking up at a man who was taller than she was. Her expression was exasperated, as if she was telling him off about something, and his face was…

Delta looked for the right emotion to describe what she saw in those features and then decided *pleading* might best fit the bill.

Or "desperate"?

West pointed at the woman. "The late Vera White." Then he rammed his finger at the screen, almost pricking into it with his fingernail. "And that is my main suspect. Your good friend's dear brother."

Delta couldn't deny it was Finn, and he looked none too happy with whatever was being said between him and Vera White.

The sheriff grunted in satisfaction. "He knew her, better than he would know a random guest at the hotel after showing them around. He had a one-on-one with her, and by the look of him, he wanted something. Something she wasn't about to agree to. And when it didn't work out the way he wanted or had hoped for, he killed her. Those things happen."

With a brisk movement West turned the monitor away from them. "We secured the murder weapon so we can analyze it for fingerprints. But even without those, you must admit I have a pretty strong case against my suspect."

Delta wondered if the sheriff was suffering from the dreaded tunnel vision Jonas had already warned her about. Once led in a certain direction, it could seem all other clues supported that first assumption, while there might be an entirely different explanation for them that wasn't even considered.

"I'm not too sure," Jonas said. "All you have is a photograph of two people talking to each other."

"And Rosalyn Taylor's testimony that Finn hit Mrs. White."

"Um..." Jonas seemed to waver between a disbelieving

smile and getting angry. "Rosalyn stated she had seen Mrs. White in the restroom at the hotel, putting makeup on what looked like a mark on her face. Miss Taylor hardly saw who dealt it. She only assumed it had been Finn."

"Yes, because she knew the two of them had been having an affair. She told me right away as I arrived." West patted the notebook that lay on the desk.

Delta pounced. "And did you ask her how she knew that? Has she actually seen them kissing?"

The sheriff snorted. "She had warned her sister before that Finn was no good for her. She made sure I took notice of that when she made her statement to me."

"So Rosalyn doesn't like Finn," Jonas said with a grimace. "First of all, that's not exactly news. Second, I don't see how that proves he was having an affair with Mrs. White. To prove that, you'd need the testimony of someone who has actually seen them being more than friendly with each other. Besides, we just talked to Ralph White, the victim's brother-in-law, and he told us that Mrs. Vera White had had an affair with Ray Taylor. Admittedly, it was in the past, but they might have rekindled their romance once she came here. Or she wanted to rekindle it and he didn't. That would make a pretty good reason for an argument."

West narrowed his eyes. "The victim's brother-in-law told you that? Just like that? Bit of chitchat as you run into each other at the police station?"

Before Jonas could reply, the sheriff stepped closer and said in a growl, "I'm warning you, Nord. Don't interfere with my investigation. Just stick to training your dogs."

He turned away from them, casting a critical look at the section of floor where the deputy had cleaned away the coffee spill. "I can still smell coffee. Wipe it again."

Delta called, "Excuse me, Sheriff, but I'm here to make a statement. I was witness to a fight between Mrs. White and another woman. The blow that left the mark on her face was a product of this fight."

West turned to her slowly, his expression incredulous. "You do realize that making a statement is official business, right? You have to sign it and stand by it. Perjury is..."

"I'm fully aware of that. I know what I heard."

"Heard? Not saw?" West looked even more critical. "I don't think your statement will be very helpful."

"I still want you to take it." Delta walked up to him. "Shall we sit down? Maybe somewhere more private?"

With a begrudging look, the sheriff went ahead of her into an empty office. "Don't you need your notebook?" Delta asked.

Without responding, West shut the door behind her and gestured to a chair in front of a desk. He seated himself behind it and leaned his hands on the edge of the desk. "Well?"

Delta told him how, during the workshop, she had taken the dogs out for a short walk and overheard the argument at the water's edge. She repeated what both women had said as verbatim as she could.

West listened with his gaze fixed on the ceiling. Then he said, "That was all? You have no idea what truth the other woman wanted to reveal about the victim or how it might hurt herself if she did? You must admit it sounds a bit fanciful."

"It's the truth, Sheriff. I can't help what I heard. I just want you to have all the information that might have a bearing on this case."

"Yes, well, I thank you for it." West rose to his feet and stretched his shoulders as if he were shaking off something unwanted. "Tell Nord I meant it about not interfering in my case. He's not on active duty anymore, and I don't share. With anyone."

He opened the door for her and walked her back to the main room. Jonas was sitting down, waiting for Delta. Two chairs away sat Ralph White with his brother beside him, white-faced and still. His fingers nervously twisted the wedding ring on his finger.

Jonas rose as Delta came over. "And?" he asked softly.

She shook her head.

They left side by side, Spud slinking beside Jonas. Outside, Delta said, "He didn't even bother to write it down."

"Told you he would think it's too vague."

"And his case against Finn is clear-cut? He never replied to my question of how Rosalyn knew Finn was having an affair with Vera White."

"I don't like the way he works, but I can't really blame him for feeling a bit of pressure. The Taylors have a lot of clout in this town, and West is up for reelection in a few months. Besides, no tourist town in the busiest season of the year wants to have the media writing there's a murderer on the loose, targeting female visitors. A quick arrest can quiet things down and limit the impact of the murder." Jonas tilted his head back and looked up at the skies. "Lots of stars out tonight."

Delta tried to wrap her mind around what he had just said. "So Herb White wasn't all wrong when he shouted that he was worried about family bribing the sheriff. I mean, West won't accept money or anything, but maybe he is leaning toward the Taylors' angle a little too eagerly. After all, Ralph White told us that Ray had had an affair with Vera and owed her money. Why isn't West following up on that right away?"

Jonas focused on her with his ice-blue eyes. "I'm

surprised to hear you say that. I thought there's not a woman in the world who thinks anything bad of golden boy Ray Taylor."

"Except for his sister, Rosalyn. She doesn't seem to like him at all and deliberately cut him out of the family photos."

"So you noticed." Jonas held her gaze, as if wanting to ask why she had been so interested in that photo session.

Delta felt her flush deepen. "Their family dynamics are fascinating. I can't help studying people. It's a habit, like you going out to see how animals behave. It wasn't just that Rosalyn didn't want him in the picture. The others didn't bother at all to argue with her about it. They all seemed to accept it right away. Just because they didn't want to contradict Rosalyn or because they actually agree with her that Ray has no place in Tundish?"

Behind their backs, the door of the police station crashed open, and heavy footfalls beat down the steps. West popped up beside them. "I'll take that camera anyway, Nord. Your memory card at least. The shots made tonight. I don't want you to be able to delete anything on it that could further incriminate Finn." He reached out a fleshy hand.

Jonas gestured at his Jeep. "It's in the back."

While he retrieved the camera and slipped out the memory card, the sheriff paced up and down. He didn't take a moment to breathe the fresh air or roll back his shoulders. He seemed full of pent-up energy that crackled in his curt steps. As Jonas handed him the memory card, he said with a huff, "Nothing private on it? Things you don't want me to see?"

Jonas retorted, "Just get me the card back as soon as possible."

West closed his fingers over it. "There's a lot to take care of. But I'll see what I can do."

Without wishing them good night, he turned on his heel and went back inside.

Jonas sighed. "I'll be lucky if I ever get it back. But I have more memory cards at home."

Delta looked him over. "Did you look through the shots? Do you know if anything worthwhile is on it?"

Jonas shook his head. "I was worried that if one of the deputies saw me with the camera, they'd conclude I was deleting something." He lifted a shoulder and let it fall again. "Sorry."

"Doesn't matter." Delta yawned. "I appreciate you driving me out here, but do you think we can head back? It's time for bed now. I'm exhausted."

But as she got into Jonas's Jeep, she wondered if she could really sleep knowing Hazel was in jail.

Chapter Five

The next morning, Delta woke up feeling like her head had been caught in a vise. She couldn't believe their first workshop had ended at the police station with an angry sheriff sending her off and placing Hazel behind bars. From glitter to murder, within hours.

She tried to recall whether she had seen anyone come from the direction of the bar the moment Hazel and she had left the boardroom, but she couldn't remember. She hadn't really been paying attention.

Where had Finn come from when he stopped them to mention the "accident" in the bar?

She narrowed her eyes to think better but it only served to tighten her muscles. Her forehead, cheeks, and neck all felt tense and uncomfortable.

Massaging her temples, Delta dragged herself to the bathroom. A look in the mirror made her groan out loud. She turned away hurriedly from the pale face with the baggy eyes staring back at her and stepped into the shower.

Twenty minutes later, dressed in her favorite jeans and sweater, and with some makeup concealing the worst signs of her late night, Delta put bread in the toaster and clicked on the coffee machine. The scent of toasting bread and ground coffee mingled on the air, giving her a bit of an energy boost. Just as she considered whether she'd boil an egg for some much-needed protein or just settle for jelly on her toast, her phone rang. She picked it up from the table and checked the screen to see who was calling.

Gran.

Delta's breathing caught. Dear Gran, who had given her a hefty sum of money to make her dreams come true. What would she think if she found out there was now a murder in the mix?

Deep breath.

OK.

Do it!

Delta answered the phone, her hand trembling with a desperate determination to sound like nothing was wrong. "Gran! How nice of you to call."

"Of course, darling. I know your first workshop was last night. At a hotel, right? Did you have a good time?"

"Wonderful. Good attendance and so much fun. I think you'd like Mrs. Cassidy. She thought up Paper Posse as the name for the group of crafters. All because she loves outlaws. She's even looking for one in her family tree. And her dog is called Nugget."

"Is it a pug?"

"No, it's not a pug. A Yorkie."

"Aren't those white? No, I think I'm confusing them with Maltese. Or bichons frises. All those breeds..."

"Yorkies have long hair, Gran, and they're kind of dark with brown patches on the face. I can draw you one quickly." Delta grabbed a piece of paper and a pen and drew a Yorkshire terrier. "You have to imagine the colors, I don't have my pencils at hand." She snapped a shot of the drawing with her phone and sent it. The silly little exercise made her feel lighter.

"Wonderful, darling, you're so talented. I'm so glad you're now able to do something with it. What time does the shop open today?"

"At ten." Delta checked her watch. "I'm just getting ready to leave. I overslept a bit after getting in so late last night."

"I'm sure you'll make it in time. You're so punctual and precise. A little perfectionist."

Delta remembered how she had observed on the day of her arrival that the counter was a bit disorganized and how she had found a set place for a tape dispenser and the scissors. In the back room where Hazel had her coffee machine and other things for breaks, Delta had immediately reorganized the drawer with cutlery and thrown out a package with one crinkled napkin no one was going to use anymore. It had been just like their college days: Hazel being happy-go-lucky, piling up junk mail until the stacks collapsed, while Delta was washing every used dish and couldn't stand candy wrappers cluttering her desk. The mess she was now in with the murder was much bigger however, and of a different order all together. How could she sort that out?

Gran's energetic voice cut through her worried thoughts. "I'll call back later then. Love you, darling."

"Love you too, Gran. I'll send you some pics of the shop as soon as I'm there. Love you. Bye." Delta kissed into the phone and then disconnected.

She felt relieved and at the same time guilty that she hadn't been honest about the murder case. But she just didn't want Gran to worry. She had sounded so happy about Delta's new life, her chance to pursue her creative passions, at last, because of the money she had given her. Delta wanted Gran to keep feeling that way.

Delta washed down her toast with a cup of coffee, grabbed an apple from the fruit bowl, and rushed out of the door just as her phone rang again. She checked the screen while opening her car door. She didn't know the number. She accepted warily. "Hello?"

"Is this Delta Douglas?"

"Yes."

"Mrs. Cassidy here. Look, I'm no good at beating about the bush, being subtle and all. Here goes. It could just be the oddest rumor, but...is Hazel in jail?"

"I'm afraid so." Delta took a deep breath to explain, but Mrs. Cassidy said, "So there really was a murder at the Lodge last night. The editor of the *Tundish Trader* had to hear it over breakfast at Mine Forever. Let me tell you: he wasn't pleased. But I guess the papers had been printed anyway. Now he's out for the full story, waiting in front of the shop."

"In front of Wanted?" Delta asked, nerves filling her stomach.

"Exactly. That's why I wanted to give you a ring. I can see him from here, pacing up and down the sidewalk, checking his watch every ten seconds. I'm quite sure he's waiting for someone to come open up the shop so he can grill them about Hazel."

"If you can see all that, where are you then?"

"Still at Mine Forever. I took a table at the window as soon as he stormed off, to ensure I could see exactly what he was up to."

Delta now recalled that Mine Forever was the name of the diner that sat across the street from Wanted.

"I'm on my way over." Delta planted her phone in the holder and started the engine. "Can you tell me how much he knows? Did *he* tell you that Hazel is being held at the police station?"

"No, Bessie did. She had it from Jane, who heard it at the

bakery when the police dispatcher came to get some bread rolls for lunch."

Delta blinked, trying to follow along. Bessie was the boutique owner she had met last night at the workshop, and there had also been a Jane there, but she had only talked to her briefly and didn't recall her last name or what she did around Tundish.

Mrs. Cassidy was already continuing. "LeDuc, our editor in chief, doesn't know a thing other than that there was a death in the hotel bar. He overheard breakfasters at Mine Forever gossiping about it, wondering whether it was an accident or foul play. That's why LeDuc is so upset. You see, there has always been one local paper in Tundish, the *Tundish Trader*. Started around 1887. Still has the same name, the same kinds of news, the small advertisements you can browse. Someone offering their surplus of potatoes or looking for good homes for puppies. It's nostalgic. A few months ago, the son of our editor, Marc LeDuc, came back to town with a degree in modern media. He was supposed to take over the *Trader* at some point in the future, but once he unfolded his plans for the paper, his father told him to drop his 'no-good modern plans' or leave, and he left. He started his own paper, which is fully digital. And ever since that day, the two of them have been competing, for scoops, for readers, for anything they can think of. Senior is at your door now, but I bet you Junior is not far behind. He has a whole network of news-hunting citizens who call in the latest at any hour of the day. I bet several of them phoned him."

Delta groaned as she turned a corner. "So this murder is already adding more fuel to the rivalry, since they both want to have the latest on it, right?"

"Definitely." Mrs. Cassidy sighed. "I have to be honest

with you, Delta. I don't know which one of them is worst. Senior is a real newspaperman who digs into a story and just doesn't let go. But Junior has access to online channels, and you know what happens when something goes…what do they call it?"

"Viral," Delta said. It sounded like the knell of death to her own ears.

In the past, bad news could only hurt you as far as local gossip could spread. But these days, stories could travel far and wide, and damaged reputations might never recover.

"I've thought about this," Mrs. Cassidy said. "And if you don't mind, I will add your phone number to our Paper Posse message group. Then we can all share what we hear about the murder in the group. As most of us work at public places, like shops, restaurants, the post office, and the museum, we tend to overhear quite a lot. You'll be in the know as soon as we discover something. We can warn you."

"That would be great. I can see Mattock Street now."

"He'll be all over you as soon as he realizes you're going into the shop. But just let him ask questions. Be careful what you say, because he will quote you."

Mrs. Cassidy seemed to cover the phone a moment and say something, her voice muffled. Then she came back on full force. "I'm finishing up breakfast, and I'll come save you."

"Thanks. I think I'm going to need it." Delta parked the car and pulled her hands away from the steering wheel. It was damp with sweat. She glanced in the rearview mirror to see how she looked.

Like a deer caught in headlights.

She took a deep breath and opened the car door, fetched her bag off the back seat, and locked the car behind her. Then she walked down Mattock Street, her eyes trained on the sidewalk in front of Wanted.

A tall man paced back and forth. His white hair was cut military short, but when he turned around to face her, she saw he did have a long, pointy beard. He wore an old-fashioned jacket with leather elbow patches and carried a notebook in his hand. As soon as he saw her, he stopped and stared.

She had already dug out her key and slipped it into the lock. Still, she had to turn it, and he was on her in a flash. "Good morning. Sven LeDuc, editor in chief of the *Tundish Trader,* a reliable news source since 1887." He pulled a card out of his pocket and handed it to her. It had a logo of two entwined *T*s inside the silhouette of a printing press, and gave his name, title, and phone numbers. No email, Delta noticed.

LeDuc asked eagerly, "Are you tending the shop while Hazel Bray is in jail?"

"I'm part owner." Delta cast him an icy look. "And Hazel is not in jail."

She stepped into the shop and wanted to turn around to close the door in his face, but he followed her in, snapping eagerly, "Not in jail? But there was a murder at the hotel last night, wasn't there?"

"I think you better talk to the police."

"Hah! As if they're going to give me anything. They're always worried that information provided will somehow interfere with their investigation. But I'm a firm advocate of keeping the citizens informed. They have a right to know what's happening in their town. Particularly when there are dead bodies appearing." He opened his notebook and scribbled something. "Part owner. So you're actually Hazel's new business partner. I heard rumors to that point. Her not being able to keep floating, having to take out an extra mortgage. And now this. You must be upset that she got herself into trouble with the law, no less."

Delta fought a rush of anger at his intrusive suggestions. Hazel had wanted her to join the store to have the freedom to create her own products, something that had been impossible in her demanding job in Cheyenne. Hazel hadn't been looking for easy money or anything. Delta wasn't quite sure what LeDuc meant about an extra mortgage. Hazel had given her figures about the store to assess its financial condition, and a mortgage had been part of those, but Hazel hadn't mentioned she had recently taken it out. Had the income from the shop been too meager to support her? Then how would the two of them live off it?

Delta shook her head in annoyance that she let LeDuc's remark drive her into worries, while she didn't even know if he was telling the truth about the mortgage having been taken out recently. Maybe he was only saying something to get her to respond, confirm, or deny it. She said to the inquisitive editor, "Hazel did nothing wrong."

"She isn't locked up?"

"She's at the police station, but only because she's cooperating in the murder case. Have you never heard of witnesses?"

His eyes went wide, and he held up his notebook to jot down more notes. "Did she see the killer? Can she identify him? Are they worried the killer will come for her next?"

Delta walked to the counter to put her bag in place before she became too tempted to slap the insistent reporter with it. She had answered one question to get him out of her hair and restore Hazel's reputation, but now he was bombarding her with a dozen new possibilities she had no intention of confirming or denying. If he started writing about Hazel having possibly seen the killer, while the killer was still on the loose, her friend could get in serious danger.

The doorbell jangled, and someone came in.

Delta breathed a sigh of relief, hoping it was Mrs. Cassidy to the rescue. With her brisk attitude, she'd see the editor out of the shop without resorting to rudeness.

But the newcomer was a man Delta's own age, with brown curls brushing the collar of his shirt. He wore stone-washed jeans and sneakers that didn't make a sound on the floor as he moved. Spotting Delta and LeDuc standing across from each other, the newcomer attempted to slink into the cell where the washi tape was kept, but the editor of the *Tundish Trader* saw him and cried, "Not you. Go away! This is *my* story."

The man came over with an eager look, holding his phone in his hand. Focusing on Delta, he said, "Marc LeDuc, NAID. *News As It Develops*." He flicked out a flashy, full-color card with the slogan *You Heard It Here First* and a long list of social media channels to follow for the latest scoops. "What exactly happened last night at the Lodge? Give me your pure, unadorned eyewitness account."

Delta realized that the phone he was sticking out to her would record everything she said. She shook her head and pointed at the phone to indicate he had to turn off the recording feature.

Senior cried, "Was the victim's throat cut?" He started to take new notes, his pen scratching across the notepad.

Junior prompted, "What time did the murder happen? How many people were at the hotel at the time?"

Delta shook her head and put both of her hands in the air in an apologetic gesture.

"Just ten?" Senior asked with a frown. "In the room where it happened, you mean? There must have been more than ten people at the Lodge's gold miners' party. It's the regional event of the season."

"Did you see the body?" Junior asked. "Is it true that your friend is in jail because she's involved? Is the real killer still out there? Should we fear a string of murders in this quiet town?"

Delta, exasperated, repeated her gesture to indicate she was not willing to answer any questions.

"At least ten murders?" Senior gasped. "Why? Is this a conspiracy? Were the victims chosen at random or with purpose?"

The door opened again, and Mrs. Cassidy walked in with Nugget on a leash. She carried a large basket full of pumpkins and butternut squashes. "Good morning," she enthused. "What a wonderful day. Ah, Mr. LeDuc. And Mr. LeDuc. What a coincidence."

She flashed a smile at the puzzled older editor and his eager, phone-toting son. "I'm surprised to see you here. I was so certain you would be at… But don't let me interfere with any of your…"

"What?" the son jumped at Mrs. Cassidy. "Is there a development? A press conference maybe at the police station?"

Mrs. Cassidy shrugged coyly. "I wouldn't want to suggest…" Without waiting for her to finish, Junior raced for the door and pulled it open so wildly the doorbell almost flew off.

His father stared after him like he didn't understand where he was going, then suddenly broke to life with an "Aha!" and followed him at a trot.

The sudden silence was like a glass of cool lemonade on a hot day.

Delta closed her eyes a moment and soaked it up gratefully.

"Just like a dog on a scent," Mrs. Cassidy said cheerfully. "Point them in a direction and off they go, baying and yapping. I did say I didn't want to suggest anything, but I guess they didn't hear." She grinned, then sobered and patted Delta's arm. "They will be back, of course. But then you'll be prepared for them."

"I doubt one can ever be prepared for that." Delta blew a lock of hair from her face. "They are each terrible in their own way, and combined..."

"Double the trouble, I know." Mrs. Cassidy nodded firmly. "We have to figure out this whole thing for ourselves. Imagine poor Hazel behind bars..."

She clicked her tongue. "The girl is good with a glue gun, but that's about all she knows about anything remotely related to crime. I guess it was an unfortunate instance of being in the wrong place at the wrong time. Look here, I have some pumpkins and squashes you can use to create a fall display. How about that table?" She pointed at a table along the wall, holding scrapbooking materials.

"Great idea." Delta picked a large orange pumpkin from the basket and went to the table, placing the pumpkin in the center and leaning some glittery paper against it. She put a row of rubber stamps in a circle around it, the stamp surface up so customers could see what the design was. Mrs. Cassidy came to stand beside her, putting some smaller pumpkins in place. "I hollowed out this one and let it dry and put a glass in it so you can put pens or pencils in."

"Oh, great, let me try." Delta collected a handful of

pens and put them in the glass. They stuck out over the edge of the pumpkin, making it look like a beautiful natural holder. "I bet people will start asking if these pumpkins are also for sale."

Mrs. Cassidy beamed.

Delta studied her from aside. She knew, especially after having faced the father-son media monster, that she could never clear Hazel on her own. She'd have to trust people, and Mrs. Cassidy seemed like the kind of person she could rely on. Someone who didn't jump to conclusions and who could also actively contribute to an investigation with clever suggestions and inside information about the people involved.

In fact, she had already been able to say a thing or two about the Whites.

Delta tilted her head. "You told us last night at the workshop that the White brothers and their wives came to the museum, and you gave them a tour there. You said you can conclude things from the way people deal with each other. Or avoid to deal?"

"Yes. The brothers were jovial, laughing and making jokes among each other and to me. Seemed like the kind of men who are quite satisfied with themselves." Mrs. Cassidy put a butternut squash in place and arranged some smaller green and white squashes around it. "The wives, however, were rather cold. Especially among themselves. I felt like they didn't get along at all and just had to endure each other's company because of their husbands."

"There's the age difference, of course," Delta mused. She draped some silk and velvet ribbons around the butternut squash's neck. "Maybe they had nothing in common? Come to think of it, last night at the station I met both Herb and Ralph White, who seemed to think they had to put in a personal appearance to ensure that the police were on top of things, but Amanda wasn't with them. I wonder if her absence says anything about her relationship with the victim. Maybe not, as she might have been so shocked after the murder that she felt unwell and stayed at the hotel."

Mrs. Cassidy hemmed and moved her head from one side to the other, as if contemplating that suggestion. "I see lots of people at the museum: families, friends, colleagues. Some want to be together, others are forced into going. It creates interesting dynamics. People who really don't like each other tend to avoid each other's company. They talk to others in the group or just ignore the other person. But these two women... They were constantly looking at each other as if assessing the other's behavior."

"Rivalry? Each trying to be prettiest, funniest?" Delta tried.

"I felt like it was more of...wariness between them. Like they didn't fully trust each other."

"Hmm. That might be because the one wasn't happy that the other was getting too close with her husband." Delta took a few steps back to study their pumpkin display. "Maybe move that big one on the left a bit more to the center? That's right. Perfect."

Mrs. Cassidy picked up the empty basket, walked to the window, and peered out. "Wild Bunch is going into the grocery shore. She's a genius at starting innocent conversations. I asked her to find out anything she could about the Whites' behavior while they were in town. They've been staying here for weeks now, so maybe someone saw an argument or overheard some significant conversation."

"Wild Bunch?" Delta asked.

"Bessie Rider. Of Bessie's Boutique. Bought this from

her." Mrs. Cassidy fingered the long necklace she wore with a gem-studded key as pendant. "Bessie's nickname is Wild Bunch, after a famous gang of outlaws. Within the Paper Posse, we all have Wild West names. It was my idea, to be honest, but now that we're in this murder investigation, it's quite convenient. We can send our messages to the group under our aliases." Mrs. Cassidy leaned down to pat Nugget. "Quite exciting." She straightened up sharply and said in a remorseful tone, "Not that I think it's exciting that Hazel is in such trouble. We'll do anything to help her, of course. You can rely on that."

Delta sighed. "It seems to all revolve around Finn. What do you know about him?"

Mrs. Cassidy took her time before answering. Delta wondered if it was just a long story or whether she was carefully choosing what to say and what to keep to herself.

Mrs. Cassidy put her hands on her back and paced the shop, Nugget darting around her. "When Finn came to town, he didn't have a job. He dropped by the museum and asked if I had things to do for him there. Repairs or other small jobs. I told him we had volunteers for that, and he seemed to be quite relieved actually. I had the impression Hazel had put him up to it, wanted for him to find something useful to do. I wondered why a young man who looked able enough to take care of himself would have his sister watching over him. Hazel never struck me as overprotective or intrusive. I concluded there was a reason she was eager to set him up here. In a place where...well, people look out for each other. Away from the distraction and, might I say, *dangers* of the big city?"

"What did you think?"

"I wasn't sure. I did notice that wherever I saw him pay

for something, whether it was a cup of coffee or repairs on his car, he paid in cash. Never with a credit card. I wondered if maybe he had been in financial troubles, racking up debt as impulsive young people sometimes do. Finn is…"

Mrs. Cassidy thought long and hard about her word choice. "He's someone who likes to be liked. If you know what I mean."

"You think that to be liked he might have spent more money than he could afford?"

"Possibly. But I don't know anything for sure. I'm just telling you what I noticed."

Delta nodded. As Mrs. Cassidy seemed perceptive and had a lot of insight into people, her observations might prove to be invaluable later on. "And have you ever seen him with the woman who died? With Vera White?"

"No. But he must have known her from the hotel. He was there often enough, not just for work, but also to see Isabel."

"Hazel doesn't seem to think they are a good match. And Rosalyn Taylor outright wants to separate them."

"Yes." Mrs. Cassidy nodded slowly. "I've told myself that there couldn't be some stain attached to Finn that might be traceable. Because I'm sure that if there was, Rosalyn would have found it already, to end the relationship."

Delta felt a rush of relief. "So, Finn can't have a criminal record, right?"

"I don't think so. To ensure the safety of the guests and their possessions, Rosalyn has background checks done on everyone applying at the hotel, even if it's a cook or a gardener, so I can't imagine her having taken on Finn without ensuring he didn't have a criminal record."

Delta was relieved, and at the same time, she wondered

what such a background check might *not* have turned up. Maybe a former policeman like Jonas could dig deeper? It wasn't nice to consider enlisting Jonas to look into her best friend's brother, but now that Hazel was caught up in a crime she knew nothing about, Delta wanted to do anything to save her.

Delta's phone dinged. She picked it up and looked at the screen. She had been added to the Paper Posse group, and a new message popped up from Wild Bunch.

Mrs. Cassidy was also looking at her phone, so Delta supposed she had gotten the message as well.

"The grocer says Vera White was in town the other day. She collected an envelope at the post office. She seemed very happy about whatever was in it. She crossed the street in such a rush that she almost got hit by a truck delivering apples. The driver grumbled to the grocer about people not paying any heed when they cross the streets these days. I wonder what was in that envelope?" Countless head-scratching emojis followed the latter remark.

Delta looked up at Mrs. Cassidy. "Could the contents of that envelope have to do with the secret Vera was keeping?"

Mrs. Cassidy pursed her lips. "Where is the envelope now? Do the police have it?"

"I have no idea if they searched her room at the hotel. Wait. That reminds me. Last night Finn asked about a box with valuables belonging to Vera White. The clerk told him it was being stored in the hotel safe. Mr. Taylor Sr. had placed it there himself. Finn seemed tense at the idea that it might have been Ray who handled it. But the clerk said only Mr. Taylor Sr. and Rosalyn had the combination of the safe. Why would Finn be interested in Mrs. White's box of valuables?"

She wet her lips. "Of course, if we assume that he had financial trouble in the past, which is why Hazel asked him to come live here..."

Mrs. Cassidy held her gaze and added, "And if we accept that, despite Hazel's precautions, he might have such trouble again, then we might also wonder if he...took a little something a rich woman might not immediately miss to pay his most urgent debts, fully intending to return it later on."

"Finn, a thief? I don't want to believe that. It would put him in a hopeless position." Delta kneaded her hands, wincing as her nails cut into her palms. If the sheriff found out Finn had indeed appropriated something belonging to a hotel guest who was now dead, he would never let him go.

Mrs. Cassidy said, "I never said it was true, just that it's an option we should keep open. An unpleasant option, I admit, not just because it implicates Finn in theft, but also because Mrs. White's discovery of the theft and her threat to report it to the police might make a very good motive for murder."

Delta's stomach felt like it was filled with ice. The photo taken during the party. Mrs. White's expression, Finn's pleading looks. The despair in his posture.

Had she accused him of theft? Had he denied it, then reconsidered and thrown himself on her mercy?

If Vera White had coldly refused to listen to Finn, to help him save his reputation, his job at the hotel, his relationship with Isabel, would that not have made him angry enough to lash out at her and kill her?

"I need to go to the Lodge," Delta said. Her voice was hoarse, and she had to clear her throat to be able to speak normally. "I need to talk to Ray and others there. I need to know more than I do now. Last night at the police station, Ralph White claimed Ray had an affair with Vera, before they came to stay here. That during that period, he also borrowed money from her and never repaid it. Isn't it possible that when they met again, at the Lodge, she asked for her money? In any case, I feel like Ray knows more about Vera than he let on. He acted to me like he barely knew her."

Mrs. Cassidy looked her over. "If he was really involved with this woman earlier, why would he tell you anything about her or about their relationship? We have no idea how it ended, who ended it, if there was tension when they met again here in Tundish. If Ray is involved in her death, he's not going to help you to clear Finn. In fact, he might do anything to ensure the suspicions against Finn stay alive and well."

Chapter Six

After Mrs. Cassidy had assured Delta she could mind the shop until she returned, Delta drove out to the Lodge. The parking lot looked very different from the night before. Most of the cars were gone, and just a few vehicles stood here and there, probably from staff who came in to work or from guests who were holed up in their rooms, not needing their car.

Delta thought back on the fishermen she had seen on the lake and wished she could bob about in a boat like that, enjoying the magnificent landscape. But she had to tackle the murder case first. If only she had some confidence that she could handle it.

As she got out of her car, the invigorating scent of pine filled her nostrils, and she inhaled a few times, steadying her nerves. She took her time crossing the parking lot, picking up a small, colorful stone and feeling the fresh air on her face. She reminded herself of the many times she had tackled something new: the first day at college, her start at the agency, going to a meeting with important clients, or traveling abroad, all on her own. The first night on a business trip to Stockholm, she remembered feeling particularly lost. But the next day she had discovered some cute little shops where they sold handmade products and spent some time sketching the colorful house fronts and talking to the passersby, who halted to admire her work.

It had all worked out fine.

This was just another something new. She would help

Hazel and Finn, she just needed a little confidence in her own common sense and the help of her newfound allies. Dropping the pebble back in the gravel, she walked up to the entrance with her head held high.

Stepping into the lobby, she spied Ray Taylor at once, standing near the elevators with Isabel, who wore cream riding pants and gleaming black boots, suggesting she had already been out with one of the Taylor horses. Ray was casually dressed in a buttoned-down blue shirt and light gray pants. He had sunglasses in one hand and a full water bottle in the other, as if he were about to go out.

They were too far away from the desk to be overheard, and besides, the clerk was on the phone, using one hand to push the phone against his ear while he used the other to type up something. A reservation probably. It was a different man than the one from last night, so Delta needn't be afraid he would recognize her as having been with Hazel when the dead body had been found in the bar.

So far so good.

Delta kept her eyes on Ray and Isabel, who stood close together, both with serious expressions on their faces. Isabel's eyes were wide and her skin pale as she listened to Ray, whose hand on the water bottle tensed and relaxed, tensed and relaxed as he spoke, as if he were squeezing a stress ball.

Curious what they were talking about, Delta sneaked up to them, moving slowly so she didn't attract attention. She heard Ray say, "Don't worry about it. I'm sure the police won't ask about it."

Delta's heart skipped a beat. Ask about what? Something Isabel knew? Something about Finn? Had he shared things about his past with Isabel? Was Isabel now worried she might incriminate him further if she told the police what she knew?

Last night she had seemed to be on Finn's side. Could Delta use that?

"Excuse me, where are you going?" The clerk had put down the phone and was eyeing her. Delta flushed.

Ray had spotted her and came over with a forced smile, waving his sunglasses. Isabel quickly backed away, going up the stairs, but halting a few steps up to look back at Delta and Ray with a worried frown.

"Welcome, welcome," Ray said, his gaze roaming her expression as if wanting to see something there, a clue perhaps that she had overheard some of their conversation? Past Delta, he said to the clerk, "It's all right, Norman. Just a friend from town."

The clerk nodded and returned to his duties.

Ray said, "So what are you doing here? Any news from Hazel?"

Delta noticed he didn't ask about Finn.

"I'm afraid she's still at the station."

Ray lowered his head. "Sorry to hear that. She must be upset." He squeezed the water bottle again. The plastic creaked under the pressure.

"Do you know anything that might help her?" Delta pushed. Full frontal attack was something an ex-football player like Ray would understand.

But Ray shook his head. "If I did, I'd have come to the station last night."

Delta studied his expression. "Really?"

It wasn't hard to put an edge of disbelief in her voice. After all, if Ralph White was to be believed, Ray had known something very important and hadn't come to the station with it.

Ray lifted his head to look at her. His dark eyes scanned

her expression, as if trying to gauge what she was thinking. "Yes, really."

Delta made a clicking sound with her tongue. She let her gaze wander to the clerk and back, to suggest she wasn't sure whether she could speak in front of hotel staff.

Ray seemed to get the message at once as he took her arm. "Come with me. I want to show you the garden." He glanced at the stairs where Isabel was still hovering and nodded at her. Delta felt almost like it was a signal, saying, "I'll take care of it." She was sorry for a moment she hadn't pounced on Isabel to see if she could get anything from her. Ray, who had led a high-profile life, seemed too experienced to give something away.

At the back of the hotel, he led her down a gravel path. The sun was shining brightly, and Ray slipped on his sunglasses. "These grounds used to be quite wild. But when Rosalyn took over as manager, she decided it had to be a cultivated garden. She hired some kind of landscape architect, who had a look and then charged us an insane fee for a few changes. An extra path, some plants, and a sun dial." He scoffed. "Not my idea of running a business."

"Do you intend to be part of the hotel's day-to-day operation now that you're back?"

Ray shrugged. "I don't know yet." He grinned. "But it sure is funny to see Rosalyn freak out over the idea that I might."

"You don't get along," Delta concluded.

"If you have brothers and sisters, you know how it is." He studied her from aside. "Or don't you?"

"I was born fourteen and twelve years after my two older brothers. While they were going to high school, I was learning to walk. Let's just say we've never been very close."

Ray nodded. "I see. Well, Rosalyn and me, our

relationship is complicated. She used to support me and my dream of playing football professionally. She talked Dad into letting me try, she came to matches, and she was my biggest fan. Or at least I thought so. Then all of a sudden I could do nothing right anymore. She didn't come to games, she made me look bad in front of Dad..."

He stared ahead with a frown, as if trying to work out what had caused that change. "And ever since I'm back here, she's been as cold as ice to me. Dad isn't much better. After all, my career failed."

"Failed?" Delta repeated. "I thought you did very well for yourself."

"I never reached the highest level. And they blame me for all the nonsense the tabloids made up. You know, of all the things they write about you, only 10 percent is true."

Delta wasn't about to ask which 10 percent and betray that, in preparation for the workshop at the hotel, she had looked at pictures of Ray online. She had wanted to know what kind of guy he was, just in case she'd run into him again. There had been quite a lot of pictures of him with tall, blond models, accompanied by speculations concerning his relationships. But then again, it was possible Ray had just been talking to someone at a party or having lunch and it had been made into a big thing.

Ray said, "Oh well, why talk about me when we can also talk about you. What did you do before you came here?"

"More importantly, what am I going to do now that I am here and my business partner is behind bars?" Delta stopped and looked Ray in the face. "Help me get Hazel out again."

"If I knew how, I'd do it." His tone was sincere, but the sunglasses shaded his eyes, making it impossible to read what he was really thinking.

"You know more about Vera White than you let on last night. Tell the police what you know."

"Why would you think I know more about her? She was a guest here. The police can get the details from our registry. The staff can testify as to where she liked to go and with whom she had dinner at night. I know the Whites shared a table with another couple one night. But I don't see how that might be relevant."

"That's not what I mean. You knew Mrs. White even before she came here."

Ray's posture tensed. "How would you know that?"

"You even had an affair with her." Delta decided to put it bluntly. She didn't have time to beat around the bush, and besides, Ralph White wouldn't have lied about this. It had been painful to mention something like that, but he had because he believed it could help the case.

Ray burst into a short laugh. "Really? Again, I ask, how would you know?"

Delta didn't flinch. "Because someone close to Vera told me. And that someone was at the police station last night. So I'm sure the police also know by now. They could be here any moment to question you about it."

"That would just be a waste of time. My statement would be like…two sentences? And perfectly irrelevant for the case." Ray looked tense but more indignant than anything else. "Yes, I did meet the woman once before on a dolphin-spotting trip, but that was all there was to it."

"You booked a trip with the White brothers?"

"Yes. Vera saw me there and…" Ray raked a hand through his hair. "She wanted to have lunch with me. It happens all the time when you're famous. I don't mind, so I had lunch with her. That was all there was to it."

"Just one lunch?" Delta tilted her head. "And you think the police will buy that? That you agreed to have lunch with a woman who asked you to, just out of the kindness of your heart?"

"OK, so maybe it was more than one lunch. Dinner, visiting an art gallery. But I never overstepped any boundaries. It wasn't an affair. I don't start relationships with married women."

Before Delta could protest, Ray said, "Have the tabloids ever exposed an affair I had with a married woman? Or even someone who was in a relationship when our contact started? No. Because it was never like that. I'd never do that to people." He pulled off his sunglasses and faced her squarely. "My lifestyle may seem shallow to you, but I do have some rules. And you don't touch what belongs to somebody else."

Delta exhaled. "And when Vera and you met up again, here?"

"Nothing. We said hi, we talked a bit when we ran into each other, here in the garden..."

"And the notebook?" Delta kept her gaze on his face, trying to read every little change in his features as she confronted him with the conclusion that had played in her mind when Ralph White had mentioned Ray and Vera's affair to Jonas and her. "The notebook you bought at Wanted. The one with the peacocks, it was for her, right?"

The twitch at his eye gave him away. "Why would..."

"She loves notebooks. She gushed over them when she wandered into our workshop last night. And why else would you buy one but for a lady friend?"

"It might have been for Isabel. She loves peacocks."

"I can go ask Isabel if you gave it to her."

Ray held up his hands. "Why the animosity? I just bought a notebook in your shop. I don't owe you an explanation of whom I intend to give it to."

"My best friend is involved in a murder investigation." Delta said it slowly and insistently to drive it home. "She's probably desperate and unsure about what her future is now looking like. And you're playing some kind of game, dodging the truth and acting like it didn't matter you knew this woman a lot better than you pretend to. Well, it wouldn't matter if she weren't dead."

Ray swallowed hard. "OK, so I bought Vera a notebook. She loves them, and why not?"

"She's a married woman, and you're giving her presents. No wonder her brother-in-law thinks—"

"Oh, it was Ralphy who talked." Ray laughed soft and disparagingly.

Delta narrowed her eyes. "Ralphy? That sounds like you know him better than the average hotel guest."

"Not at all. He's just a pathetic little man, Vera told me. She didn't like him at all, but she pretended they were the best of friends."

To spite her sister-in-law, Amanda? Delta wondered. She was building an image of Vera in her head: an outgoing personality with an opinion on everything and everyone, not caring much for what people thought of her in return. Refocusing on Ray, she asked, "How about the money?"

"What money?"

"The money Vera lent you and you put into some business enterprise. You promised to repay her, but the enterprise tanked and you didn't keep your word."

"What?" Ray jerked back his shoulders, as if wanting to make himself physically broader under these accusations.

"Ralph White told that to me at the police station right after he had revealed your affair."

"That's a blatant lie," Ray fumed. "Slander. I never took any money from that woman."

"But..." Delta fell silent. According to Ralph, Vera had borrowed money from him, claiming she was in a tight spot because her own money had been taken by Ray and never repaid. But what if she had been lying? Making up a reason for her financial troubles so Ralph would feel sorry for her and give her what she wanted?

It seemed he had been pretty much under her spell, anyway, continuing with their dancing sessions while his wife, Amanda, didn't like it.

She said to Ray, "I need to know everything you know about Vera White. However small or insignificant it might seem to you. It could help Hazel's case."

"I'm not sure anything can help Hazel's case."

The flat tone of his voice punched Delta in the gut. "How do you mean? You don't think she murdered... That can't be. She was with me the entire time when we cleaned up after the workshop. We left the boardroom together and then..."

"She didn't kill anyone, of course. But she did decide to cover for Finn. And Finn could be guilty." Ray rubbed his hands together.

Delta felt a little doubt niggle inside her own heart. She didn't know Finn at all.

"Isabel must know Finn better than most of you," she tried. "What does she think about the murder?"

Ray looked past her. "Isabel wouldn't tell me anything."

Then what were you two talking about when I came upon you? Delta wanted to ask but realized Ray wouldn't reveal that to her anyway. Where he was obviously not close to Rosalyn, he was just as obviously protective of his little sister, Isabel.

She spread her hands in a pleading gesture. "Is there anything about last night that you noticed, anything odd or...that you can tell me?"

Ray shook his head. "It was a perfectly nice little party. Too many people asked me what I intend to do now that I'm back in town. I tried to avoid them, as I have really no idea yet, but I didn't want to tell them that. I danced too much and drank too little. That champagne Rosalyn managed to get was quite good."

He pointed a finger at Delta in feigned excitement. "Hey, that could be it. Maybe Vera White was trying to steal our champagne when someone caught her and killed her."

"Not funny."

"Seriously, though, what was she doing in the bar when it was closed for the night? Why wasn't she with her husband or dancing the night away? Why leave the party, on your own, and wander into a closed room? I mean, the door into the bar probably wasn't locked or anything, but it was clear that people weren't supposed to go there during the party."

Good point, Delta admitted. So far, no one had asked what Vera had wanted in the hotel bar. But Delta bet that if she raised the point with the sheriff, he'd claim Finn had lured her there somehow.

She looked at Ray again. "And the box with valuables your father put in the hotel safe?"

"What?"

"The hotel safe. Your father put some valuables in there for Vera White. I overheard the hotel clerk mentioning it when I was in the lobby."

"Oh, Dad might have. Nothing special. Guests often put larger amounts of cash, jewelry, etc. in the safe. Dad or Rosalyn puts it in and gives it back by the time the guests leave again, or earlier if they need it. They don't"—he smiled at her—"investigate what is inside those boxes or pouches the guests hand over. I bet you want to know what was in Vera White's, huh?"

His tone piqued Delta. He was being way too frivolous about something that could ruin her best friend's life. "Not because I'm nosy or anything. Only because it might help the case." She didn't want to say Finn had specifically asked about it, had even seemed anxious about it.

"I don't see how." Ray shrugged. "But anyway, the police have the box now. They took it away this morning."

Delta narrowed her eyes. "Not last night, right after the murder?"

"No, how come?"

"Between last night and this morning, someone might have opened the safe and taken something from the box."

Ray shifted weight. "Who would do that? And why?"

Before Delta could say anything, he continued, "Regardless, I suppose the police won't be able to determine what was in it when Vera handed it in. She's the only one who knew, and she can't tell anymore."

Was there a certain grim satisfaction in his voice, or was that just Delta's imagination?

She took a deep breath. The lingering pine scent calmed her high-strung nerves once more. She shouldn't have gone head-to-head with him in quite this fashion, but what else was she to do? Rosalyn would certainly not want to talk to her and tell her anything, so she needed Ray's help to sort out what had happened at the hotel during Vera's stay there.

Even if he wasn't honest about his own role in everything, he might reveal things about others that were important.

Maybe a different approach would do the trick. Not being confrontational but acting helpless. It wasn't really Delta's style, but it might just work with a man who was confident about his own abilities. She smiled ruefully. "I'm sorry. I'm just out of my depth with this whole situation. I have to run the shop now, and I know next to nothing about retail. I had counted on Hazel showing me the ropes during my first few days out here, and suddenly I'm left to do it all alone. There were two reporters waiting for me as I arrived, asking all of these questions and..."

"Never tell them anything." Ray leaned over and took a confidential tone, "Believe me, if you do say something, it just gets twisted around and thrown back into your face. You better not comment at all. Let them write what they want. It will die down."

Delta held his gaze, eager for more, but Ray pulled back and stretched himself, rolling his shoulders. "I have an engagement to go boating. And no, not with a woman, but with five teenagers. See you later."

He put the sunglasses back on and walked off, with the same controlled elegance Delta had observed earlier. Here was a man who knew his own body inside and out. Who watched his step and wouldn't soon slip up.

A man who would kill if it could save him from disaster?

But why? His career was over anyway. A revelation about an affair with a married woman couldn't harm him anymore.

Still, it was odd he had given Vera a present. Why had she come here? Had she known this was the Taylor hotel, and Ray was staying here now? Had her husband and brother and sister-in-law not known, but she had? Had it been a setup? The seemingly coincidental meeting...and then?

It didn't seem to make sense. Unless Vera had been the kind of woman who couldn't accept Ray turning down her proposition and who had decided he had to be punished for his refusal.

A metallic snipping sound made Delta turn her head. Isabel stood at a hedge, randomly cutting off protruding twigs. Her gestures were frantic and her choices illogical. She was still wearing her riding outfit. Delta wasn't sure when Isabel had appeared and how much of the conversation she might have overheard, or at least tried to overhear. Apparently, she hadn't been fully confident that Ray would handle it.

Determined to use this opportunity to talk to her, Delta walked over quickly. A little chat about the garden could serve to break the ice before she introduced herself. "You'd better leave that to a gardener. I cut a box hedge wrong once and it was totally ruined." Gran had been furious, then had laughed until tears ran down her cheeks.

Gran! She had promised to snap some pics of Wanted for her. She should do it as soon as she was back at the shop.

Isabel looked at her. "I know what I'm doing." Her voice was unstable.

Delta waited a few moments while the erratic pruning continued. She wasn't quite sure how to handle the situation. She supposed everyone was upset about the murder, how it had destroyed what should have been a carefree night of fun. But where was their sympathy for Finn, some eagerness to help prove his innocence?

It seemed like everyone was going about as normal without even asking about Finn and wondering how he would get out of the predicament he was in. Finn hadn't just been an employee at the hotel, he had been about to become part of the family. In Isabel's place, Delta would have been at the police station, working to get her boyfriend released. But here Isabel was, pruning the shrubs. Not even asking Delta how Hazel and Finn were, although she had seen Delta with Hazel last night when Hazel had been taken along to the station and, even without introductions, could deduce she was a friend of hers and would know more about Hazel's position and Finn's.

Delta felt a rush of anger at Isabel's dismissive attitude. How about just skipping the nice introductions and small talk, and cutting right to the core of the matter? Maybe a little provocation could put a crack in her 'business as usual' facade?

"Do *you* want to know how Finn is, or don't you care either?" Delta asked, on edge.

Isabel threw the tool down with a clang. "I do care!" she cried. "I'm not allowed to go see him. And you might think that's rather odd as I'm a grown woman and I can go fetch a car and drive out to the police station, but I'm afraid of the consequences if I do so. Rosalyn said…" She fidgeted with her hands. "You didn't grow up here, you don't know how it works. Taylors must stick together."

"I don't see how speaking up to help Finn could hurt your family." Delta tried to sound firm. "A murder happened at your hotel. It would be best for everyone if it's solved quickly."

"It's solved now, isn't it?" There were tears on Isabel's lashes. "And none of us are involved."

Delta looked her over. "So, you…you think that…" Her mind raced. "If Finn is acquitted, the blame might shift to one of you."

Isabel wiped a tear away from her cheek. "I love Finn. Honestly, I do. But I also love Ray. He came back home at last and…"

"You think Ray is involved in the murder?"

"No. But Rosalyn will make it look that way. She hates Ray." Isabel hid her face in her hands. "Rosalyn said in so many words it wouldn't be bad if Ray went to prison for what he did to her."

"Her being Vera White?"

"No! To Rosalyn. Don't you see? It's all about something in their past and…Rosalyn thinks the murder is a chance to get rid of Ray." Isabel collected the pruning tool and turned away. "I've already said too much. Please tell Finn I love him, but I can't help him. I know he will think I'm a coward, but…"

She burst out sobbing and fled across the path.

Delta looked after her with narrowed eyes. Her prior assessment that Isabel was the weak link seemed to have been correct. Under the first bit of pressure, she had cracked and become emotional, accusing others to make up for her own lack of involvement to plead for Finn.

Still, her outburst also left Delta with an uncomfortable feeling. If Taylors did stick together, why would Isabel point the finger at Rosalyn, suggesting she hated Ray for a thing from the past and now she saw a chance to get rid of him? That could make perfect sense when you considered Ray was a threat to Rosalyn's leadership at the hotel.

If Ray ended up in prison, Rosalyn could keep the hotel away from him, not just now but in the long run.

But if that was the case, why hadn't Rosalyn said anything to that end last night? She told the sheriff that Finn had an affair with the victim, not Ray. She had accused Finn of all kinds of things—being aggressive, abusive, and a hard drinker. Not a bad word about Ray, though.

That didn't make sense at all.

If Rosalyn had wanted to incriminate Ray, she should have done so last night, first chance she got. Right now, Finn was about to get charged and then Ray would stay around here and...

Unless he would go down as an accessory? Was that possible?

Delta rubbed her forehead. Isabel's revelations had shifted the picture and left her with an uneasy feeling that something wasn't quite right here. She had to get back to Wanted and put all the information people had provided, last night and this morning, into a neat overview.

Chapter Seven

Back at Wanted, Delta found Mrs. Cassidy helping two friends who wanted to build their washi tape collection. They sat on the floor of the old cell with about forty rolls laid out between them and gently bickered about the best choices. "No, pink is so loud. You can never quietly combine it with anything."

"I think it's lively. It adds a splash of color to anything you make. Use plain wrapping paper and then add a bit of that tape and you have a stunning present."

"I don't use my washi tape on ordinary gifts!"

Mrs. Cassidy grinned at Delta and nodded in the direction of the door leading into the small kitchen in the back. Delta suddenly felt a mad sense of expectation that Hazel had been released and was waiting for her there. She rushed in, only to find one of the women there who had been at the workshop the other night. She wore an orange dress with long sleeves and a broad gold belt decorated with French lilies. Her black hair was pulled to one side of her head and threaded into a loose braid that reached all the way to her belt. She was just taking a bite off a large piece of cake.

"Oh." Holding a hand to her mouth, she prevented crumbs from flying all over the place as she mumbled, "Carrot cake. New recipe, with lemon frosting, so I need second opinions. Want to be my first tester?"

After her meager breakfast, Delta's stomach growled,

and she nodded eagerly. "I've always wanted to be cake tester, or chocolate tester."

"You're hired." The woman cut off a large slice for her and put it on a plate. "How's Hazel?" she asked as she handed her the plate and a paper napkin.

Delta grimaced. "I don't know. The sheriff wasn't forthcoming last night, so I put my energy toward delivering him another suspect. It didn't really go as planned." After her fruitless trip to the hotel, she felt totally deflated and sank onto a wooden chair in the corner. Hanging her head, she said, "I did talk to Ray and Isabel Taylor, but… I don't know what I was thinking. That a killer would just slip and reveal themselves? Or that they would suddenly share something incriminating? If they were going to do either of those things, they would have done it last night, right?"

"Well, you don't know that. They might have seen something without realizing it." The woman smiled at her. "I don't think you remember my name from last night. I'm Jane Buckley, alias Calamity Jane. The idea with the Wild West names may have been Mrs. Cassidy's but this has been my nickname ever since I was a kid. You see, I tend to be, uh…" She slid the carrot cake back under its glass cover, unbalancing the weight and nearly dropping the entire thing. "Clumsy," she added with a rueful smile.

Delta grinned. "Pleased to meet you. I guess I'll also need an outlaw name now that I'm part of the posse. I'll look online to see if I can find something inspiring."

Her moment of relaxation flooded away again as she continued, "I did ask Ray and Isabel a few questions and got a few answers, but…on the way back, I really started to doubt this approach. I mean, I'm a stranger to this town and these people. Why would they tell me the truth?"

Jane nodded. "Well, usually people only tell you what they want you to know."

Delta pointed her fork at her. "Exactly. That's the feeling I had after Isabel ran off in tears. That she would never let herself go to a perfect stranger. It was almost like...she told me exactly what she wanted me to know. Pretending it was a slip up, under emotional strain." Delta stared ahead. "What can it mean? Is it her way of giving me something to help Finn, even though Rosalyn forbade her to get involved? Or is she diverting attention away from herself?"

"The bad relationship between Ray and Rosalyn is hardly news," Jane said, leaning against the sink. "The entire town knows about that. Ray came back and, well, Rosalyn wasn't eager to take him back into the family fold. She doesn't like to share the helm."

"It's more than that. Isabel suggested there is an old matter Rosalyn blames Ray for. Do you have any idea what it can be?"

Jane frowned, fingering her braid. "I've only lived here for two years. It might have happened before my time. You could ask Mrs. Cassidy. She might know."

Delta felt a little better now and bit into the carrot cake again. "Delicious. I love the lemon frosting. The tartness is a perfect contrast to the spices in the cake itself."

"Recipe from my mother-in-law. I wasn't sure it would work, as not everyone likeſ the zing of lemon." Jane pulled herself away from the sink, taking along a tea towel that slithered to the floor. She picked it up just as Mrs. Cassidy breezed in.

The opening door almost hit Jane in the head.

Mrs. Cassidy tutted. "Sorry about that. I should have looked before I barged in."

"No harm done," Jane said, gingerly touching the top of her head. "It only brushed my hair, I think."

Mrs. Cassidy said to Delta, "In the end they each bought five rolls of tape. They were still arguing about the colors as they went out. How did you get on at the hotel?"

"I'll man the shop," Jane said and left them discreetly.

As Mrs. Cassidy helped herself to a slice of carrot cake, Delta told her everything she had learned from Ray and Isabel, explaining her doubts about Isabel's revelations. "I don't see why she would first underline that Taylors stick together and then tell me something that puts both her siblings in a bad light."

Mrs. Cassidy nodded. "Most astute. Isabel is the youngest, yes, and quite impulsive at times, I daresay, but she is still a Taylor. She has been raised with this idea that you don't spill outside the family circle. That you keep your back straight at all times and your chin up. Why would she suddenly fold and tell on Rosalyn to you?"

Mrs. Cassidy wiped some crumbs off the sink. "I agree she could be eager to divert suspicion from herself. Think about it this way. Rosalyn claimed to the police that Finn was having an affair with Vera White. Had she already mentioned this to Isabel in private, for instance to have her end her relationship with Finn? Imagine how Isabel would feel, confronted with such an allegation. If it became known Finn was cheating on her, with a hotel guest at that, it would be tremendously hurtful and embarrassing. Humiliating, even. I think Isabel might, in a fit of rage, have lashed out at the woman responsible."

Delta nodded. "If you put it like that, it does sound possible. But we should verify if Isabel knew about Rosalyn's claim before the murder took place. But how? I can hardly ask her and expect an honest answer."

"If Isabel knows that Finn cheated on her," Mrs. Cassidy mused, "she might consider the fact that he got arrested as a form of justice. That it was, after all, his fault, as he betrayed her. She won't feel the need to clear his name."

"True as well. But why then throw suspicion on her own sister?"

"She and Rosalyn never got along well. Rosalyn is very domineering and always tries to control Isabel's life. Tells her what jobs to do at the hotel, what people to meet, what contracts to close. To Rosalyn, Isabel is still the little girl she could take by the hand and lead wherever she wanted. No doubt she means well… It's all rather difficult."

Mrs. Cassidy sighed. "You see, Delta, when Mrs. Taylor died, the children were practically left to fend for themselves. Mr. Taylor immersed himself in his work, and Rosalyn played the mother role. She was there for the others. I think she did a wonderful job but it also…gave her this idea she's entitled to determine things for them. That's understandable, but it doesn't make it right. And it doesn't mean they like her any better for it."

"I see. Rather sad when you think about it. Rosalyn must have wanted the best for everyone, and now everybody hates her for it."

"Which makes her even more determined to prove that her way of seeing things is the right one," Mrs. Cassidy added.

"You think she's happy now that Finn is locked up, because it proves he was never the right man for Isabel?"

"Might be."

"But how about Isabel's feelings? What if she doesn't have anything to do with the murder herself but she's not sure about Finn? What if she has to face the devastating idea her boyfriend really is a killer?" Delta shook her head. "Rosalyn should be there for her instead of telling her 'I told you he was no good.'"

Mrs. Cassidy laughed softly. "Rosalyn has come so far in life because she's a hard worker with a clear, analytic mind. She doesn't allow herself to be distracted by feelings."

"Not even where her own family is concerned?"

"*Especially* not where her family is concerned. Leading a family business is no easy thing. You might be persuaded to give someone a job he's not suited for or entrust someone with money he can't take care of. Rosalyn had to take on all of those decisions. She tried to keep the family together." Mrs. Cassidy stared at the floor with a frown. "I wonder if anyone ever gives her credit for that."

Delta pulled the sketchbook and pencils she always carried out of her bag and turned to the last sheet in the back. "I'm going to make an overview of information. I can then add to it as I go along. I'm taking this book everywhere I go, so it should come in handy for additions as they become available."

In the center of the page, she drew a body outline as she had seen it in crime series and wrote inside: Vera White, from Miami, hotel guest at the Lodge. Above, she wrote: *Body lay in hotel bar. What was Vera doing there?*

To the left, she drew an envelope and wrote inside it: *Picked up at the local post office, Vera so excited she almost got hit by a truck.* To the right, she drew a big box with a lock on it, noting inside it: *Kept in safe, valuables?, taken along by police morning after the murder.*

Then around the body, she sketched the people involved in their party clothes from last night: Rosalyn with her elbow-length gloves, Isabel with the expensive bracelet on her arm, Ray in his tuxedo, the White brothers, looking alike, but Ralph in a dancing posture.

Mrs. Cassidy followed everything she was doing with interest. "I know what you need," she enthused and disappeared into the shop. She came back carrying some washi tape in pale pink. "You can use strips of this to connect the various persons and write their connection on it."

"Great idea. Let's do it." Delta set to work, connecting Herb and Vera with the note *married*, Ralph and Vera *dance partners*, Ray and Vera *Ralph said they are exes and Vera lent Ray money, Ray denies*. She connected Vera to Finn with a note *affair according to Rosalyn, conversation at party proven by photo*, her throat tight again when she thought of Finn's expression in that photo of him and Vera.

Mrs. Cassidy also brought her a stack of small, sticky notes in neon colors. "You can write questions on those and paste them beside the person who might have the answers. Then when you have talked to them or have otherwise found the answer, you can remove the sticky note and write the answer down permanently."

"Great idea!"

For the body, Delta wrote on an orange note: *Murder method? Weapon found on spot? Fingerprints on it?*

A lime-green note with the box kept in the safe got a question: *Who put it in the safe? Has anyone touched it between the murder and the police taking it along the next morning?*

Both Rosalyn and Ray got a yellow sticky note reading: *What happened between Rosalyn and Ray?*

The White brothers got pink sticky notes, asking: *In town for business, what business?*

For Ralph, Delta also asked: *Did he really believe Vera needed money to repay Ray?*

Delta's phone beeped. She pulled it up and studied the screen. Unknown number. With a wriggle of nerves that it might be the press, she answered. "Hello?"

"Delta? Jonas here. I wondered if you'd be free to go boating tomorrow morning. I'd love to show you the lake. I might also have something to discuss."

"To discuss?" Delta repeated.

"Yes. Case-wise."

"Oh, I see. That sounds good." If Jonas had answers to a few of the questions she had just written down, she could make real progress. "Yes, tomorrow would be perfect. The shop is closed then. What time?"

"Eleven? You can meet me at Deer Point. Everyone knows where that is. I have a boat there."

"OK. Looking forward to it." Delta disconnected and said to Mrs. Cassidy, "That was Jonas Nord. He says he has something to tell me about the case."

Mrs. Cassidy seemed lost in her thoughts, and Delta had to repeat herself before her companion responded. "What? Oh, Jonas Nord. Yes. He should have something. He's a former policeman, after all. No way he'd have gotten it from the sheriff, though. They don't see eye to eye."

"Did they work together before?"

"No, not at all. But Sheriff West feels that a former big-city policeman might, uh...think he knows better, and Jonas interferes with the way he handles cases. I remember a while back there were some issues with teens making trouble in town. Jonas had a wonderful idea how to defuse the situation, but the sheriff wouldn't hear of it. It only got worse. Windows broken, mailboxes demolished. That sort of thing. Even a car stolen for joyriding."

Mrs. Cassidy shook her head. "It could have ended

terribly for those kids. They could have crashed the car, hurting themselves or someone else. But Sheriff West has his own ways, I guess."

Delta put her phone away. "Well, I'm going boating with Jonas tomorrow, and then he can tell me whatever he has found out. I'm looking forward to it already. But right now, I want another slice of that delicious carrot cake, and then I'll better snap some shots of the shop for my gran. Your fall display is just the thing she'd love to see."

As she said it, a spark of joy replaced the sad feeling that had haunted her all morning as she had considered her position. She *did* have a shop, she was making new friends, and she'd get Hazel released somehow.

Who knows, the sheriff might see the lack of evidence and release her of his own accord at any moment.

Yes, things would get better. She just had to believe it.

Chapter Eight

"AND THEN YOU PRESS THIS BUTTON AND THE CASH REGISTER adds all sales for the day and spits out a receipt with the total amount earned. You need that for your bookkeeping." Mrs. Cassidy smiled at Delta. "It's so easy now. My parents had a grocery store, and they had to write everything down in a ledger. Not just sales, but also people buying on credit. I still have some of those old ledgers at home. Every now and then I leaf through them and smile at my mother's diligence in keeping everything organized to the last cent."

"I must admit that when I pictured myself having a store, I never saw myself bookkeeping," Delta said with a grimace.

Mrs. Cassidy laughed, tilting her head back. "At least the cash register does most of the work for you. And you'll get used to it, I'm sure. Well, I'd better be off. I have to cook dinner, and my country-line-dancing group is giving a demonstration at eight."

Delta checked her watch. "I hope I didn't keep you too long."

"Nonsense, it was my pleasure. But now I have to run." Mrs. Cassidy pulled Nugget along, who also seemed eager to dive into Saturday night. "See you later. And have fun boating tomorrow."

"Thanks." Delta sighed as the door fell to a close. Helping customers had distracted her for the rest of the afternoon, but now that it was time to go home, the idea of an empty cottage pressed upon her. She ambled about, taking some wrapping paper with tree silhouettes down off the rack and giving it a more prominent place. A new package of collectible erasers had come in, but Delta didn't feel like opening it without Hazel and put it under the counter.

With a heavy heart, she closed the store and dragged her feet to her car. It was one of the last ones left in the lot. Everyone seemed in a hurry to get home and do something with family or friends. Maybe she should have asked Mrs. Cassidy where this country-line-dancing demonstration was so she could go there instead of sitting around an empty house—worrying.

Delta slid into the car and turned on the radio, but not even singing out loud to the country classics on the local station could cheer her up. She wished she had Spud with her to rub his head across her knee, or Nugget to jump from the car and dart up the path ahead of her.

She felt like she had to tell Gran about the murder to prevent her from finding out some other way. Gran was active online and would keep an eye out for news from Tundish now that Delta made her home there. But how to best share the news so Gran didn't think it was disastrous to the shop and Delta's prospects in town?

Gran was smart enough to deduce at once that the suspicions against Finn and Hazel could have serious repercussions for Delta's own future.

Having parked the car in the driveway, Delta took a deep breath and took the phone from her purse. Gran's cheerful voice came on after the third ring. "Delta! How are you? Saturday night, are you going to do something fun? You have to get to know your new hometown, not just hide out in the store."

"I know. I got invited to go boating tomorrow. Jonas is a wildlife guide, and he has a great dog."

After some chatter about the dog and his owner—Delta definitely sensed some interest from Gran, which was unsurprising, since it wasn't a secret that Gran wanted to see Delta find someone nice to date—Delta took a deep breath to come to the point. "Gran, something happened at the hotel on Friday night. A party guest was murdered."

"Darling! Are you all right? And how about Hazel?"

"It happened in the hotel bar, so we were nowhere near the murder. But unfortunately, Hazel's brother discovered the body and...the police don't fully trust his story. Because Hazel believes him, they're also suspicious of her and...it's a bit of a mess right now."

"But it will be sorted out, won't it? The police can discover so many things these days. With DNA and all. They must be able to find the killer."

"There were hundreds of people at the party."

"Not all of them can have had a motive to kill the victim."

"That's true enough. Unfortunately, someone claimed that Hazel's brother was close to the woman who died and—"

"Oh." Gran fell silent a moment. "And is that true? I suppose Hazel would know about that."

"Actually, I haven't been able to talk to her about anything since it happened, because she's been held at the police station, along with her brother."

"Your new business partner is in jail?"

"The police station is not a real prison," Delta said to make Gran and herself feel better. "She's just being held there because"—she took a deep breath—"I don't know why exactly. But you really needn't worry about that. I wanted you to know because the murder might be on local news sites, and I bet you've been looking online to see more about Tundish."

"Oh, yes. I've seen lovely shots of the fall colors. And I found the site of this gold-mining museum. They have the cutest little gift shop."

"I made friends with someone who works there. I should go have a look soon."

"You do that, darling. Don't worry too much about that murder business. It'll be sorted out by the proper authorities, I'm sure."

Delta agreed and promised to call again soon. "Love you, have a wonderful evening at the bridge club." For as long as she could remember, Gran's Saturday nights had been all about bridge. Delta had never managed to understand the rules, but even as a child it had fascinated her to watch people play it. The concentration, the drive to outwit each other, the elation of the winning duo when they had beaten the others. It was a game of tactics and a bit of bluff, perfectly suited to Gran's character.

With a grin, Delta lowered the phone and got out of the car. She had to think about dinner. Maybe a pizza? She didn't feel like cooking an elaborate meal just for herself.

Rounding the cottage, Delta had to duck underneath the long trails of wisteria that grew against the side of the house.

She stopped abruptly when she thought she heard a scraping sound coming from up ahead. From Hazel's back veranda.

Was someone there?

In a flash, Delta had a vision of someone trying to break into the house through the back door or the kitchen window. But why on earth? There was nothing worthwhile in there. Hazel didn't have expensive things like a brand-new TV set or a jewelry box.

Delta picked up a shovel sticking out of a heap of earth and carried it ahead of her as she approached the veranda. The scraping sound had stopped, and she wondered if she had even heard it correctly. Maybe her tight nerves were playing tricks on her?

But then, as she turned the corner and could catch a glimpse of the veranda, she did see someone moving. Her breath caught, and she clutched the shovel's handle harder. What to do? Confront the intruder? Call the police?

But what could she tell the police? That she had seen someone prowling around the house? She didn't even know if it was an actual stranger.

She sneaked closer, on her toes, determined to get a better look. The figure squatted down, disappearing from her line of vision.

Delta exhaled without a sound. That meant the figure also couldn't see her as she came closer. *Perfect.*

She closed the last few feet, poked her head around the veranda's supporting pillar to look. Then she dropped the shovel in a clatter and raced up the steps. "Hazel!"

Hazel turned to her. Her eyes were red rimmed. Her fingers clutched some dead flowers she had plucked off a plant on the veranda. She released them, and they drifted to the floorboards. "Delta! I assumed you were at Wanted, but I didn't want to come there and risk being seen by half the town.

"I wanted to call you, but my phone is still at the station." Hazel's voice was brittle. "They didn't return it to me, and I was so glad I could leave, I forgot to ask for it. I was almost afraid West would change his mind again and keep me anyway."

Delta grabbed her friend's shoulders and squeezed. "Are

you all right? I don't understand why Sheriff West thought he could keep you after you made a statement."

Hazel sniffled. "It was my own fault because I lied about having heard noises in the bar. I should have told him Finn asked us to go look, but it seemed so...incriminating. Finn isn't cooperating at all, one of the deputies told me. He refuses to make any kind of statement, not even after a lawyer talked to him, explaining the seriousness of the charge he could be facing. I don't know what has gotten into him."

Her face contorted, and new tears welled in her eyes. "I'm just so afraid for Finn."

Delta wrapped her arms around Hazel and held her tightly. "It's OK now. You're free again, and we'll find the real killer together. Trust me."

She patted Hazel's back awkwardly, then said, "I've been doing some work already. Jonas is helping me and Mrs. Cassidy. The entire Paper Posse. You can trust them to see and hear everything."

Hazel pulled back a little to look Delta in the eye. "It's not just Finn. It's also..." She swallowed hard. "I was so happy to be out. I came here and went to the back door. Then I saw that."

She nodded at the door. Delta, in her excitement over Hazel's return, hadn't noticed anything peculiar. But now she saw it.

An envelope was pinned to the doorframe with a pen knife, like a butterfly in a collection. A shiver went down Delta's spine just looking at it. Nobody delivered an innocent note or invitation that way.

"Have you looked inside?" she asked in a trembling voice.

Hazel shook her head.

"Maybe we shouldn't touch it and let the police remove it. They can see if there are fingerprints on it. Determine who did this."

"I'm not calling them. I just got out of there, and I don't want them coming here or me having to go back to make a statement." Hazel rubbed her eyes. "I just can't do it, Delta."

Delta nodded. "I understand. Wait a sec."

She looked around and found a pair of thin gardening gloves. She put them on and removed the pen knife from the envelope. Putting the blade on a small wicker table on the porch, she turned the envelope over. It wasn't glued shut. She could just lift the flap and pull out the note.

It was a sheet of simple, white, letter-size paper, on which someone had pasted letters cut out of a newspaper or magazine. They danced across the page, almost taunting Delta with their careless assembly.

Stop poking your nose where it doesn't belong or you'll join Vera White.

"It must have been put up there by someone who knows that the police were going to release me," Hazel said in a small voice. "Someone who is close to the investigation somehow." She stifled a sob. "I just wish I could…really leave. Leave town, forget about the murder until it is all over. The killer apprehended and Finn set free."

"I'm afraid it won't be that easy." Delta put the paper back in the envelope. "I'll take this to the police station. I'll pretend I found it. And I about did, right? I won't say anything about you."

Hazel stood with her head down, her shoulders slumped. She looked smaller, thinner, and totally dejected.

Remembering her happy friend when they had met up a few days ago to start their adventure, Delta felt a terrible anger rush through her veins. The killer, whoever he or she may be, wanted to solve their problem by dragging other people into this big mess.

"The Taylors are determined to protect each other," she explained. "I talked to both Ray and Isabel and I couldn't get much from them. Vera White's brother-in-law Ralph is certain Ray is behind it, because he knew the victim much better than he pretends and also borrowed money from her, which he never paid back. Ray denied this to me, but of course he would do so if he is trying to cover up something. And what about the fight I overheard? Oh, you don't even know about that yet. I have so much to tell you."

Hazel didn't look like she was up for a long talk about murder, and Delta put an arm around her shoulders. "Tell you what. I'm taking this to the police station. You don't have to come. Just go inside and make us a nice pot of tea. When I return, I'll cook us dinner. Then we can talk it over."

Hazel looked at her. "The person who pinned this to the door came to the house while no one was here. Is it even safe to...be here alone?"

"The door was locked. He or she hasn't been inside." Delta went over to check as she spoke. "See. Not a trace of an attempt to enter. I'll also check the front door and the windows before I leave. Please don't be afraid."

Hazel wrapped her arms around her shoulders. "But I am afraid. I don't understand why..." She licked her lips. "Finn knew about the dead woman in the bar. That's why he sent us in to look. He didn't want to be the one discovering the body. But how did he know she was there?"

Delta sighed. "I don't know. The sheriff showed me a

photo taken at the party where Vera and Finn are talking. Maybe he was supposed to meet her in the bar so they could discuss something in private, and when he came in, she was already dead. The killer could have used the appointment of the victim with Finn to ensure that someone else would be blamed for the murder right off the bat. I don't want to say the police won't be looking at all the information they get, but West started to suspect Finn right away, and then everything just seemed to support that. It's only human, I suppose, to believe that what you assume to be the truth is actually the truth, without asking yourself what real facts you have to support it. Anyway, I'll take this to the station, and I'll be back as soon as I can."

At the police station, Sheriff West didn't seem eager to check into the threat, eyeing Delta as if suspecting her of cutting out those letters and pasting them on the paper. Delta didn't press the point, as she wanted to get back to Hazel and put together a hot dinner for her, creating a relaxed atmosphere where they could forget about the murder for a bit and spend some quality time together.

Once Delta returned from the station and popped two pizzas into the oven, they kicked off their shoes and curled up on the sofa side by side to leaf through some catalogs and find stock for Wanted.

Having no previous retail experience, Delta was surprised to find the most recent catalogs full of heart stamps for Valentine's Day, notebooks decorated with daisies and blue tits, washi tape with swallows, and glitter pens advertised as perfect for making Mother's Day cards.

"This is all spring material. I thought we'd do Christmas first," she sheepishly said to Hazel, who burst out laughing.

"That was done in early summer. Some of this stuff comes from the Far East or Australia, and I always order well in advance to make sure I have it on time. Christmas sales really start in October, so all that stock is already in. You don't want to disappoint people and have them go elsewhere when they start their shopping early."

Hazel pushed a velvet pillow behind her lower back. "I've rented a booth at the upcoming Tundish Harvest Craft Fair, where we'll present Christmas stock and run a design contest. People can hand in their personal design for a notebook, and the grand winner will have his or her design put on actual notebooks that we will sell in the store and online. Limited edition."

"Oh, that sounds like fun. Have you already thought about decorations for the booth? Mrs. Cassidy was in Wanted with pumpkins this morning, and she had hollowed out one to make it into a holder for pens. It looks amazing."

"That's a great idea. We could also use a hay bale, and then we can put items against and on it."

The oven dinged, and Delta went to get the pizzas, plates, cutlery, and napkins. She even snatched a few scented candles off the mantelpiece and lit them, while Hazel cut the pizzas. The invigorating scent of rosemary and pineapple from the pizza mixed with the sweet cinnamon and cranberry of the candles.

"Here." Delta put a blanket over Hazel, tucking it in around her knees.

"Thanks. This is just like college." Hazel dug into her slice. "You won't be looking for your own place right away, will you? I kind of like having you here."

"I'm in no rush if you're not. It's also better money-wise to stay with you for the first few months so we can split the rent. I've never had a business before, so I need to see how everything is going to pan out. You have to explain bookkeeping to me so I can understand all the financial details. I know what we made today, but I have no idea if that figure means it was a good or a bad day. There's still a lot you have to teach me."

Delta reached out and squeezed Hazel's arm. "And I do intend to pull my weight."

Hazel smiled at her. "You already are. You took care of everything while I was at the station. You…didn't even say you were angry at me."

"Angry?" Delta echoed, puzzled. "Of course I'm not angry. It's not your fault. You had no idea that Finn even knew this woman, right?"

Hazel's pale features and reluctance to confirm made Delta's heartbeat stagger. She hadn't forgotten LeDuc's suggestion that Hazel had wanted a partner because the shop was in financial trouble. He had even mentioned an extra mortgage. Simply rumors, going around in a small town? Or the truth? She hesitated a moment, unsure how to breach the subject without making Hazel squirm. She had been through enough already, having been held by West. "You did say before that Finn was rebuilding his life. I'm not quite sure what you mean by that." She fell silent, scrambling for what to say next. Outright ask about the mortgage? Or give Hazel time to bring it up herself? Delta decided to let the silence linger and picked up a slice of pizza like she wasn't tense at all about this conversation.

Hazel looked down and plucked at the blanket. "It won't look good when the police find out about it," she said in a small voice.

"About what?" Delta lowered the pizza she was about to bite into. Suddenly her stomach squeezed.

"A while back, some friends invited Finn on a luxury vacation. He couldn't afford it, but he didn't want to say so. He went online, to one of those sites where you can play poker, and to his surprise he won a lot of money. He just thought it was a one-time thing. For the vacation. Then once he was back—"

"He figured it was an easy way to make money," Delta supplied.

"Yes. He meant well. He wanted to give me a vacation too. Do something special for Mom and Dad, for their anniversary. But unfortunately, he started to lose. And lose. Once he had lost over twenty thousand dollars, he came to me. At first, he claimed he needed money for a new car because the old one had broken down. But when I asked more questions, he told me the entire story. I promised to help him if he quit playing. He said he might never be able to as long as he stayed where he was. He was living in an apartment complex in Los Angeles where he hardly knew a soul; he had lost touch with his friends from college. He worked fifty hours a week at the insurance agency, which he had never really liked but chose only because Dad had pushed him into it. I had already let Dad down, you know, not choosing to major in something he thought sensible, like English lit. He'd never wanted a daughter with a stationery shop."

Hazel bit her lip, then continued, "Finn felt like all the pressure to make Dad proud was on him. He worked way too hard and was too tired to do sports or go out and meet new people. Basically, he felt alone and anxious if he'd ever make it the way Dad expected him to. I guess gambling didn't just bring money but also a thrill, substance to his life."

Hazel took a deep breath. "It was so hard on Finn to admit to me what had happened. And he was so afraid Dad would find out about it and would never want to see him again. I had to do something to make it better. Yes, Finn leaving LA would have been a blow to Dad, but at least he need not know about the debts."

"So you asked Finn to come here."

"Yes. I wanted him to turn his life around, quit the long hours, be active again, hike, jog, forget about what he had done. I took out a mortgage on Wanted to get him the money he needed to pay off his debts. He had borrowed the money from a colleague who had pointed him to the online gambling sites to begin with. I suspect he hoped Finn would fall into it, and he could put the squeeze on him, asking for a ridiculously high interest. The good thing about it was that Finn's debts weren't registered with a credit authority, so they wouldn't show up in a background check. That's also why Rosalyn and the rest of the Taylors don't know a thing about it."

Hazel exhaled slowly before continuing. "I told myself they had no need to know, as Finn's past was over and done with, but now I realize how odd it will look when it all gets out. West can check Finn's résumé and see he transferred from insurance to wildlife guide. People do make career changes, but West is the type to immediately smell a rat."

She hung her head even more. "I've been honest with you about the financial situation of the shop, you have to believe that, and when I mentioned the mortgage before you signed on, you just assumed it had been necessary to keep things going, but…I was worried that telling you about Finn would dissuade you from coming here. And I really wanted to work with you. I've got the business side down pat: buying stock, doing admin, but I missed someone to bounce ideas off and develop the artistic side of the business. Create workshops, design our own products. There is no way I could ever draw like you can. I need you."

She fidgeted with the blanket again. "I'm sorry, Delta. I should have told you so you could decide whether—"

"I would have come anyway." Delta tried to catch Hazel's eye. "This is what I've always dreamed of doing. Wild horses couldn't have kept me away."

"But West told me as he let me go that Finn was in deep trouble. That there's proof, tangible proof, that he knew the victim and that he had argued with her. He didn't give details, but I was suddenly worried when I was in the cab home that Finn had started gambling again and that maybe he had asked this woman for money or...tried to blackmail her."

"Blackmail?" Delta asked, her head tilted in surprise. Theft had occurred to her, no matter how unpleasant that idea had been, but blackmail?

"Yes," Hazel insisted. "Finn is out and about all the time. He sees people coming and going, notices who they are with. I thought that maybe the woman was up to something furtive and Finn had found out about it and tried to get money to keep his mouth shut."

"West showed Jonas and me a photo of Finn speaking with the victim at the party. She seemed to be exasperated and ready to walk off. Blackmail in progress?" Delta pursed her lips. "The expression on Finn's face was pleading and almost sort of desperate, which doesn't fit with a blackmailer knowing he has his victim cornered."

Delta's phone dinged, and she pulled it out. It was a new message from the Paper Posse. Rattlesnake Rita reported: "Just seen Ralph White meeting someone in town. He got into the car with this person and they drove off. I snapped a pic."

The picture attached to the message was obviously made in a rush, not completely sharp, and the car was already moving away. Delta could see only that it was a dark-blue station wagon; there was no way to tell the make or read the license plate.

Calamity Jane had already responded to ask what make it had been.

Rattlesnake Rita replied that she had no idea, as she was so bad with cars.

Mrs. Cassidy asked if there had been anything special about it. "Something stuck behind the window? A sticker on the back? Anything?"

Hazel, who looked over Delta's shoulder, asked in a whisper, "Why would Ralph White meet someone in town? Does he have friends there?"

"No idea. The White brothers do seem to be here on business, so maybe it was to discuss a business opportunity?" Delta stared at the phone's screen, waiting for the next message to pop up.

"I think there was a sticker on the back with a moose in it." Rattlesnake Rita added almost as an afterthought, "Santa's sleigh is pulled by moose, right?"

"No, by reindeer, darling," Calamity Jane retorted at once. "Moose have different antlers."

"I'm so bad at this." Rattlesnake Rita underlined the conclusion with several embarrassed and laughing-crying emoji.

Delta lowered the phone. "At least we have a pic of the car. I'll add this information to my overview. Could be unrelated, but might also come in handy later in the investigation."

Chapter Nine

Maybe it was too much pizza, or their tiramisu dessert, or the heavy duvet Delta crawled under for comfort, but she had a night of wild dreams in which she was arrested by Mr. LeDuc Sr. and his son, who tied her wrists with pink washi tape and put her on a dappled pony to take her into an abandoned gold mine. Somewhere inside, Hazel was being held captive, and Delta had to look for her through an endless maze of passages.

At last she saw something glittering in the passage wall. It was the notebook with the peacock pattern. It came loose and fell in front of her feet, opening. Scribbled on the page was the name of the killer. It read—

Delta awoke with a start, blinking up at the ceiling. She tried to remember what had been written on the page, then laughed at her frantic efforts. It had been nothing but a dream.

She got out of bed and took her time getting dressed and preparing a full breakfast for Hazel and herself. Scrambled eggs, yogurt, plenty of fruit and nuts, and a large pot of fresh ginger tea. The tea inspired her to draw up an assortment of tea cups and tea glasses with tea bags in them and snacks beside them that she might use for a design for tea lovers.

"Doodling at breakfast is the perfect way to start the day," she said contentedly to Hazel, who came padding in, her dressing gown with its fluffy collar turned up around her ears. She yawned and immediately reached for the bowl with almonds. Taking a handful of them, she dug up a bar of chocolate from a drawer and melted the chocolate over the hot ginger tea to dip the almonds into.

Delta grinned at her. "You know how to dress up the healthy stuff."

"Chocolate is healthy as well," Hazel mumbled, leaning back against the chair. She seemed to shiver for a moment and ducked deeper into her dressing gown.

Delta studied her friend's worn features for a few moments and then said reluctantly, "I can't lounge here with you much longer. Jonas invited me to go boating today. I can cancel if you don't want to stay here alone. Or you could come with us, I suppose. I don't know how big his boat is, but..."

"Nonsense. If he asked you to go, he wants to take you. Not me." Hazel winked at her.

Delta shook her head. "He mentioned information, case-wise. So it's all business."

"Of course."

"How do I get to Deer Point anyway?"

"You can take my mountain bike. I'll draw you a little map." Hazel pulled Delta's notepad toward her. "Don't worry about me. You set me up perfectly with this breakfast. After I finish it, I'm going to lie on the sofa and start a new book I bought. Victorian paper crafting. They made amazing scenes. I wonder if we can use the techniques for a workshop sometime."

Delta was glad to see Hazel lively again as soon as she started thinking about paper crafts. "Great. You can tell me all about it once I'm back. I'll get my things together."

Five minutes later, carrying a light fleece in case it was chilly on the water, a bag with her sketching material, and a water bottle, Delta waved goodbye to Hazel. Cycling fast, against the wind, drove the lingering dream images from her mind and put new energy into her body. Gold leaves whirled around her as she whooshed down the sloping path that got narrower as it approached her destination.

Deer Point turned out to be nothing more than a wooden platform along the lake's clear blue water. A few boats lay docked there, bobbing on the waves. The sun warmed the platform's wood, which radiated upward against Delta's bare ankles above her sneakers as she walked out to meet Jonas, who was loosening the rope that tied his boat to a pole. He wore a dark-blue tee with gray jeans, giving him a sporty, outdoor look.

Spud stood beside him, watching everything with his alert amber eyes. When he spotted Delta, he came to her in long bounds.

She leaned down to rub his head. "Hey, boy. Good morning. How are you?" The feel of his soft fur under her fingertips calmed her heartbeat.

"Hello." Jonas grinned at her. "You are dressed exactly right. Have you done this before?"

"Not really." Delta glanced down at her purple sweater, jeans, and ankle boots. "I was a bit of a workaholic where I used to live."

"Don't apologize for that. I was the same." Jonas stared ahead a moment, his brows drawing together. Then he smiled at her again. "Let's go."

He helped her into the boat. Spud jumped in after her and settled himself in front of her, leaning his head against her.

"He must know you're new to it," Jonas said. "He wants to make you more comfortable."

He sat down opposite her and took the oars in hand.

"I'm sorry this is not a luxury yacht. Or at least a motorboat. But I like to make as little noise as possible when I go out on the water. Then you have the biggest chance of seeing wildlife. And I don't mind the exercise."

"The bike ride over here was wonderful." Delta sighed. "I really needed that. I had a bad night with all the murder stuff. But at least Hazel is out now."

"I know. I have a source at the station." Jonas winked, dipped in the oars, and away from the platform they went. The sky overhead was clear blue, and in the trees at the water's edge, countless birds chirped their tunes.

Shimmering bugs shot past the boat, hovering for a moment before breezing on. Dragonflies with their multi-faceted wings. Some were green, others blue. Delta tried to follow them with her eyes, but they were so fast. Especially when the sunshine hit their wings. There one moment, gone the next.

"Can you hear it?" Jonas asked.

"What?" Delta turned her head, trying to pick up a distinctive sound.

"The silence. No talking, no music, no car engines. Nothing. In the city, there's always noise, you know. A constant hum in the distance. Here there's nothing. I admit I had to get used to it in the beginning. It felt like a sort of… emptiness. A vacuum I got sucked into. But soon enough it started to grow on me. Now I wouldn't want to have it any other way."

He looked her over. "You bought half of Wanted. But did you just want the shop or did you also bargain for small-town life?" Delta blinked. It was a question she hadn't really considered when she had decided to take her leap of faith. She had just asked herself if she wanted to work for someone else or be her own boss, and whether it would be great to exchange long hours in an office for giving workshops with Hazel. Creating her own designs and seeing them come to life in her own line.

She hadn't really considered small-town life. And now, it seemed, she was caught up in it.

Jonas said, "People keep an eye out for each other. That can be a good or bad thing. There's a fine line between concern and curiosity. Or even intrusion. Especially with the murder, be careful whom you get close to."

Delta tilted her head. "Anyone particular you have in mind?"

"I heard that LeDuc was at your shop yesterday."

"Which one?"

"Junior. He probably promised you that his online community could help solve the crime. But all he wants is to score at his father's expense."

"He didn't mention anything about an online community," Delta said.

"They're called News Hunters. They deliver him the scoops he can share. And not even for money. Just for a mention in the byline." Jonas shook his head.

"Concerned citizens?" Delta suggested.

"More like sensationalist citizens. They manage to heat up the town and turn people against one another. Let's say that to LeDuc Jr., normal journalistic practice doesn't mean anything. He believes he can write what he wants as long as he has readers clamoring for more."

"So his stories are not based on fact?"

"I doubt he understands what that word even means. He asks for people's opinions, and he does present them like that. Mr. X said this, Mrs. Y said that… But when people read the news, they believe it's the truth. I mean, when he has someone tell their opinion, people repeat that opinion like fact. Because they are led to believe it represents the actual situation."

"Well, I can assure you that I didn't speak with Mr. LeDuc. Junior or Senior."

Jonas sighed. "Senior has kept the *Trader* alive. We owe him for that, I suppose. A local paper provides lifeblood to a community. But when his son came and started to compete with him, he completely lost his head. I can only hope things will calm down again."

They were on the middle of the lake now, and Jonas rested the oars.

"Is Spud yours or just a temporary charge?" Delta asked.

"Spud is mine. I'll keep him for as long as he lives. But I employ him to rehome K-9 officers. When they retire, they need to go into normal homes. But that can be a challenge for them. They have a high work ethic, which means they don't just switch off and become pets. You have to train them first and then find a home perfect for their character and needs. I do that, and Spud assists me. He can show the other dogs what their behavior is supposed to look like. We delivered a Rottweiler to his new home just last week and now we're waiting for a new family member. Hey, Spud?" Jonas brushed the dog's head.

Spud shook himself and then stood, looking at the shore. Jonas followed his gaze. There was nothing to see underneath the trees, but after a minute or two, a group of children appeared. Jonas smiled. "Their senses are so much better than ours. Hearing, smell. Spud heard those kids long before we ever did."

"I couldn't keep a dog in the city, but I've been thinking

about getting a puppy now that I live here. However, a grown dog is nice too." Delta tapped her hand on her knee to attract Spud's attention. He was watching the children and not paying any heed to her.

Jonas said, "He still turns into work mode every now and then. Complete focus. I just let him. It has been tough to adjust to civilian life."

Delta wondered if it had also been tough for Jonas. To exchange his busy life in the city, his career in the force, for the peace and quiet out here. Had he done it by choice?

Or had something driven him away?

Delta said, "You mentioned over the phone you knew something pertinent to the case? I have a couple of prominent blanks. Such as murder method."

Jonas grimaced. "Vera White was stabbed with an ice pick that came from the bar. Clean as a whistle, I heard, so no fingerprints to help West along."

"A weapon picked up on the spot… Meaning it wasn't premeditated?"

"*Suggesting* that it wasn't premeditated," Jonas corrected her. "We can't be sure of course. Why did Vera go into the bar in the first place? Had someone asked her to come there? Was there an altercation? The doctor who looked at the body established that she had a cut on her hand. A shallow cut but made shortly before she died. Was she in an argument in that bar?"

Jonas gestured with both hands as he continued, "That she met someone might become more likely if you consider what else I heard."

Delta's heart beat fast waiting for him to go on. Would it incriminate Finn? Involve Hazel? Make everything even more complicated?

"There was a box left in the hotel safe," Jonas began. "It belonged to Vera White. She had it put there for safekeeping. The police took it along to have a look at it. It seemed Finn had asked the hotel clerk about it, and they were curious as to why he had done so."

Delta licked her lips. "And?"

"They opened it at the station and went through the contents. Part of it was jewelry, part money and checks. Things you would normally have the hotel store for you so it can't get stolen if you keep it in your room."

"Yeah, yeah, I know how that works. What else was in it?"

"There were some purchases she had made in town, souvenirs from the museum shop, and notebooks."

"Notebooks? It can't be the ones she purchased on the night she was killed. Hazel handed those to the clerk at the desk when Vera was already dead in the bar."

"I don't know about the origin of the notebooks. Seems all of them were in wrapping paper, like they were gifts."

Like the one Ray had bought at Wanted.

Jonas said, "There was an envelope on the bottom. It contained paperwork. From a lawyer."

Envelope? Delta sat up. Could that be the envelope that Mrs. White had picked up at the local post office? According to Wild Bunch Bessie of the Paper Posse, the grocer said she had been giddy with joy when she received it, right? Had almost walked right in front of a truck with apples because she hadn't been minding her surroundings as she crossed the road… Interesting.

Jonas said, "It was about the possibilities for divorcing her husband. The lawyer had looked into her marriage contract and was confident that she could walk away with half the guy's fortune from that dolphin-spotting company of his."

"Oh. So their marriage wasn't doing well? I wouldn't have expected that. Friday night at the station, her husband seemed so devastated by her death."

"Well, it seems she had kept the idea of divorce strictly to herself. When asked about it, her husband, her brother-in-law, and her sister-in-law all denied knowing anything about it. They were questioned separately, in quick succession, so they didn't know from one another what the other had said."

"Unless they had agreed on their answer even before they were asked. I mean, the box was removed by the police, so they must have realized the contents would be scrutinized."

"But did any of them even know what was in it? It was Mrs. White's personal property. She had the keys on her. The police took them off her dead body the night before."

"She had those keys with her while she was at the gold miners' party?" Delta pursed her lips. "That does suggest she kept the secret of her upcoming divorce close to her chest. I wonder..." She stared in deep thought at the gold trees lining the lakeshore.

"Yes?" Jonas studied her.

"I have to write this down." Delta turned to the back of the sketchbook with her overview and added to the washi tape connecting Vera and Herb: 'Vera getting a divorce, not wanting anyone to know'.

She also used a red pencil to connect the envelope to the box and added the contents Jonas had mentioned: jewelry, souvenirs, notebooks in wrapping paper.

Jonas grinned as he watched what she was doing. "Your version of a case file?"

"Portable case file," Delta said cheerfully, adding the

ice pick as murder weapon and noting there were no fingerprints on it. She also wrote beside the body: *shallow cut on hand*. "I can add to it as soon as I have another clue. Now what does this upcoming divorce tell us? I mean, often people get divorced because they have fallen in love with someone else. Does the divorce strengthen Rosalyn's claim that Finn was having an affair with Vera?"

Jonas shook his head. "Not likely. Vera had engaged this lawyer before she came here. His report mentioned having looked at all options, which took time. Unless we assume Finn and Vera had already been having an affair before she came here, we can exclude him as the new love interest."

"Ray then," Delta mused. "Ralph White was so certain there had been an affair between Vera and Ray. Did they not come here by accident, but on purpose to allow Vera to spend time with her lover?"

Jonas said, "I might have something for you there. I asked my fellow wildlife guides about the couple."

"Guides, plural? Does the hotel employ that many guides?"

"No, but there are a number of independent guides working in the area. They all offer different services. Some take people birding, others take them out at dusk to see deer or even after nightfall to study night hunting creatures like owls. I asked all of them and I heard from several that they had seen the little blond lady, meaning Vera White, walk around by herself. Over the past three weeks, she has been seen a dozen times going up the path to a birding hut that gives a view of a small pond where animals come to drink. Now I ask you: What business has a woman who is more interested in fashion and dancing than in wildlife at a birding hut? Alone, several days in a row sometimes."

"You think she met her secret lover there?"

"Exactly. Question is: Who was it?"

Delta hmmed. "Have you been to that birding hut? Is it popular? I mean, if birders walk in and out, it isn't a very good place to meet a secret lover."

"On the contrary, it's a perfect place. If you do get seen there, you can always claim you were just bird watching together."

"Did those nature guides you talked to mention someone else going up frequently?"

Jonas laughed softly. "Let's say they don't pay as much attention to other men as they do to pretty women. They all noticed Vera because she's the kind of woman you notice."

"They might not have noticed her sister-in-law either if she had gone up some time. Suppose Amanda White followed Vera and discovered she was betraying her husband, Herb. Was that the truth she referred to in the argument I overheard? But why would revealing Vera's infidelity hurt Amanda too?" Delta toyed with her pencil. "Amanda has been completely invisible so far. I should really find a way to talk to her and gauge how she feels now that Vera is dead."

"Good idea," Jonas said. "The hotel organizes a high tea starting at one. You could go there."

"I doubt that someone who just lost a relative is sitting at a high tea." Delta stared down on her case overview, feeling that, despite the connecting tape stripes between the people listed, there were still far too many unconnected pieces.

Jonas said, "You can at least try. The murder will be the talk of the day, also at the high tea, so you might hear something useful."

Delta had to admit he had a point there. "I think I'm

going to call Mrs. Cassidy and ask her if she'll come with me. She's a star at extracting information."

Chapter Ten

Because of the fine weather, high tea was served on the terrace, waitresses flitting to and fro between tables decked out with stylish, dark-red covers and silk napkins. Large, shiny, three-tier servers were placed on each table, filled with macarons, cakes, cupcakes, and sandwiches. Grapes dripped from the top layer while separate bowls held huckleberry jam and whipped cream. Tea flowed into cups from the porcelain teapots carefully handled by the waitresses.

"Those handles get hot," Mrs. Cassidy whispered from half-behind Delta. She had just gotten back from taking pumpkin soup to an elderly friend when Delta had called her, and she had agreed at once to come out for the tea. "I'll bring my knitting to feel even more like Miss Marple."

As Mrs. Cassidy knew what Amanda White looked like, Delta let her take the lead and detect the object of their interest among the many ladies present at the tea. Some had persuaded their husbands to come, who looked decidedly uncomfortable. A few hid behind newspapers or worked on their phones, while others followed the waitresses around with their eyes. One man kept drumming his fingers on the table, suggesting it was already taking too long for his liking.

"There she is." Mrs. Cassidy motioned discreetly to a table at the edge of the terrace close to a stone railing. The woman sitting alone was working on an embroidery ring, counting the stitches with her needle. Everything about her was immaculate: from her flawless makeup to her brushed-back brown hair.

Comparing her to the vivacious Vera, who had crashed the workshop, Delta understood immediately why Amanda had faded into the background as soon as Vera was near. Amanda was good-looking, but Vera had been striking. Amanda seemed pleasant enough, but Vera had been bubbly and engaging. Amanda could probably make good conversation, but Vera had wound people, especially men, around her little finger. Amanda had a lot going for her, but Vera had always had more. That must have been very frustrating.

While Delta hung back, observing, Mrs. Cassidy approached the target, holding her knitting bag up like a shield. Close enough to Amanda to be heard, she said, "What lovely roses. Do you mind me sitting with you?"

Without waiting for a reply, she pulled out the unoccupied white chair opposite Amanda and sat down with a sigh. "That's better. I've been on my feet all morning. We had our harvest service at church. Everyone brings something to share. Pear pie, sweet potato brownies, walnut cake. I made pumpkin soup with corn bread. Took what was left to a friend who is stuck at home with a bad ankle. She twisted it while gardening. Not broken fortunately, just needs to rest up for a day or two. I pulled out a few weeds for her while I was there. She does hate her garden looking unruly. The weather is lovely, don't you agree?"

She gestured to Delta, who had hovered nearby to allow her to break the ice. "My friend Delta Douglas."

Delta hurried over to shake Amanda's hand. "You've chosen the best spot on the entire terrace. What a view."

Mrs. Cassidy reached out her hand as well and shook across the table. "Mrs. Cassidy. And that's Nugget."

The Yorkie sat up, tilted her head, and held out a paw to Amanda White.

Her face relaxed into a genuine smile while she leaned down to take the little paw into her hand.

"Hello there. You're cute. Yes, you are." Glancing up at Mrs. Cassidy, she said, "Amanda White, pleased to meet you. My mother had a little dog just like that. She died a few years back. Mom never wanted to have another."

Amanda scratched Nugget behind the ears. "What a doll. Are you staying here as well? I don't think I've seen your dog before."

Delta felt her heart skip a beat. She fidgeted with the pillow on her chair so she didn't have to look at Mrs. Cassidy as she tackled this potentially awkward moment.

"No, I'm not staying at the hotel," Mrs. Cassidy said, sounding perfectly at ease. She extracted her knitting from her bag. It was a large affair in yellow and white, with four needles sticking out. Turning it over and taking two needles to hand, Mrs. Cassidy said, "I was at the party on Friday night, though."

Amanda's eyes darkened. "Then I suppose you know? I still don't understand it. How something like that can happen inside a hotel. Where you believe yourself to be safe!" She threw a scorching look at the hotel as if it were to blame for the murder. "Vera so wanted to stay at this lodge. She had read about it online, about the grand twenties atmosphere of it and that annual gold miners' party. She was so excited to come and experience it all for herself, and then this happens."

Delta's heart beat even faster. So Vera had chosen the destination. The hotel run by the family of the man whom Ralph White had named as her secret lover and the recipient of a large sum of money.

Had Vera demanded her money back? And had Ray killed her because he couldn't pay up?

Amanda said, "Vera was impulsive like that, and Herb

usually indulged her. After his first wife died, he was very lonely, and Vera brought the light back into his life." She smiled for a moment. "It was good to see him so cheerful again. Ralph used to say he wasn't sure Herb would ever get over his first wife's death, but then he did." Her expression contorted. "And now this. Now he's a widower all over again."

Delta reached out to the teapot. "Shall I pour you some more tea?"

Amanda nodded gratefully. She pulled a hankie out of her sleeve and rubbed her eyes. "I just can't imagine how it happened. Not a mugging in the street, but cold-blooded murder in a hotel. I told Ralph I wanted to leave right away, but he said we can't. Not until the police say we can. There's so much to do, to take care of, but they won't even let us have the body."

Mrs. Cassidy said, "I'm sure they will release it to you as soon as they can. But they need to investigate—"

"They're treating her like an object, a thing." Amanda waved the hankie. "And what good will it do? She's dead anyway."

"They have to determine who killed her."

"I thought they already knew. That young man. The guide. He did strike me as rather…free with people. Someone who puts a hand on your shoulder when you didn't ask for it, that kind, you know."

Delta pointed at the filled teacup. "Better drink something. I'm sorry this is such an upsetting time for you."

Amanda picked up the cup and sipped. "I knew it was crazy to come here. All the way from Florida. Why couldn't we have vacationed nearby? I hate flying. All the weird sounds the engines make. And if you get caught in turbulence…" She shivered.

"I never fly if I can help it," Mrs. Cassidy sympathized. "My children live near enough for me to drive out to them, so I avoid planes where I can."

Delta said, "Vera wanted to come here because she had read about the place online? I thought she knew Ray Taylor. From his football days?"

Amanda looked at her. Was there a moment's flash of suspicion in her eyes?

"Didn't Ray take a dolphin-spotting trip with your husband's company?" Delta pushed. "I think he mentioned it to me. It was the best trip he ever went on."

Amanda seemed to relax again under the compliment. "Yes, we hear that a lot. Lots of companies promise you sightings, but we always deliver. Whatever the weather."

"Vera knew Ray Taylor?" Delta asked again.

Amanda shrugged. "Could be. Vera went on some of the trips. I never do. I don't like a rough sea."

"Maybe Ray and Vera knew each other from before Vera married your brother-in-law," Mrs. Cassidy said in an innocent tone. She kept her eyes on Amanda.

Amanda looked into her teacup. She didn't seem to have heard the remark.

"I mean," Mrs. Cassidy said, busily clicking her needles, "you just said Vera married your brother-in-law after his first wife passed away. You can't have known her for very long."

"Two years." Amanda put the teacup back on the table and studied the three-tiered server with treats. "Those macarons are awfully sweet, and artificially flavored, I bet. How else do they create those bright colors?"

"Well, it's lucky your brother-in-law met another woman at all," Mrs. Cassidy mused. "Men tend to bury themselves in work when they're grieving. It can be so hard for them to meet someone socially." She sat up and studied Amanda across the table. "It must have happened at a dolphin-spotting trip then. Vera and some friends coming to see the dolphins. Or maybe it was a trip with her colleagues? Don't they do such trips for team building?"

"It was at a birthday party at my home, actually. I insisted Herb at least attend birthday parties back then. Else he'd be sitting by himself every single night."

"Some people do need a bit of help to come out of their shell again." Mrs. Cassidy pulled at the yarn threading up from the bag she had put beside her. "So you knew Vera before she actually met your brother-in-law? I'm sorry. I was under the impression he had brought her along."

"No. I, uh… Vera was a friend of a friend. She only tagged along to the party because they wanted to go someplace afterward. In a single car."

It sounded vague and half-made-up.

Delta narrowed her eyes as she studied Amanda's pale face.

"It must have been meant to be," Mrs. Cassidy enthused. "I had the same thing happen among my friends once—"

"Now I remember," Amanda cut her off. "You work at the museum in Tundish. I didn't recognize you at all. At the museum, you were dressed like it was 1880."

"All part of the act, my dear. I hope you did enjoy having a little look around. Tundish's history is fascinating."

Amanda shifted weight in her chair as if uncomfortable.

Mrs. Cassidy called Nugget, who had strayed toward another table. The Yorkie returned reluctantly, glancing back at the table where chicken sandwiches beckoned.

Delta picked up a huckleberry cupcake, which was decorated with white-chocolate slivers.

Turning over the knitting in her lap, Mrs. Cassidy observed, "Your husband and his brother are clearly a great team. At the museum, they were laughing and joking the entire time. Vera seemed a bit silent, though."

Mrs. Cassidy took her time to count stitches, then continued in a thoughtful tone, "I wonder if someone was threatening her."

"Threatening her?" Amanda echoed. "Why would you think so?"

"Well, now that she's dead, you can't help but think she must have been threatened. I mean, you don't just go to a party full of strangers and get killed. It must have been someone she knew. Someone she was afraid of, maybe?"

Amanda seemed dismissive. "We don't know anyone here."

"I heard"—Mrs. Cassidy leaned forward and lowered her voice—"that Vera was seen in the hotel garden on Friday night, arguing with someone. Another woman. It was quite a fierce argument too. Vera was struck in the face, I heard. Imagine that."

Amanda's expression seemed even paler now. She raised a hand to her forehead. "The sunshine is giving me a terrible headache. I think I'll go lie down a bit."

Mrs. Cassidy looked at her. "The woman arguing with her wore a distinctive gown. The police are looking for it."

Distinctive gown? Delta tried to keep her expression from betraying her surprise. She had heard nothing about this. Did Mrs. Cassidy know more, or was she merely bluffing to provoke Amanda into a response?

"I don't see why they would look for a dress, since a man killed her," Amanda said fiercely, shooting to her feet. The embroidery ring fell to the terrace tiles in a clatter.

Nugget jumped at it. Mrs. Cassidy made a grab for the collar, but it was too late already. The Yorkie had the ring in her mouth.

Amanda and Mrs. Cassidy almost collided as they both leaned in to separate the dog from the ring. Nugget was twisting to keep away from their grabbing hands, determined to keep her new toy to herself.

"I'm so sorry about this," Mrs. Cassidy said. Nugget wriggled backward, half under the table, and Mrs. Cassidy crawled after her, cooing that she had to be a good girl and let go.

People at other tables were watching with amused expressions, and a waitress approached and stood a few steps away, apparently unsure if her assistance was needed.

"Bingo!" Mrs. Cassidy's head and shoulders reemerged from under the table, and she held up the ring to Amanda, who accepted it with barely a glance at how it had fared in the dog's mouth.

Mrs. Cassidy said, "I'm more than willing to replace it if it's damaged."

"It's fine. I just need to get inside, lie down." Amanda clutched the ring and walked off, unsteady as she zigzagged between the tables. She almost ran into a waitress, who had to hold her tray to the left to avoid everything falling off. She seemed to mutter something less than complimentary as she stared after the panicked woman, who dashed through the terrace doors into the hotel's dim interior.

"Are the police looking for a distinctive dress?" Delta asked Mrs. Cassidy in a whisper.

"I doubt it. After all, Sheriff West didn't believe your story about the argument between two women, and no one actually saw the woman who fought with Vera. But the idea that the police are onto that particular woman seemed to spook her. I wonder if she's right now rushing to her hotel room to get rid of the dress she wore that night. She was in such a hurry to get away she didn't even check if Nugget had damaged her embroidery ring. If she puts a lot of hours into that hobby, she should have cared, right?"

"So you were only bluffing." Delta sighed as she sank against the chair's back. "The whole talk didn't deliver a thing."

"On the contrary, it was very instructive." Mrs. Cassidy pointed a finger at Delta. "I told you before that I had the impression, at the museum, that those ladies didn't like each other. That they were watching each other all the time. Now, when we combine that with the knowledge that Herb White met his wife at a birthday party at Amanda's place… Maybe Amanda was originally happy that Herb had met a new love because of her. That he had been pried out of the shell of his grief and that he could start life all over. But once she got to know Vera better, she must have noticed she was…self-centered, not caring for Herb's opinion about her behavior. At the gold miners' party, she was dancing with other men, drinking too much, and overall making a spectacle of herself, without caring what people thought about her."

Delta nodded. "And in the argument I overheard, Vera sounded dismissive and callous."

"Right. There was a…coldness about her, and it's very well possible that over time, Amanda felt worse and worse about having introduced them. She watched Vera, waiting for her to make such a serious mistake that…the marriage would end in divorce?"

"Even if that's true, how does it help us in the murder case?" Delta rubbed her forehead. "I didn't want to say out loud that I was the witness who had overheard her fighting with Vera. It would have sounded like an accusation."

"I think we learned all we can from her." Mrs. Cassidy picked up a yellow macaron. "Contrary to what Amanda White assumed, these are not artificially colored and flavored. After all, they are made by our very own Calamity Jane."

"Really?"

"Yes, all these sweet treats are. Her husband runs the bakery on Mattock Street and she does catering for parties, etc." Mrs. Cassidy lifted the macaron to toast Delta with it. "Light as a feather, French to the core." She popped it into her mouth and closed her eyes with an expression of pure bliss.

Delta picked up a pink one and bit into it carefully. Raspberry jam rolled across her tongue, not too sour, not too sweet, just perfect.

The sun reflected off the three-tiered carrier, and despite all the upheaval, Delta couldn't deny that life in Tundish wasn't all that bad.

Chapter Eleven

On Monday morning, Delta drove out to The Lodge, strictly for business, as the next workshops had already been scheduled, and Delta wanted to discuss with Rosalyn whether they could continue as planned. But deep down inside she hoped she could also use the opportunity to gauge Rosalyn's feelings about the murder and find out if she was, like Isabel had suggested, eager to implicate Ray in it.

Upon arrival, she saw three police cars parked in front of the building and the last deputy just going inside. Were they going to do another search?

Delta parked her car and hurried to get inside and hear what the commotion was all about.

At the reception desk, Sheriff West was talking to the clerk while the deputies had fanned out through the lobby. One of them stood at the elevators, also keeping an eye on the nearby staircase, while two were entering the breakfast room. It seemed they were looking for someone.

The clerk reached for the telephone, but West stopped him with a curt hand gesture. The clerk sank back in his chair, his face pale and worried-looking.

Delta stayed out of West's direct line of vision, retreating to the far corner of the entry hall where a large display held flyers with information about local attractions, including the gold-mining museum, a wildlife refuge, and the restored nineteenth-century mansion of a copper king. Delta let her gaze wander, pretending to contemplate what to do for the day, while her ears strained to pick up any threads of conversation.

"You can't do this!" a sharp female voice cried.

Delta peeked around the display.

The two deputies came from the breakfast room, holding Isabel between them. As they drew nearer, Delta could see her hands were cuffed behind her back.

"Really, Sheriff." The clerk stood up and banged his hand on the counter. "Do you have to do this in front of the guests?"

West looked at the deputies. "You could have asked her to come along of her own accord."

"But you said she had to be apprehended at all costs. We thought..." The deputy looked at his colleague, bewildered.

West waved a hand. "Yes, yes, it's all right. Take her outside and put her in the car. Do it quickly, so we don't get more of a fuss."

"Where's Rosalyn?" Isabel cried. "I want a lawyer. Rosalyn has to call a lawyer for me. Ray! Where's Ray?"

She sounded like a frightened little girl.

Delta watched her struggling figure as she was led outside. Her mind raced to work out what this could mean. Did West believe Isabel had been involved in the murder with Finn?

Or could this new arrest mean that Finn was actually off the hook?

West said something to the clerk in a low, almost threatening tone, leaning heavily on the counter. Then he straightened up and walked off.

Delta waited until he was gone and then darted to the counter. "What a rude man," she exclaimed. "If you want to ask someone a question or two, you can do it right here in the privacy of the office. Why take someone along in such a fashion? Terrible. If I were the Taylors, I'd complain."

The clerk shook his head. "Nobody complains about him," he groused. "Thinks he about owns the town."

"He must have a good reason for taking her along..." Delta said just as the elevator doors opened and Rosalyn came out. She wore a dark-red pantsuit that emphasized her height. Her hair was styled into lush, wet waves. She carried a clipboard under her arm.

Delta waved at her. "Your sister has been arrested."

Rosalyn looked at her as if she didn't believe her for one moment, but then she looked outside and apparently spotted the police cars, for she broke into a trot through the doors.

Delta followed her in a rush.

Rosalyn was at the car, putting her hand against the glass. On the other side of it, Isabel's pale face was visible. West was just about to get into the driver's seat. Rosalyn called across the roof of the car, "Sheriff! What are you arresting her for? If you don't tell me at once, I will have a whole army of lawyers marching into the station within minutes."

West hesitated, then declared in a gruff tone, "When we arrested Finn Bray on Friday night, we searched his person. There was a heavy gold bracelet in his jacket pocket. We had it tested for fingerprints. There were three sets on it. The victim's. Finn's. And your sister's."

Rosalyn stared at him. "And? I don't see why you'd have to arrest her for something so trivial."

"Trivial?" West scoffed. "It wasn't hard to put two and two together. Finn Bray is Isabel's boyfriend, right? He also happens to have been in financial trouble before he came to live here."

Rosalyn's nostrils flared. "I knew nothing about that."

Delta's heart skipped a beat, and she clenched her hands.

The sheriff smiled in grim satisfaction. "But we do. We assume the following: Finn Bray was in financial trouble. He shared this with his girlfriend, Isabel, asking her for help. Isabel didn't want to ask her father or you for money, so she took Mrs. White's bracelet out of the jewelry box in the hotel safe and passed it off to Bray so he could sell it and use the money to pay off his debts."

"My sister wouldn't steal anything." Rosalyn looked appalled. "Certainly not from our guests."

West huffed. "If your sister never touched it, how can her fingerprints be all over it?"

"I have no idea, but I do know you're making a terrible mistake."

"Miss Taylor, I told you my reasons, and not to prevent an army of lawyers descending, because I'm quite sure you will have lawyers over anyway to clear your sister. I told you because I want you to know, upfront, that your sister is guilty. Fingerprints don't lie. She handled the bracelet belonging to one of your hotel guests, and that bracelet ended up in the pocket of her boyfriend. Now you tell me how to interpret that differently."

As Rosalyn struggled to reply, the sheriff nodded with determination, ducked into the police car, and drove off.

Rosalyn stood frozen, staring after it.

Delta walked up to her. "Did Isabel have access to the safe?" Ray had told her that only his father and Rosalyn had, so how would Isabel have been able to get the bracelet out of Vera White's box of valuables?

Rosalyn turned to her with a jerk. "What? What are you doing here?"

"My best friend was in a cell overnight," Delta said. "She's been released, but people will speculate about her involvement until the real culprit is caught. I'm trying to determine who that might be."

"Not Isabel." Rosalyn shook her head. "She doesn't have the stamina to argue with anyone, let alone kill them. And she wouldn't steal either. Contrary to what the sheriff seems to think, she has her own money. If Finn had asked her for some, and I suppose he might have, as I never trusted him, Isabel could have given him money from her own funds. This whole bracelet thing is a misunderstanding. Isabel might have handled the bracelet because the guest asked her to fetch it from the safe before the party began."

"So Isabel did have access to the safe?"

"We all do. Ray, Isabel, me, our father."

Delta stood motionless, her mind racing. Ray had lied. He had access to the safe as well. He could have looked in Mrs. White's box. He could even have removed items from it after the murder and before the police came to take it the next morning.

"What does it matter who had access to the safe?" Rosalyn challenged Delta with her eyes. "We're not in the habit of stealing from our guests. This hotel has been in the hands of a Taylor since the mid-nineteenth century, and we've never had anyone complain."

"Come on," Delta said. "Things go missing in every hotel. You can't vouch for the staff or other hotel guests or even thieves coming in to steal."

"Not from the safe. You heard the sheriff say he believes the bracelet was taken from the jewelry box Mrs. White had us place in the safe."

"Yes, that does reduce the number of viable suspects."

Rosalyn narrowed her eyes. "I can't blame you for feeling a bit of satisfaction now that the sheriff is looking at someone else other than your friend Hazel or her dear little brother. But that satisfaction will soon wash away, believe me. I never liked Finn; I never wanted him for Isabel. And now that I know about his past… I'm going to make sure Isabel breaks it off with him and Finn pays for what he did to us, to our good name."

She leaned closer. "And if I discover that Hazel knew about Finn's financial troubles and she let him come here and go after my sister, I will also make her pay. You can bet on it."

She turned away and walked off in an indignant clatter of her high heels.

Delta swallowed. Hazel had told her that she had taken an extra mortgage on Wanted to help Finn pay off the gambling debts. If Rosalyn found out about that, she'd have her irrefutable proof that Hazel had known about his financial troubles and not spoken up about them. That she had let her brother cozy up to Isabel without warning the Taylors about his past. Rosalyn would be livid and come after Wanted, whatever way she could.

Delta exhaled slowly to regain her bearings. Isabel's arrest hadn't really made anything better. It didn't mean Finn was off the hook for the murder, and Rosalyn's anger would only heat things up for Hazel and the shop.

Great, just great.

She pressed a hand to her forehead. How had the bracelet ended up in Finn's pocket? Had he seen it lying somewhere and picked it up to put it in a safe place? Then find out whose it was later?

But if he had, he would have told the sheriff right away. Hazel had said Finn refused to cooperate in any way, and she didn't understand why. There had to be something else going on.

"Hey." A hand landed on her shoulder. Ray stood beside her. "What did I hear? Did the police take Isabel? What on earth for?"

Delta looked up at him. His usually jovial face was now worried, and his dark eyes searching her expression with serious insistence. Having sensed before that he wanted to keep Isabel out of trouble, she hoped she might get some cooperation from him now that Isabel was in the sheriff's spotlight.

"The police found a gold bracelet on Finn," she said.

"That's probably Isabel's bracelet. She wore it to the party."

Delta recalled having seen a bracelet on Isabel's arm when they had been taking the family portrait. Delta had even drawn it on Isabel's character in her portable murder case file. "But that can't be. If it was Isabel's bracelet, Finn would have said so. And how would Vera White's fingerprints have ended up on it?"

"Vera's prints? On Isabel's bracelet?" Ray tilted his head. "That makes no sense at all."

"No. But if you're right and the bracelet does belong to Isabel, the sheriff's story doesn't hold water. He claims the bracelet was stolen from the jewelry box in the safe. That Isabel took it to give to Finn so he could sell it and pay off his debts."

"Debts? Ridiculous. Finn doesn't need money. I know for a fact that he has been saving every dime he earns here to support his sister's shop. He told me Hazel supported him when he was in college, and he wants to pay her back. I can't see him stealing... I mean, that would risk everything he has here: the job, his relationship with Isabel. And West thinks Isabel would have helped him to steal?" Ray shook his head in bewilderment. "I can't imagine." He fell silent and looked pensive, as if he had suddenly thought of something unpleasant and was considering the repercussions.

Delta put a hand on his arm. "Ray? What's wrong?"

Ray focused on her. "What? Oh, nothing. I have to go to the police station to ask West to show me that bracelet. I'm sure we can easily establish if it is Isabel's. Then he can drop his theft story and let her go."

"I'll come with you." Delta was eager to find out, firsthand, if the bracelet had been Isabel's or not, as it could also exonerate Finn, who, in West's scenario, had been an accomplice in the theft of the bracelet. Hazel would be so upset to discover her brother was under new suspicion. The sooner they could clear it up, the better.

To convince Ray to take her, she offered quickly, "Jonas gave West the party shots he took that night. In the family portraits he took before the party started, Isabel is wearing the bracelet. West can easily establish that it's hers by a look at those photos. We should try and convince him to do it right away."

"He should have done that before he came out here to arrest Isabel in front of the guests," Ray groused. "That man is like a bull in a china shop. Come on. Let's go."

At the police station, they had some convincing to do to get the deputy to call West away from questioning Isabel. But once he had come out to them and heard their story, he did ask the deputy to dig out the memory card with Jonas's photos, and soon they were all watching as he clicked through them. "There, that's it," Ray said. He pointed at the screen. "That's Isabel's bracelet."

The sheriff leaned in, then zoomed in on Isabel's arm to see better. "It could be the same one..." he said begrudgingly.

"You arrested my sister for her fingerprints being on her own bracelet," Ray said. "If Rosalyn were here, she'd threaten you with a lawsuit for damages. I won't...if you just let Isabel go right now."

West shook his head. "I can't do that just yet. I don't understand what Vera White's fingerprints were doing on the bracelet. Your sister's, all right. Her boyfriend's, maybe; after all, the thing was in his pocket. He could have kept it for her or whatever. But the victim's? Combined with the photo of Finn pleading with her..."

Ray sighed. "I don't believe this. What new theory are you coming up with now?"

West gestured with both hands. "Let's not forget that Rosalyn said right after the murder that Finn had had an affair with Vera White. What if Isabel knew about this and asked Vera to end it? To persuade her to do so, she gave her the gold bracelet. When Finn found out, he asked to have it back, but Vera didn't want to give it. Then later that night, Vera turns up dead and the bracelet is found in Finn's pocket."

"You're basing all of that on the fact that Finn spoke with Vera White during the party and the bracelet was found in his pocket afterward?" Ray shook his head. "Thin ice, Sheriff. Very thin ice."

West scoffed, "If Finn is so innocent, why doesn't he want to tell us what the bracelet was doing in his pocket? He isn't cooperating in any way, and I find that very suspicious."

Suddenly he fell silent and stared into the distance, his eyes getting a strange glow. "That's it," he muttered. "That's it. Protecting someone. That makes perfect sense!"

Ray groaned, but Delta kept her eyes on West's expression as he seemed to have hit the theory jackpot.

West banged his fist in the palm of his other hand. "That's it. He's protecting her. Isabel gave her bracelet to Vera. Vera had it in her hand when she died. And then Finn came upon the body, and he took the bracelet away to protect his girlfriend. He slid it into his pocket and he told you to have a look in the bar, meaning to slip away himself and dispose of the bracelet. But he didn't manage it."

Delta had to admit that this sounded almost plausible. Finn had looked furtive when he had met them and said they had to look in the bar. He had been eager to get away.

West continued. "It also fits with what the doctor told me about the dead body. There was a shallow cut on her hand, like something had caught there. The bracelet! I bet if we have it analyzed, there will be minuscule traces of the victim's skin or blood on the bracelet."

He rubbed his hands. "Finally, we're getting somewhere."

"Didn't the doctor say the cut was made *before* the victim died?" Delta asked.

West glared at her, as if he wanted to know how on earth Delta knew about the doctor's findings.

Before he could grill her about it, Delta said quickly, "Even if you can prove that the bracelet was in the dead woman's hand and Finn took it from there, that doesn't mean he killed her. He saw the dead body, recognized the bracelet in her hand, and picked it up to prevent his girlfriend from getting entangled in the murder. He hasn't been cooperating for her sake."

A bit of relief washed through Delta that Finn might have acted the way he had only because he loved Isabel.

West said, "I'll determine that. I need to talk to Isabel

now and see what she knows about the bracelet." He turned away from them.

Ray called after him, "Is there a lawyer present?"

"Yes, your sister made sure one was waiting for us when we arrived."

Ray said to Delta, "I'm staying here to see what's next. I can't imagine Isabel actually being involved in the murder, and I don't want that oaf of a sheriff locking her up."

Delta looked him over. "You never came here when Hazel was being detained. Or to plead for Finn."

Ray averted his eyes. "They're not family."

"Oh yes, like Isabel told me earlier: Taylors stick together." Delta nodded slowly. "It sounds nicer than it is."

"How come?" Ray asked, visibly piqued.

"Finn may have refused to cooperate with the police to protect Isabel because he loves her. But you Taylors only love yourselves. And your good name, the hotel's reputation."

Ray scoffed. "The hotel means nothing to me."

"Then why did you come back home and make Rosalyn feel like you're ready to take over?"

"If that's her conclusion..."

"You enjoy making her worry."

"Rosalyn is always so self-assured. Knows everything. I don't mind her doubting herself for a change. Wondering if Daddy dear won't give the hotel to me." Ray flexed his fingers. "You know how Rosalyn and I used to get along fine. She came to my games, she supported me. Then all of a sudden, it was over. She even acted like playing football was something inferior. She was actually glad my career ended and..." He bit down hard, his jaw tensing.

"Do you know what made her change?" Delta asked.

Ray shook his head. He drew a deep breath, as if he had

to force himself to relax again. "I have no idea. I never asked either. She would just say it's my imagination and nothing had changed between us. But I know."

"Something did happen. Isabel mentioned to me that... Rosalyn hates you for something that happened in the past. Something she blames you for."

Ray stared at her. The color drained from his face. "Isabel said that?"

"Yes. She doesn't know what it is. Just that Rosalyn said to her that...she wouldn't mind seeing you in jail for the murder. That you'd deserve it."

Ray flinched. He stepped back and stuck his hands into his pockets. "I can't imagine she'd say that. Or maybe merely in a moment's anger. She doesn't mean it, you know." His words didn't carry conviction, and he shuffled his feet.

"But you have absolutely no idea what past incident she is referring to?" Delta probed.

Ray shook his head. "Not at all." He studied the floorboards.

Delta wasn't sure whether to believe him or not. Something so serious that another hated you for it couldn't just have slipped your memory, right? How could you not know whether you had done anything so terrible?

Ray turned away from her and sat on a chair that was beside a table holding a few newspapers and old magazines. He pulled out his phone and started to swipe through screens.

Delta hesitated a moment and then went outside. She pulled out her own phone, which she had put on silent mode before going to the hotel, and checked the messages from the Paper Posse.

Rattlesnake Rita reported that she had checked an

assortment of deerlike creatures on the internet and was quite sure now that the animal depicted on the dark-blue station wagon that had picked up Ralph White in Tundish had been a moose. "Not a reindeer or a red deer or anything. A moose. Keep an eye out for such a car and we can figure out more."

Delta typed, "How do you know what Ralph White looks like anyway?"

Calamity Jane responded while Rita was still typing. "The White couples have been all over town. Everyone knows them. They've been to the diner and the shops. The ladies argued over a handbag they both wanted to have. Leah said they almost hit each other over the head with it."

Rita chimed in, "You all type faster than me. Now I don't have to explain anything anymore. But I'm sure it was him. I saw them pretty well at the museum."

"Museum?" Delta asked. "You work there, too?"

"Manning the gift shop."

Calamity Jane explained, "Rita also makes the little mining carts we sell. They look just like the ones they used to have in the mines. They are filled with little stones that shine like gold."

"Just gold paint on pebbles," Rita cut in. "But I love making them. Ralph White bought one for his grandson. He even showed me a picture of the little guy on a pic in his wallet. I had every opportunity to see his face and the way he moved. He's also the better dresser. More stylish. Herb is more of the garish one."

Delta had to smile. But that smile vanished as she typed, "Am at the police station. Isabel Taylor was arrested because her fingerprints are on a bracelet found in Finn's pocket when he was arrested Friday night. The sheriff initially believed the bracelet was Vera White's but when he looked at pictures of the party, he had to admit Isabel had been wearing it when the party began. Now he thinks maybe Vera White had it in her hand when she died."

"But how did Vera White get ahold of it when Isabel was wearing it?" Rattlesnake Rita asked.

Delta typed hurriedly, "I don't know yet. Either way, the sheriff is convinced both Isabel and Finn know more about it than they're willing to admit."

She clicked away from the message screen and called Hazel, who was restocking at Wanted. As soon as her friend answered the phone, she said, "I can't say much, but please be aware that the sheriff has found out about Finn's financial problems. He told Rosalyn, who's livid and determined to find out if this was known to you before Finn came to the hotel."

Hazel groaned.

"Just be careful in case you're contacted with questions about it."

"Wait! Where are you now?"

"Outside the police station."

"Can you meet me at the hotel? I'll go there to tell Rosalyn myself. Offense is the best defense, right? You don't have to be in on the conversation, but I'd like the moral support afterward."

"Sure. We could grab lunch there."

"I doubt I'll have an appetite after my talk with Rosalyn. But hey, why not? See you later then."

Delta lowered the phone, happy that at least Hazel had her fighting spirit back. It was indeed best to tell Rosalyn how things had come about and ask her for her understanding. Having a brother and sister, Rosalyn had to know the feeling of wanting to help out.

Chapter Twelve

While Hazel was in the office with Rosalyn, Delta walked through the lobby, looking at all the old photographs on the walls. As Mrs. Cassidy had pointed out to her earlier, they gave a brilliant impression of the time periods in which they had been taken. The twenties with the tassel dresses and feathered headbands during the party nights. The thirties with families coming into town for the first time. The fifties when outdoor wear became more practical and tennis tournaments were organized. The seventies with giant hairdos and miniskirts.

Circling the room, Delta ended up near the hearth where the family portraits were. She compared them, the faces, how everyone had changed as they grew up.

In the very old ones, where the children were little, Mrs. Taylor was there too. By the time Rosalyn was about twelve, she had disappeared. Delta felt a stab of pain for the three kids looking at her from the silver frame, so suddenly left without a mother. They grew up quickly, Ray turning from a scrawny boy with serious eyes into a muscled young man who seemed to challenge life with his chin up.

In a photo from more recent years, Rosalyn had a young man by her side, leaning into him with a radiating smile. He was also in the next portrait, but after that he was gone. Rosalyn's expression had become emotionless, her posture tight. This was the Rosalyn Delta had come to know in the past few days.

But who was the man? Another loss in her life? A broken

relationship? Delta heard footfalls and turned around, hoping it might be Hazel coming to fetch her for lunch. But it was Jonas, all dressed in dark green, with binoculars dangling on his chest. "I'm taking a group up to the birding hut," he said. "Why don't you come along? If you have the time."

"I'd love to, but I promised Hazel we'd have lunch together. She's had a rough week." Delta took a deep breath. She didn't know if it was smart to tell him, but she needed to talk to someone about it. Someone other than Hazel, who was worried enough as it was. "There was a threatening note left at the cottage Saturday afternoon. Hazel found it just when she had been released."

"You didn't mention that when we were boating."

Delta shrugged. "You started talking about the envelope in the jewelry box revealing that Vera wanted a divorce, and I just forgot. But Hazel is nervous about it. She doesn't say so, but I can tell." She held his gaze. "Do you think it's serious or some...prank?"

"That depends. Any clues as to who might have written it?"

"No. It was a standard envelope, the kind you can buy everywhere. The paper was printer paper, like you use at home. Then the letters had been cut out of newspapers or magazines, like a ransom note in a movie."

"Cut out letters? How old-fashioned." Jonas grimaced.

"But smart. A typewriter or printer might be traced. I took it to the police, but the sheriff looked at me like he figured I had put it together myself to distract him from the murder case."

"You can't do a lot with an anonymous threat," Jonas said, fingering the binoculars. "Still, why would someone want to threaten Hazel? What did it say anyway?"

Delta grimaced as she repeated the offensive words. "Stop poking your nose where it doesn't belong, or you'll join Vera White"

Jonas narrowed his eyes. "So it wasn't directed at Hazel, but at you. *You* are poking your nose where it doesn't belong, going around asking people questions. Someone must have seen you talking to people or..."

"Talking to the press? I told you that both father and son LeDuc were at the shop on Saturday morning. But I told them nothing. They didn't come back, so they must have figured they wouldn't get anything from me. If they've been writing about the case, it wasn't on my authority."

"Who would be nervous about your involvement?" Jonas mused.

A grandfather clock on the far wall struck one, and Jonas jerked upright. "I have to go meet my group."

"OK. Oh, one more thing. I'll walk with you." Delta fell into step with him on his way outside. "Do you know who owns a dark-blue station wagon with a bumper sticker that has a moose on it? Or something that looks like a moose?"

Inwardly, she apologized to Rattlesnake Rita for doubting her identification of the antler-bearing animal, but not everyone could know everything about wildlife, right?

"Sure," Jonas said. They were outside now, him ready to turn left in the direction of the parking lot. A young man in riding clothes came across the lot on a gorgeous chestnut. With a mere click of the tongue, he coaxed the animal from a walk into a trot. Muscle rippled under the horse's smooth skin as he passed Jonas and Delta, his hoofbeats making the ground tremble.

"I'd like to go riding sometime," Delta said with a

longing sigh. "Haven't done it since I was a kid. My best friend at Gran's had a pony."

Jonas laughed softly. "Riding a pony in a meadow is a bit different from riding a horse out in the open here. The Taylors aren't likely to lend their horses to inexperienced riders."

Before Delta could protest against his judgment of her riding skills, Jonas added, "But I know a few people who have horses, so if you're serious about riding, I can take you there and we can see how well you do. Now, about that station wagon with the animal sticker on the back..." Jonas gestured across the parking lot. "I've seen it here in the lot a couple of times."

"Could it belong to a guest?" Delta asked with a sense of deflation, as Ralph White going out with another hotel guest probably had no bearing on the murder case at all.

"Then it's a guest who's practically living here," Jonas retorted. "I saw it for the first time maybe six weeks ago? I don't know the exact date, but I do remember the trees weren't turning color yet."

He smiled half-involuntarily. "As a police officer, even a former one, you're always paying closer attention to your surroundings than average people do. Gotta run now. Talk to you later. And if you get more threats, let me know. Be careful."

With a wave to underline the latter words, Jonas rushed off.

Delta looked around the parking lot. There were only a few cars there now, and none of them were dark blue. But it was interesting that it might belong to someone who stayed here.

Or worked here? That would explain why he was here often, over a longer period of time.

Delta turned back inside, seeing the door into the office open and Hazel come out with Rosalyn. Hazel said, "I hope that it has cleared up a few things."

"I never was a fan of the relationship," Rosalyn said in a prim tone. "And this isn't making it better. But I suppose Isabel can do what she wants. As soon as she hears he lied to protect her, she'll think it's romantic and fall into his arms again."

She huffed. Then she looked Hazel straight in the eye and asked, "Are you 100 percent sure your brother isn't the killer?"

"Yes," Hazel said without flinching. "I know Finn. He's not violent."

"Not even when he's desperate?" Rosalyn tilted her head. "People are different under pressure."

You should know, Delta wanted to say as Rosalyn's reddish face and hurried manners on the night of the murder came back to her, but after Hazel had just gone out of her way to build bridges, Delta could hardly barge in and ruin it again for her friend.

The sensation that Rosalyn was a little too eager to keep the focus on Finn lingered uncomfortably in the back of her mind. However, there was nothing to connect Rosalyn to the crime. No fingerprints, no witness statement. Nothing.

Delta wished she had asked Jonas if he had noticed anything odd about Rosalyn that evening. Like he had said, former policemen did notice more than average people, and perhaps an observation he had made could shed light on it.

Then again, if he had noticed anything important, he would have mentioned it himself, she supposed.

Hazel shook Rosalyn's hand again, saying she hoped

things were cleared up now, and then waved Delta along to the doors leading onto the terrace.

Taking a table far away from the building, Hazel let herself down onto the chair with a sigh. "I did my best to smooth things over, but it was awkward. I would be mad in her place. You don't want someone with…well, an issue in your business. Or getting close to your sister." She wrung her hands. "Finn should never have started working here."

"But he did," Delta said briskly, "and we have to make the best of it now. Come on, have a look at the menu and decide what you'd like. I could have gone bird watching with Jonas, but I said no to have this lunch with you, so I intend to enjoy it. Maybe the fall salad with beets, cheese, and walnuts?"

Hazel picked up the leather-bound menu with gold leaves emblazoned on the front. "Jonas asked you out?" she queried casually, leafing through the pages.

Delta gave her a sharp look "Just bird watching with a group he was taking. It wasn't going out as in…" She felt a flush coming up. Jonas had also asked her to go riding together. Did he want to spend more time with her? Or was he just being nice to a new arrival in town? "I guess he just wants to show me around."

"Sure. Nice. Too bad you said no." Hazel leaned over the menu. "I think I'll have freshly squeezed orange juice to begin with. How about you?"

"Iced tea for me."

The waiter came, and they ordered their drinks and asked for a few more minutes to make their choices for the meal. Hazel flipped from one page to the next and back. "I think that this leaf-peeping cheese platter sounds delicious.

Brie, Manchego, goat's cheese, and several chutneys, nuts and grapes..."

"I'll have the peppered beef wrap. That will have a nice strong flavor I can then douse with my iced tea."

They put the menus away and let their gaze wander the view of the lake. Bright canoes shot across the water as the canoers raced each other.

"The water seems greener today," Delta observed. "I'm always surprised how water changes depending on the weather. It can be bright blue or almost inky black. I should draw this." She reached into her bag and extracted her sketchbook and pencils. "I could do a design for wrapping paper with outdoor activities on it. Canoeing, skydiving, skiing, and snowboarding. What do you think?"

"I hope Finn and Isabel can make it work despite this trouble," Hazel said, nervously fidgeting with the laces that tied her cardigan. She had obviously not been listening at all to what Delta was saying.

Delta glanced at her. "I thought you considered them a bad match. Isabel the career woman, Finn the outdoor man. I had the impression that if they broke up, you wouldn't mind."

"Not personally, no, but...Finn was in a relationship before, in college, and when it ended, he was really down for weeks. Months even, if I remember correctly. I don't want him to go through that again."

The waiter brought their drinks and took their orders, retreating on his soft soles. The iced tea came with lemon slices in it and a long spoon with a decorated handle depicting the mountain view across the lake.

Between sips, Delta sketched the vivid greens of water, the yellow of canoes on it, the reddish trees, and the dark green of pine dotting it. As always, her mind calmed down as she worked, transferring the image in front of her to paper. After all those years of practice, much of it was done semiautomatically without her having to make conscious decisions about lines, perspective. She didn't have to stop constantly to see if it was right, but followed her gut, adding colors and shapes in quick succession.

Hazel leaned across the table with a grin. "I have a surprise for you. We're going to an antique fair tonight."

"Really?"

"A Western antique fair. I want you to help me buy some stuff for Wanted to give it even more of an authentic atmosphere. And if you see something nice for the cottage, we can get it. You brought so few things. You should make it more your own, especially since you told me you have no intention of moving on right away. I've been to this fair before, and they have amazing bargains."

Delta started to reply, when she heard laughter from below. Leaning over the terrace's railing, she spotted a woman and a man walking on the path that came up from the lake. The woman leaned over to the man and laughed again, touching his arm with a certain familiarity.

Her simple sundress and the hat she wore made it difficult for Delta to place her until she could clearly see her face. With a shock, she realized that it was Amanda White.

There was no trace of the sadness over her sister-in-law's death that had been so prominent the day before. In fact, Amanda looked perfectly carefree, as though she were having a splendid time rather than being embroiled in a murder case.

"Who's that man?" Hazel asked in a whisper.

Delta shrugged. "I don't know." She let her pencil hover

over the paper and observed the couple as they approached. Her mind was working overtime. Was Amanda White seeing someone without her husband knowing about it? Had Vera found out and threatened to tell? Had Amanda lashed out to silence her? Not just with a blow to the face but with something more...permanent?

Still, she was walking here in full view of the people on the terrace, apparently not caring who saw her with her companion. That made no sense if you assumed the man in question was indeed a secret lover.

Delta called out, "Mrs. White!" She waved her sketchbook in the air. "Delightful day for boating."

She had no idea if Amanda had been boating, but since she was walking back from the lake, it was a good guess.

Amanda looked up at them and waved. "Excellent," she called back. "Are you drawing?"

"Yes. Do you want to see? Why don't you join us for lunch? Both of you?"

Amanda seemed to hesitate. The man said something to her. She laughed and nodded. "We're coming!"

As the pair disappeared from their view, Hazel said, "How odd to be enjoying yourself while..."

"Well, if we can trust Mrs. Cassidy's judgment, Amanda and Vera didn't like each other much. Apparently, Amanda doesn't feel the need to constantly play the grieving friend she never was. I wonder who that guy is. Guess we'll find out in a moment." Delta barely got the last sentence out of her mouth before the two in question appeared on the terrace and came over to their table.

Delta rose to her feet, extending her free hand. "Delta Douglas, pleased to meet you."

The man took and shook it. "Fred Halliday. Boating

instructor." He wore a red shirt and beige pants, spotless white sneakers, and a rather ostentatious gold watch. Delta wondered if it was real or gold-plated. Would a boating instructor make enough to afford an expensive watch?

Halliday also shook Hazel's hand. "If you ever want some lessons on how to sail or row or paddle, I'm your man."

"He's really good," Amanda said. "This was just my second lesson, but I managed to steer the boat all by myself." She looked at Halliday. "I did all right, didn't I?"

"Better than all right." He winked at her, then gestured at a chair. "Do you want to sit here?"

"Please." She sat down, and he pushed the chair in place before seating himself. "You have already ordered?" He nodded at their drinks. "What are you having, Mandy?"

Amanda half closed her eyes. "White wine. Chilled."

"Great idea, I'll join you. And what to eat?" Halliday studied the menu. "Chicken is filled with protein. Very healthy."

"I'll have whatever you're having." Amanda smiled leisurely.

Delta didn't want to stare and focused on her drawing again. Maybe she was reading too much into a few words, a look? Surely a married woman wasn't overtly flirting with her boating instructor?

Hazel and Delta's orders were served, and they began to eat while Halliday told them about the charms of the lake in all seasons. Amanda interrupted him every now and then with a question, nestled into her chair as if she never wanted to leave again. The sun sparkled in a ring with countless small diamonds she wore on her left hand. The gemstones built a flower in two tiers, with emeralds forming the leaves. Delta had never seen anything quite like it.

She was just toasting Halliday with the chilled white wine the server brought when her husband charged up to their table. "There you are," he said brusquely. "Come along."

"Ralph!" Amanda looked mortified. "We've just started lunch. I'll come up later."

"You're coming right now." Ralph's broad neck seemed to widen as he pulled up his shoulders. "It's not right sitting here toasting like it's some happy occasion. Herb just lost his wife. *Again.*"

"I do have to eat."

"You needn't make such a spectacle of it. Come along."

Halliday said, "Just let the lady eat her lunch."

"I don't want to hear anything out of you." Ralph pointed a finger at Fred as if wanting to stab right through him.

His hand swooped down and arrested his wife's shoulder. "You're coming with me, right now." He tried to pull her to her feet.

"Ralph." A red flush mottled Amanda's face. "Everyone is looking at us."

"That wouldn't have happened if you had done as you were told right away. Now move it."

Amanda stood up and went ahead of her husband, who shepherded her with his arms wide, as if driving geese inside.

Halliday cleared his throat.

Hazel gave him a wide-eyed look. "That man has a nasty temper."

"Always did have a strong opinion about everything," Halliday admitted. "He never liked me and Mandy being friends."

"Oh, you know each other? I had the impression you had just met here at the hotel."

"No, we were at high school together. I took Mandy to

the prom, but Ralph put a ring on her finger. He always did know how to sweep in for the kill."

Delta frowned at the word choice. "And you just ran into each other here?"

"Yes. Mandy told me that it had been her sister-in-law's idea to come to Tundish. She had no idea I was working here now. A wonderful surprise."

"Not to her husband," Hazel said. She nodded at Amanda's wine glass abandoned on the table.

"Well, can't let good wine go to waste," Halliday said and pulled the glass toward him. "Cheers."

Within the next fifteen minutes, he managed to drink Amanda's wine and his own, while also polishing off both chicken dishes, which were served by a waiter who seemed surprised by the sudden empty spot at their table.

Delta said, "You have a healthy appetite, Mr. Halliday."

"Being outdoors all the time does that to you. Please call me Fred." He scraped the last bits of chicken together with his fork. "Poor Mandy. She doesn't seem to be very happy."

"That's logical, considering her sister-in-law was murdered last Friday. Were you at the party?"

Fred laughed. "The Taylors don't invite their employees to their parties."

It wasn't really an answer to her question, Delta noted.

"Finn was at the party," Hazel said.

"Yes, but he managed to snare the boss's daughter." Fred clicked his tongue. "Pretty Isabel never looked my way."

Which isn't odd, considering he's old enough to be her father, Delta thought.

"So you missed the murder?" Delta glanced at him. "How did you find out about it then?"

"I wasn't at the party, but I did find out soon enough." Fred pointed at the lake. "I was out boating."

"In the dark?"

"There was moonlight."

Delta tilted her head. She had seen a boat out on the water when she had walked Nugget and Spud. She had assumed it was a fisherman, but what if it had been Fred? She couldn't imagine him having boated for hours, so at some point he could have come up to the hotel. Had he met up with Amanda, who was in an emotional state after her altercation with Vera?

Fred was just saying, "I came up, and I saw the police were at the hotel. I asked the clerk what was up, and he told me. He had even seen the dead body. Stabbed with an ice pick." Fred grimaced. "Must have been a pretty gruesome sight."

"I bet the ice pick was from the bar," Delta mused. "So the killer didn't bring a weapon but picked one up on the spot. Not premeditated." She kept her eyes on Fred to see how he took this suggestion. If he had lied about coming up to the hotel after the murder, he could have been there before it had happened. A weapon available on the spot would also have been available to him.

"Self-defense, even?" Fred asked. "I heard she was a mean little cat."

"Did Mrs. White tell you that? I mean, as you were old high school friends, she might have chosen you to confide in."

"She didn't have to. I saw the way they were around each other. Watching and waiting. Who would be first to..." He fell silent and played with the wine glass.

"Would be first to what?" Delta asked.

Fred laughed and waved his hand. "Make a stingy remark or buy a new thing. You know how women are among each other."

Delta had the distinct impression he had meant something else.

"Did Mrs. White tell you anything while you were boating that can throw light on the murder?" Hazel asked. She added, after a few moments, "My brother, Finn, has been accused, you know, and I want to help him."

Fred nodded. "Of course, of course. I don't know Finn well, but he certainly doesn't seem to be the violent type. Too bad he was arrested."

"Did Mrs. White tell you anything?" Delta pressed. She had the impression Fred Halliday was an expert in saying a lot but revealing very little.

Fred shrugged. "No, I can't say she talked much about her sister-in-law. Or her life at home. I guess she wanted to be away from it all."

"That's understandable," Delta said, although she wasn't sure she believed him. Wouldn't Amanda have dropped something about her relationship with her sister-in-law? Fred could also have seen they differed like day and night. Wouldn't he have asked about it, how she dealt with it?

Did he know something he wasn't about to tell because he liked Amanda?

"That was delicious." Hazel pushed her plate away.

"I'd better get going," Fred said. He jumped to his feet.

The waiter came over to their table at once. "Do you want to pay separately or together?"

Fred said, "You can put the two chickens and the two white wines on Mr. Ralph White's bill." He winked at Delta and then left with a cheerful goodbye.

"He has got some nerve," Hazel said after the waiter had left to get their bill.

Delta stared at the empty plates. "He's a strong man too. He could kill a woman with an ice pick." She turned to the pages in her sketchbook that held the notes about the murder and added Fred Halliday, connecting him to Amanda with a note: *friends in college, met again at the Lodge.*

Her gaze lingered on the notes she had made about Amanda after the high tea with her: *Introduced Vera to Herb* and *Seemed upset when altercation in garden was mentioned and Mrs. C bluffed about a distinctive dress.*

Where Amanda had earlier been almost invisible, she now seemed to take on more relevance in the investigation. How close was she with Halliday? And…had Halliday been at the hotel before the murder?

Delta wrote the latter question on a yellow note she placed beside Halliday.

Hazel was following everything she did with interest. "Why would Halliday want to kill Vera White?" she asked softly.

"No idea, but he didn't seem to like her while also claiming Amanda had told him almost nothing about her. Isn't that odd?" Delta leaned back with a sigh. "And I should have asked him if he knew who owns the dark-blue station wagon with the moose on the back. Jonas thinks he saw it before, here in the hotel parking lot. Maybe it belongs to someone on the staff?"

The waiter brought the bill, and Hazel paid. She waved off Delta's offer to pay her share back. "You're doing so much for me, let me treat you."

They sat for a few more minutes, looking at the lake and the canoes cutting across the water. The tranquility of the place soothed the anguished questions in Delta's mind. Going to an antique fair with Hazel would just be like the old days in college, when they had hunted for bargains to decorate their rooms or give to friends. They had always hoped for that one elusive find that would turn out to be worth a fortune. A vase or painting that didn't look special at first but proved to be a diamond in the rough. So far, it hadn't happened. But it was nice to speculate about it. Maybe tonight…

The wind seemed to carry the cold off the snowcapped mountain peaks in the distance. Delta focused on its touch on her face and felt her breathing become deeper. Her eyelids turned heavy, and she was close to falling asleep. What a wonderful place to sit and just let time tick away.

Before Hazel and Delta left the Lodge to get back to Wanted, Delta stopped at the reception desk. "Excuse me, do you happen to have a copy of the *Tundish Trader* here? Most hotels offer a newspaper to their guests."

The clerk turned red. "We normally do have a copy, but, uh…not today. I'm sorry. Excuse me." He got up and hurried into the back.

Hazel stared after him. "He seemed eager to get away from us."

"Well, the *Trader*'s front page is probably full of news about the murder, and as it happened here, it would be awkward to have it lying here with a splashy headline or something. His response suggests the *Trader* might carry something of interest. Can we buy it in town?"

"Sure, at the grocer's or the diner. But what do you

expect to find in it? The sheriff won't have told the media much about the case. Whatever the paper has must be hearsay or, even worse, speculation."

"Still, speculation can be very interesting. Suppose we ask ourselves, for a change, not who does the sheriff suspect, but who does the town suspect? And foremost, why."

Hazel seemed unconvinced. "You know that the editor of the *Trader* is in a fierce competition with his son. They probably think that whoever solves the murder first is the grand winner."

"All the better. They'll work hard to unearth something. Anything." Delta nodded in satisfaction as she got into the car. "Into town then."

Once they were in the heart of downtown Tundish, while Hazel went to Wanted, Delta crossed the street to Mine Forever. The large sign on top of the building was adorned with old mattocks and sieves that had rusted under the influence of the Montana seasons. The door handle looked like a clump of gold, sparkly with glitter paint. Delta touched it with a finger to see if it stained, then had to laugh at her own reluctance. She was worried about Mr. LeDuc Sr. lurking somewhere inside, as it had proven to be his breakfast spot the other day, and he might be a frequent diner. But spying through the door's glass pane, she just saw a lot of ladies milling about. As she entered, the noise of female voices and laughter hit her like a hurricane.

A waitress, decked out in a Stetson and a suede jacket with fringes, waved at her from behind the counter. "Take any table you like. Coffee and cakes coming up."

Delta elbowed her way to the counter anyway. "I'm not with the group," she said, gesturing at the women. "I guess they're here for the museum?" Her eye fell to the *Tundish Trader*, put ready on the counter. The headline seemed to say something about "missing and why?" What was that about?

The waitress was just explaining. "The huge turnout is for the leaf-peeping photo contest. They're all amateur photographers." She leaned over the counter. On her jacket was a name tag reading Terry. "Beats me why we need eleven more shots of gold trees along the lake. But I'm not complaining about the business it brings."

"Ah, the *Trader*," Delta said. "Can I have a quick look at it?"

"That's what it's there for. Coffee?"

Delta didn't really want any after her large lunch but realized it would be rude not to buy something and nodded. "Espresso, please."

"Coming up." Terry turned away to one of the three hyper-modern coffee machines lined up along the wall. Delta picked up the newspaper that was already worn from being leafed through by countless customers. On the front page was a photo, a family portrait of the Taylors, with the headline: *Who's missing here and why?*

Delta thought for a moment that it was the most recent portrait, taken on the night of the party and the murder, and wondered how on earth the newspaper editor had managed to lay hands on it, since Jonas's memory card was with the police. But then she realized it was an earlier portrait.

And was that blur on the left-hand side the not-quite-removed silver edge of a frame? Had the clever editor used his phone to snap a pic of a photo standing on the mantelpiece at the Lodge?

"That's old news," Terry said in a disparaging tone, pushing the espresso across the counter.

At once, the invigorating scent rose into Delta's nose.

Terry snorted. "We all know who's missing in the picture. Rosalyn's fiancé. And he isn't coming back either."

Delta looked at her. "Who was her fiancé? Did he leave a long time ago?"

"Two years, I think. It was quite abrupt. He had gone to Europe for the company he worked for. He was an engineer, I think. Or an architect. He never showed his face here, he considered himself too good for that. We only saw his Jaguar breeze through town. Seemed he was always flying across the globe for work. France it was that time he ended it with Rosalyn. She had asked him to find some new wines to serve at the Lodge. From the Rhone valley, or something? I don't know all those foreign places. Rosalyn even planned to join him there for the last few days of his stay. But he wrote her a letter out of the blue, ending their relationship."

"A letter?" Delta said. "He didn't tell her face-to-face or call her to break up with her?"

"No, it was a letter all right. The mailman noticed because it had a French stamp and all. He collects stamps, so he even asked Rosalyn if he could have it. But you can imagine that after her reading what it said, she was in no mood to think about stamps."

"I see." Delta took a sip of the espresso. The strong taste rolled across her tongue. "Delicious."

"We use the best ground beans around," Terry said with a proud grin. "People don't expect it in a small town like this. But we've won prizes with our coffee." She gestured over her shoulder to where some ribbons and certificates sat on the wall.

Delta nodded. "Impressive." She tapped her finger on the newspaper photograph. "Had Rosalyn and her fiancé been together long?"

"About a year, I think. The wedding date was set and all. She had already ordered her dress. There was going to be a big party at the Lodge with all of her friends from college coming over. It was quite the blow to her when it ended." Terry tutted. "I think it's tasteless of the *Trader* to bring it all up again. It can't have anything to do with the murder."

"Do you have any idea who committed the murder?" Delta asked. It was a blunt question, but it might bring something.

Terry laughed, brushing back her auburn curls. "I couldn't say. I hardly knew the victim."

"I thought the Whites have been all over town? That they even ate here."

"That may be true, but when it's busy, I don't have time to talk to the guests. I did see them, and I remember she was wearing a really fancy ring with a lot of little diamonds forming a flower and emeralds for leaves. It twinkled whenever she moved her hand."

"No, that's her sister-in-law, Amanda, I think. She was just wearing that ring when I saw her at the Lodge for lunch."

"It was the petite woman with the blond hair," Terry said with a determined nod. "She had these killer lashes. I wanted to ask her where she got them, but my boss doesn't take kindly to us asking guests such things, you know. Her sister-in-law is the older one, right? I'm sure she didn't have the diamond ring. I remember thinking her husband was probably too stingy to buy it for her. Didn't strike me as the generous type at all."

Considering Ralph's behavior when he had spotted his wife having a good time with Halliday, Delta had to admit Terry was probably right. Not generous, even if it was also understandable, as there had just been a death in their family.

But the ring itself posed the most interesting revelation. If the ring had been Vera's, then why was Amanda now wearing her dead sister-in-law's jewelry? How odd.

Terry excused herself, as she had to pour coffee for the photographers, and Delta thanked her, paid for the espresso, and took her leave.

Crossing the street to Wanted, she mused about the fiancé who had suddenly broken it off with Rosalyn from abroad. Why then? Had he been a coward who had waited for a chance to end it while he was far away so Rosalyn couldn't confront him?

Or was there more to it?

Just from studying the photographs at the Lodge, Delta had gotten the idea that Rosalyn had been extremely happy when she had been engaged and had become bitter and cold after it had ended. Was this the thing from the past she blamed Ray for? But why would Ray have had anything to do with her broken engagement?

Back at Wanted, Delta found Hazel demonstrating some calligraphy pens to a woman and her daughter. She had spread a large sheet of paper across the counter and used the different pens to show how the lettering turned out thicker or thinner and what different tips one might insert to reach yet another effect. Delta made a mental note to ask Hazel to go through this with her as well, to ensure that if she had to sell them to customers, she'd know what she was talking about.

Delta waved in passing and disappeared into the back

room. She pulled out her phone and got online, searching for a history of Ray Taylor, football star. It wasn't hard to find an overview of his career. *Two years ago…*

Delta stared at the information for the summer in question. Ray had been in training camp in Europe. In France, to be exact. So Ray had been around when Rosalyn's fiancé had decided he didn't want to go on with her. Was that why Rosalyn believed Ray had had something to do with it? It did seem like a curious coincidence.

But why would Ray want his sister's engagement to end? Just spite? Ray had said that, at the time, they were rather close, with Rosalyn coming to see games and cheering for him, acting like his biggest fan. Why would Ray suddenly do something to hurt her?

Delta lowered the phone. Of course, the thing from the past that Rosalyn blamed Ray for could be something else altogether. Still, she pulled up her portable case file and drew a male figure beside Rosalyn. She dug up the role of washi tape she also carried in her bag and connected Rosalyn and the man, writing on the tape *Why did it end?*

She connected the man to Ray as well, writing *both in France at the time of the breach.*

She put her sketchbook and the phone away and went into the store, where a newly arrived customer was studying the offer of wrapping paper with a look of utter concentration on her face. She explained to Delta that she had to wrap presents to make up five gift baskets they were raffling off for a dog rescue, and she hoped they had something appropriate, with dogs, but nothing too expensive. "There are nine presents in each basket, so I'd need to wrap forty-five in all."

"But you might not have to wrap every item in the basket. It could be nice to have people see what some of the items are. Then you can wrap others in this paper with dogs." Delta pulled out a roll of wrapping paper decorated with little dachshunds chasing each other. "There's a lot of paper on each roll." She checked the measurements on the label. "I think if you have an idea how large the presents will be, we could calculate exactly how much you'd need. You could also decide on plain wrapping paper and use a section of this with the dogs to wrap around a part of the present. Like this." She took the woman to a corner where they had a selection of wrapped-up presents to demonstrate the possibilities.

"Oh, that's nice. And I love those labels."

"You could put them on the baskets and customize for the winners. Or merely thank them for participating in the raffle, on behalf of the dogs. Add a paw print or something by way of signature? We have paw print stamps." Delta pointed to the display table with the pumpkins where she had put a selection of rubber stamps.

"That sounds lovely. You have such good ideas."

"Since you're buying this for a charitable event, we can also give you a discount." Delta hadn't discussed this with Hazel, but it seemed like a good idea.

The woman clapped her hands together. "Then we will also mention you on our list of sponsors of the raffle. We have a local news station coming over to produce a short segment about the raffle, so it would also mean a bit of publicity for you."

"Wonderful," Delta said. Finally, a bit of positive publicity to boost the shop's image and Hazel's mood. Tonight, they'd unwind and have fun at the antique fair, not mentioning a word about murder. Then in the morning, she'd contact Jonas and ask him if he had anything new to add to the puzzle pieces she was collecting in the back of her sketchbook. The images of the people involved were getting clearer and clearer, and she knew she'd just have to keep going until she found the center piece that would suddenly make her see the full picture.

Chapter Thirteen

"There it is!" Hazel pointed enthusiastically through the windshield at the large building up ahead. A sign read *Western Antiques, every Monday 7–11 p.m. Entry free.*

Delta couldn't help grinning at the prospect of a relaxed night out antique hunting. Hazel was a master of negotiation and had often persuaded a seller to give her something she really wanted for much less than the asking price. As Delta parked the car, excitement flooded her veins, and she guessed the gold miners of old must have felt that exact same way.

They walked to the entrance, which had a giant cowboy hat hung over it, the rim lit with blue and red flashing lights. Inside, country music blasted from speakers, and to their right stood a bar where cowgirls served beer and wine.

Delta tapped her foot to the rhythm of the lead guitar while Hazel studied the floor plan to see which booths she wanted to visit first.

Hazel squeezed Delta's arm. "This is so much fun. I haven't been here in ages. I guess it's different when you're on your own. Just not as exciting."

"Couldn't Finn have taken you some time?"

"He doesn't like 'old junk' as he calls it."

"But he does know you like it. He could have done it for you." Delta wanted to add that a relationship shouldn't be a one-way street, but realized her friend wanted to have a good time, not be reminded of her tenuous bond with her brother. So, she put an arm around Hazel's shoulders and ushered her into the main room where the booths were.

Some vendors were selling cowboy hats and boots, crackled pairs with old, rusty spurs on them. Others had silver candlesticks with running horses and bulls worked into the patterns or entire candelabra of bulls' horns to hang from the ceiling.

One seller had brought in a mechanic bull, and potential buyers were testing it, hanging on for dear life as it bucked and counting the seconds until they were thrown off.

"Might be a nice addition to Wanted," Delta said to Hazel with a wink.

Hazel rolled her eyes. "I was thinking more about some old books or maps of the gold fields. And the extras for the cottage are all up to you. How would you like to put your own stamp on the place?"

Delta had already made up her mind about this. "I think I'd like a sheepskin to throw in front of the fireplace or across the sofa for when it gets colder at night. Oh, and if you want books, how about adding some book ends with a western vibe? Maybe a running horse or a sheriff's figure?"

"Have you seen any like that?"

"Not yet, but we're just starting out."

They wandered from booth to booth, picking up some handblown glass ornaments for the porch and a small side table with a tree silhouette burned into the surface. Delta could already picture it beside the sofa, holding a tray with scented candles or, when Christmas approached, a nice piece of evergreen with glittery baubles, cinnamon, and red ribbons worked into it.

Then Hazel ran ahead to a booth. "Look! What a great clock."

She pointed at a wooden-encased model with a painted clock face depicting horses and riders.

"Real 1830s," the seller assured them.

Hazel pulled up her phone and snapped a shot of the clock, sending it off right away. "I have a friend," she explained to the seller, "who is really good with these things."

The seller looked a little hurt, as if his expertise were being questioned, but Hazel studied the clock closer and asked if it still worked.

"Not at the moment, but you can have it repaired."

Delta was doubtful and tapped Hazel's foot with her own, their old signal of *let's forget about this one and move on.*

But Hazel stood her ground, checking the message that came in on her phone. "My friend says it won't be 1830s, but more likely 1870s."

"That's still nineteenth century." The seller leaned back on his heels, jutting his chin up. "I'm not going to lower the price."

"What do you want for it?"

"One hundred bucks."

Hazel looked appalled. "And then we have to have it repaired as well?"

"Maybe that expert friend of yours can do it for free."

Hazel took Delta's arm. "Let's move on." She added in a whisper, "Maybe he'll change his mind and come after us."

"You really want that clock? I think it's rather tacky. And it doesn't even tell time."

"Not yet, but I can find someone to fix it." Hazel glanced over her shoulder. "Looks like he isn't following. Too bad." She suddenly grinned at Delta. "This is just like old times."

Delta returned her grin. Arm in arm, they strolled past booths and listened to people haggling over a few dollars' discount.

Hazel dove into stacks of old books and managed to dig

out a few big, impressive-looking tomes bound in leather to put on the shelf in Wanted. She also found an old map. "It's a bit torn at the edges, but perfect to put a glass slab across and put it on the counter so buyers can look at it while I wrap their presents for them. See, this is a supposed gold field."

Delta leaned over and followed Hazel's guiding finger. "Fascinating. Does every cross represent a stash?"

"Or a place where they've already dug and didn't find anything?" Hazel had to laugh.

Suddenly Delta thought she heard a familiar voice. Turning her head, she saw Fred Halliday in a bomber jacket, black pants, and shiny leather shoes that shouted *handmade*. To the lady by his side, he pointed out a hope chest with elaborate woodcarving on the lid.

Delta arrested Hazel's arm and nodded in the direction of the eager boating instructor. "Seems he doesn't mind spending his night off entertaining hotel guests."

"How do you know that woman is a hotel guest?" Hazel asked in a whisper.

"I think I saw her at the high tea yesterday. With her husband. There was this man drumming his fingers on the table as if he couldn't stand to be at the tea for another minute. I only glanced at his wife, but she was a platinum blond and wore rather long, conspicuous earrings. The same ones she's wearing now."

"Oh. If Halliday is friendly with all the ladies at the hotel, maybe it's not so strange for him to be close to Amanda White."

Maybe he isn't involved in the murder either, Delta added to herself. Perhaps the boating instructor just enjoyed female company and adoration? That woman was smiling up at him like a sixteen-year-old with her first crush.

Hazel paid for the map and the books. The seller put

protective bubble wrap around them. Hazel said to Delta, "Let's call it quits and have a snack. I saw a chalkboard advertising pumpkin soup when we came in."

"Just what I need after all this ambling about," Delta agreed.

A few minutes later, they were at a table surrounded by their purchases, warming their hands on the bowls of pumpkin soup. Between them on the table was a plate of fresh bread with small bowls of butter and toasted bacon beside it. A tea light in an orange holder spread a warm glow, and the hum of voices and laughter around them increased the coziness.

Delta lifted her spoon in a toasting gesture. "To our enterprise and our friendship."

Hazel smiled. "To us."

The repeated beeping of an alarm clock dragged Delta from an enticing scene where she was accepting an award for having made the best photo in the leaf-peeping contest. In reality, she was lying on her stomach, facedown in her pillow, not quite ready for another day. Her muscles were sore, and she dug through her memory for a reason why.

Oh yes. After they had come home from the antique fair, they had spent time going through old stuff in Hazel's attic, as Hazel had been certain she had a glass slab somewhere that would fit perfectly across the old map they had bought for Wanted.

But no matter how many unpacked cardboard boxes they had moved around, they hadn't been able to find anything close to a glass slab. Before they knew it, it was after midnight.

Delta groaned and rolled onto her back. A hot shower

would be bliss. While she let the water do its restorative work, she already heard sounds from the kitchen. Hazel was up and about, fixing them breakfast. Delta's stomach growled, and she imagined hot toast with scrambled eggs, fresh coffee, and a yogurt with banana and figs to top it off. Hadn't Hazel mentioned she had coconut flakes in the house? Those would be great on top of the fruit yogurt.

But just as Delta ran downstairs, Hazel came out of the kitchen. Her face was pale, and she was clutching her phone in one hand. "Mrs. Cassidy just called. There's a problem at Wanted."

"What?" Delta asked, bewildered. "How do you mean?"

"Someone vandalized the shop last night. We have to get over there now." Hazel was already at the door.

But Delta grabbed her arm. "Did you turn off the stove? Otherwise, the next call we get will be about our cottage having burned to the ground."

Hazel sighed. "You're so right. Could you do it? I'm just shaking in my boots."

"I can imagine. Wait a sec." Delta breezed into the kitchen and turned off the stove and the coffeemaker.

After a quick look around to ensure everything was in order, she grabbed two bananas from the fruit bowl and went back to Hazel. "Here." She handed her a banana. "You eat something. I'll drive."

As they came into town, a group of people had gathered on the sidewalk outside the shop. A deputy was just unrolling the crime scene tape.

"What on earth happened?" Hazel asked. "I can't see

the shop properly with everyone in the way." Despite Delta's encouragements, she hadn't taken a single bite of her banana.

"We'll know soon enough." Delta parked the car, and they jumped out and ran over.

Forcing herself through the crowd, Delta came up to the deputy. "Excuse me, but this is our shop." She gestured half behind her, where she suspected Hazel to be hot on her heels. "What happened?"

The deputy pointed behind him at the shop front. "Broken window. Might have been a break-in. We haven't been inside yet. We hoped you'd show up and could let us in, before we broke down the door."

"Thanks," Delta said and asked Hazel for the keys. She unlocked the door with trembling fingers. What if half their stock was gone?

But who would want to steal notebooks and washi tape? It was nice stuff, but not exactly easy to sell quickly and make a bundle... The first thing that struck Delta when they stepped inside the shop was that everything looked orderly. Not at all like someone had gone through their things. In fact, everything was just as they had left it last night at closing time, except for the brick on the floor amid a sea of shattered glass.

Delta exhaled slowly. "I think Mrs. Cassidy told me about other incidents like this in town. Local teens breaking windows, damaging mailboxes, and joyriding. This must just be a case of that. Of course, it's sad that it was Wanted this time, but..."

At least it didn't have anything to do with the murder and the threatening note left at the cottage.

The deputy put on gloves and gingerly stepped over the broken glass to retrieve the brick.

Delta turned to Hazel. "It doesn't look like anything was stolen. We'll just have to get the window replaced. Was it insured?"

Hazel shook her head. "I thought about insurance after the other incidents in town, but it's an extra bill to pay and... To be honest, I just hoped the kids would get smart and stop doing it after the police got involved. Some of them were identified and their parents notified, so I assumed the kids had been getting an earful at home and would be more careful next time."

Delta nodded. "I see. Well, we'll just have to pay for the window." She looked at its dimensions, trying to estimate what something like that might cost. "I wonder if we can get it replaced today or if we'll have to have it boarded up first. Do you know a carpenter here in town who might do that? I could give him a call—"

"Nobody is doing anything right now." The deputy's tone was grim as he cut her off. "We'll need to look closer at this." He held up the brick.

Delta didn't see at first what he meant, but when he turned it around toward them, she caught sight of the white paint on it. It read in tall, bold letters: *LEAVE.*

So, it hadn't just been kids breaking windows because they were at an age where you liked to do forbidden things. Hazel gasped and Delta reached out to wrap an arm around her friend's shoulders. "It'll be OK. We can deal with it together."

"I should never have asked you to come here. Now you're caught up in it too. What a mess." Hazel started crying.

The deputy edged closer and held out an arm as if to shepherd them out of the shop. "It's better if you leave. We have to do work here. We'll see if we can get information from the neighbors about suspicious sounds last night. Maybe someone saw something."

Delta nodded. "All right." She squeezed Hazel's shoulder. "Are you up to facing the people outside? I bet they'll all want to know what happened."

"I don't want to talk to anyone right now."

"Is there a back entrance you can use?" the deputy suggested.

Delta nodded. "Good idea." She didn't want to give anyone a chance of snapping a picture of Hazel with red-rimmed eyes.

The deputy leaned closer and cleared his throat. "I'm, uh...not supposed to tell you this, because the sheriff will call about it later, but as you're so upset about this mess here..." He lowered his voice. "Your brother will be released this morning. The sheriff says there is no more reason to hold him. He made a full statement about how he found the body and took the bracelet off it so it couldn't incriminate his girlfriend. He still has to stay around town, of course, keep himself available, should there be more questions."

Hazel smiled through her tears. "That's wonderful news." She looked at Delta. "We have to meet Finn as soon as he's out."

Her expression contorted again as she added, "I don't want him to hear about this right away. He'll be so angry at whoever did this."

The fear in her eyes resonated in Delta's own heart. Finn would be mad that someone was after his sister...and what would he do then? He was only just being released and still a suspect in the investigation, so he had to be extra careful not to land himself in hot water.

"Look, I have an idea. Why don't you go meet Finn and take him out to breakfast? Keep him away from Mattock Street as long as you can. Just say that I'm at the shop. In the meantime, I'll talk to Jonas and see if he can help clear up who did this."

Apparently, the deputy had overheard, for he said with a sour expression, "Nord is no magician. He can't just see by the look of a brick with a painted word on it who threw it through this window."

Delta bit her lip, sorry that she had let him catch her words. The police and Jonas weren't exactly seeing eye to eye, and further fanning that fire wasn't going to do them any good. She wasn't quite sure what she could say to make it better.

But the deputy didn't seem to want to wait for a response. He turned away and looked around as if assessing something.

Delta took the chance to drag Hazel into the back. "Do what I just said. I'll call you later. OK?"

Hazel looked her over. "We came in my car. How will you get around?"

"I'll call Jonas and see if he can pick me up. Don't worry about it. It will be fine."

Hazel gestured over her shoulder at her shattered shop window and sniffed. "Right now, nothing feels fine to me."

Jonas answered his phone on the third ring.

"Good news," Delta said. "Finn will be released this morning. Hazel is going to meet him and take him to breakfast. I guess the media will be jumping for a chance to talk to him, but it's better if he stays out of the limelight."

"That's sensible." Jonas sounded distracted, like he was doing something that required focus.

Delta hesitated. Could she just impose on him? "Look, uh, there is also some bad news."

"Another threat?" Jonas sounded razor sharp and almost indignant. "You can tell me right away. I promised I'd help you if I could."

Relief flooded Delta. "Yes, well… Wanted's window was smashed overnight. Someone threw a brick through it with the word LEAVE painted on it."

Jonas scoffed. "I don't believe it. Are the police doing something about it?"

"Yes, they're at the shop now. We can't be present there while they work, let alone open up for the day, which is also why I sent Hazel off with Finn. She needs the distraction. She's pretty upset about this."

"And you?" Jonas's voice was sharp. "Are you going after whoever did it?"

"I have no idea who did it."

"But I bet you intend to find out."

"I can't just let someone terrorize my friends. Or damage what is now also my property."

Jonas exhaled. "Of course. I tell you what. Remember that my wildlife guide colleagues said the victim had been visiting the birding hut a number of times? Let's go up there together and see if we can find out why she was so eager to go there."

Delta hesitated. "That hut is used daily, by groups as well. You even went there after the murder, with a group. Why do you think we can find anything? If there had been traces of some kind, they must have been trampled by now."

"On site, a bright new thought might strike us. If not, we'll at least have a good time. How about it?"

Delta figured Jonas wanted to keep her away from potential trouble, or give her some distraction as well, so she could hardly refuse. She did look forward to seeing the birding hut and maybe sketching some birds that came to show themselves off.

"All right. I'm in town without transportation. Can you pick me up?"

"On my way. Wait in front of the library. See you."

Delta decided there was time to pick up a few croissants and things to take along by way of an early lunch and crossed to the bakery. The delicious smell of freshly baked bread was in the air, and the counter had a plate with brownie samples to try. Delta took a big chunk and popped it into her mouth. Rich chocolate rolled across her tongue, followed by the tang of salted caramel.

Calamity Jane leaned across the counter toward her. Her braid was pinned up around her head like a wreath, and she wore a dark-green dress with a broad leather belt studded with fake gemstones. "It's so terrible about your smashed window. Must be the same kids who did that before. I wish the police would take them in and lock them up for a few hours just to give them a scare. They'll never learn otherwise, you know."

Delta decided not to mention the threat, aware that other customers were present and probably listening in. She asked for two croissants, two Kaiser rolls, a chocolate bun, a cinnamon twist, and a pecan-caramel braid. Jonas might like something to eat, and she could take the rest home for later.

Jane put everything in paper bags, added some napkins with a flowery pattern, and rang up the total on the old-fashioned cash register that gave the otherwise modern bakery a bit of nineteenth-century glory. "I'll keep an eye out, you know," she said with a wink, handing Delta the change.

Delta nodded, picked up her purchases, and left.

Jonas was waiting for her in front of the library, leaning against his Jeep. In the back, Delta spotted not only Spud, but also a big black shepherd.

Jonas gestured. "Just looking after him for two days while a friend of mine is visiting his parents. They live in a small apartment with a no-pet policy, so she couldn't take him along. King is a former K-9 too. Search dog. And that might come in handy now."

He held up a plastic bag. "This is a shawl that belonged to the victim. She left it in the lobby the day of the murder, and the clerk had meant to give it back to her but never did. He was willing to let me have it when I told him it was important for the murder case. He is upset that it's affecting the Taylors so much. He worked at the hotel all his life, so he feels like they are family. I'll let our buddy sniff it and search around the hut."

"You believe he could still find a trace of her there, even after several days?"

"It's worth a try."

Jonas opened the passenger door for her. "Hop in."

Once they were driving, he asked, "How are you?"

"Not too bad."

"Don't you want to run away screaming? I mean, you moved here to build a beautiful business, not face dead bodies and broken windows."

"I moved here mainly to build that business with Hazel.

I wanted to do something that is really my handiwork, together with someone who's just as passionate about paper crafting as I am. I'll support her, whatever happens. Besides, I put all the money I got from my grandmother into Wanted. It's got to turn into a success."

Jonas threw her a glance from aside. "Your grandmother? Is she, uh… I mean, was it her inheritance you put into the shop?"

"Oh, no. She wanted me to have it while she's still alive. So she can see what I do and…cheer for me." Delta bit her lip. "That's the thing. I want it to become amazing, just to make her happy."

"I see." Jonas turned the wheel to round a corner. "I can't say I'm very close with my grandparents. Not that there is any conflict, just that we don't see a lot of each other."

Delta said, "My gran raised me for a couple of years when my parents were on the road a lot with my brother Greg. He's a gymnast, and even competed for a place on the Olympic team. He didn't make it, but he did compete at many major events all over the world. My dad coached him, and my mom supported them, planning the trips and making the dietary schedules. I'm a lot younger than him and my other brother, Zach. Zach was already in college, and they decided not to take me along but leave me with Gran. I loved it at her place."

"Still, it must have been hard that they were away with Greg all of the time. Putting their time and energy into his sports career and not into being there for you."

Delta shrugged. "I was proud of him when I saw him on TV."

She could still feel the thrill of the moment when Dad lifted Greg so he could grab the rings and balance his weight properly before the exercise began. How she held her breath when he had to hold a pose for seconds on end and she could see his muscles shaking with the exertion. How she clenched her hands, waiting to see if his landing would be perfect or he was unbalanced and had to make a little hop to avoid falling. That meant a subtraction of points toward his total.

"They made a choice to support Greg when he had a chance to go to the Olympics. It was then and there or not at all. Athletes can't compete forever. Greg didn't make the Olympic team because of an injury. After that, he never got back to where he had been. That meant his career was effectively over, and he hadn't even gotten a college degree. He had to sit down and figure out what he wanted to do with his life. It wasn't easy."

Delta looked at Jonas and continued thoughtfully. "I don't envy him. I did miss my parents every now and then, I won't lie, but...Greg made so many sacrifices for his sport. He had a dream of competing at the Olympics and maybe even winning a medal, and it fell through. We're not talking about a few months of training or even a few years. It was his entire life."

Jonas nodded. "I see. So, what's he doing now?"

"He really loves traveling, so he became a motivational speaker. One week he's in Tokyo, the next in Sydney. Large companies ask him to talk to their staff or do a presentation at a company anniversary. His wife takes care of all his bookings, flights, hotels, etc. She writes for a travel blog, so while he's doing his presentations, she tours the city where they are staying and writes up her entries for the blog. Last year, they had a baby, and Olaf is traveling with them now. That baby has been to more places in the world than I have."

Delta pulled up her phone and clicked through a few

pics until she had the one she wanted. "Here they are cuddling kangaroos. Olaf isn't afraid of anything. According to Greg, he'd even pick up a snake if they'd let him."

They were on the quiet road up to the Lodge, and Jonas could throw a quick look at the screen. "Australia is great. I spent a few months there, traveling around, herding cattle, and taking hikes up mountains."

"I'd love to go there sometime." Delta lowered her phone. "I guess I could have used Gran's money to travel. She might have expected that. She knows how I drool when I see Greg's pics. But I'd wanted to do something creative for so long and…this money seemed like the perfect opportunity to quit my job and become my own boss. Hazel already had Wanted, so it seemed like a no-brainer to join her here."

"And now the murder has messed everything up," Jonas said. "I guess it would have been bad if it had just been Finn getting accused and the town talking about it, about Hazel by association, but these threats against her, against the both of you…"

He shook his head, muttering, "It must mean we're onto something. I just wish I knew what it was."

They drove into the parking lot at the Lodge, and Jonas parked the Jeep. Delta got out and balanced the paper bags of pastries in her arms. Then her gaze fell on something, and she walked over quickly. It was a dark-blue station wagon with a moose on a bumper sticker. "Here it is!" she called out to Jonas. "This is the car I asked you about earlier."

Jonas looked and nodded. "Told you it's parked here often."

Delta studied the moose. "It's not just an animal sticker. It seems to be the logo of something."

"Maybe a national park the driver has been to?"

"Do you know it?"

"No, but you could look for it online."

Jonas let the two dogs out of the back of the Jeep and told them to stay. They sat and watched him as he put on his backpack and slipped the strap of his binoculars over his head. "You can use these," he said to Delta, holding out an extra pair.

Delta looked down at her full arms.

Jonas said, "I'll carry them for now."

With his free hand, he collected the dogs' leashes and they set out from the far edge of the parking lot, following a dirt path wide enough to walk side by side.

The tall pines moved in the breeze coming from the lake. Far away, a predator bird cried, a high, eerie sound that lingered a moment.

Spud didn't pay attention to it, but the other dog turned his ears in all directions, trying to pick up every sound.

Jonas hummed a tune as he walked with long paces. Delta had difficulty keeping up. Her sneakers were fine for walking, but the soles were so thin that every now and then she could feel a twig or stone underneath. If she wanted to do this more often, it would probably pay to invest in a pair of sturdy hiking boots. Tundish had a large outdoor store on a side street off Mattock Street where she could get some.

"Squirrel," Jonas said, pointing at a tree.

Delta squinted. "Where?"

"Third branch. Now going up. They're so quick. I've never gotten a good shot of one. Yet."

"I don't even see it now." Delta waited a few more moments, then she hurried after Jonas, who was already moving again. The eager dogs trotted by his side.

"Is it far to the birding hut?" Delta asked.

"Not that far." Jonas glanced at her. "Am I going too fast?"

"I'm low on energy. This is breakfast." Delta nodded down at the paper bags in her arms.

Jonas shook his head. Then he frowned. "I guess the news about the broken window reached you before you could have any."

"Unfortunately, yes. I'm hoping Hazel is with Finn now, making up for her lack of calories with a gigantic breakfast to celebrate his release."

Jonas halted and slipped the backpack off his back. "Give me some of those bags and you eat something."

Grateful, Delta selected the pecan braid and gave the rest to Jonas, who packed it away. They continued walking. The fresh air made the taste of the nuts and caramel even more intense, and Delta felt instantly better. Her fingers got a bit sticky, but the sun was caressing her face, and her step seemed to fall in with Jonas's at last, finding a natural rhythm.

As they enjoyed the silence of the forest together, it seemed like they could walk on for hours, just feeling in place.

"There it is." Jonas pointed. A glimpse of a wooden structure was visible through the trees. A sign warned people that a wildlife observation point was up ahead and it wasn't permitted to talk loudly or make noise.

Delta accepted the binoculars from Jonas and put them around her neck.

The hut was a structure with a heavily mossed roof, dark and low, just high enough for a person to stand in. When Delta turned left, she discovered an opening in the side. It led into a narrow passage that kept the light out of the main room. There, a few wooden benches allowed a seated person to see through the narrow slits made in the wood. That way, the animals who came to drink from the water in front of the hut couldn't see the people inside.

Jonas said, "Now that we're here, you might as well have a look and see if you spot anything. I'll have King search for Vera White's scent."

Delta sat down and looked out, narrowing her eyes as the light outside appeared very bright compared to the dimness inside the hut.

The water seemed abandoned. Delta searched the tree trunk directly opposite them and the brush beside it. But there were no animals in sight.

"There will be birds soon," Jonas assured her. Plastic rustled as he unwrapped the shawl. "You can also see mice coming to drink." He leaned over to her. "Sometimes they get into the birding hut as well. I was here with a group when a mouse ran right across a participant's foot. She screamed loudly enough to have been heard back at the Lodge."

"You're kidding me."

"No. They run across the ledge you're resting your feet on." Jonas nodded downward.

Delta pretended she didn't believe him or care, but after a few more moments, she did lift her feet and tried to keep them away from said ledge. She wasn't afraid of mice per se, but still…

Jonas pulled out the shawl and offered it to the black shepherd. The dog sniffed it from all sides, his tail starting to wag.

"Search, boy." Jonas gestured around the hut. "Search."

The dog put his nose to the floor and started to sniff the boards, covering inch after inch in careful consideration.

Delta watched with a wriggle of excitement in her stomach. What if they found something crucial to the case? Vera White had come up here often, alone. She hadn't seemed like a woman who enjoyed being alone. Or studying the birds that came by.

The dog made his way to the far end of the hut and then came back, covering the side. He was completely engrossed, ignoring Spud, who barked at him. Jonas touched Spud's snout to signal silence and then scratched him behind the ears as they both watched King work.

Delta's excitement faded as the minutes ticked by and nothing happened. She glanced at Jonas and caught the same disappointment in his features. Then suddenly the dog began to bark and dance, pushing his nose to the floor.

Jonas jumped to his feet. "Easy, boy." He pulled the dog back and let him sit, then knelt over the place where he had shown interest. He studied the floorboards, ran a hand over them. "Hey..."

He leaned down farther, saying to Delta, "Could you dig into my backpack and find a brown leather pouch for me?"

Delta opened the pack, searching quickly between a raincoat, plastic-covered map, apple with bruises, and water bottles. There. That felt like leather. She drew up the pouch and handed it to Jonas, who zipped it open and took out tweezers. He leaned down again and used the tool to grab at something between the floorboards.

Delta held her breath. "What is it?"

The black shepherd moved in again, and Jonas wrestled him back with his shoulder. "Sit. Come on, King, sit. Let me work."

The dog sank back on his rear, his ears forward in eager attention.

Jonas moved the tweezers up slowly. Caught between them was a small snippet of a something colorful.

Delta got up and closed in to see it better. "Paper."

Jonas nodded. "Wrapping paper." He looked up at her. "Isn't a birding hut a bit of an odd place to unwrap a present?"

"Unless you're meeting your secret lover here." Delta looked more carefully at the paper. A shiver went down her spine. "I recognize it. It's wrapping paper we use at Wanted to wrap purchases for our customers."

"You mean, it was around some stationery or something?"

"Yes, around a gift Vera White touched. Otherwise King wouldn't have detected her scent on it, right?"

"Paper soaks up scent, for instance from a person's perfume, and can retain it for a long time."

Delta nodded. "Ray Taylor bought a notebook at Wanted the day I came to town. He admitted to me later that he had bought it for Vera White." She studied the paper with a frown. "But I think I gave him another pattern. Not this one."

She closed her eyes a moment to go back to her first-ever customer in her very own shop. She had chosen blue-and-gold wrapping paper because it matched the peacock's colors. And this paper was pink and purple. The silver streak was probably the leg of the *Y* in happy. She could picture the paper in her mind. It had the words *Happy Day* printed across it. "It was a different wrapping paper. Not this. But this does come from Wanted. I recognize it."

"Maybe Ray bought more notebooks at Wanted for Vera White."

"Or it wasn't Ray." Delta produced her phone. "I'll give Hazel a call to ask if she can recall someone involved in the murder case getting this wrapping paper around their purchase."

She waited impatiently as the call connected.

Hazel answered on the fifth ring. "Delta? Is something wrong?"

Before Delta could reply, Hazel added, "I walked away from the table to prevent Finn from… I didn't tell him about the mess at Wanted yet. He was so happy to be released, I didn't want to ruin it for him."

"Fine, just let him sit and eat a nice meal. You can always tell him later. Now listen," Delta said. "Do you remember wrapping a present at Wanted, somewhere before last Friday, in the bright-pink-and-purple paper with the words *Happy Day* on it? You told me the other day it was a recent addition, so I assume you can't have used it very often."

"Yes, it was in new inventory that arrived a few days before you came to town. Who did I use it for? Phew, let me think. It's rather thin, and it tears easily when you try to put it around items that are irregularly shaped." Hazel thought long and hard. "I know for sure I gave it to Finn. He bought a notebook, and I gave him that particular paper because I thought it was a gift for Isabel, and her favorite color is purple. How come?"

"Finn?" Delta repeated, glancing at Jonas. "You sure it was Finn?" That was bad news. Bad news indeed.

"I must also have used it for other customers, I'm sure, but I don't recall exactly. Does it matter?"

"No, not really. You two have a good time."

"Finn isn't about to sit around for long." Hazel sighed. "He wants to repair the boathouse where all the Lodge's boats are docked. He said he promised that to Isabel before he was arrested, and he wants to do it right away now that he's out."

Delta said, "Oh, OK. I guess it can't hurt for him to keep busy. Talk to you later."

She disconnected the call and told Jonas what Hazel had said about wrapping a notebook in that specific paper for Finn.

Jonas pursed his lips. "It's a very thin lead, but we can use it to start a conversation. Finn is coming to repair the boathouse, right? We could meet up with him there and ask him about the notebook he bought."

Delta nodded. "If he did give it to Vera, he can also tell us why. I mean Ray also gave her a notebook. Obviously, Vera liked notebooks, but that doesn't explain why two men at the hotel where she was staying would give her one. And..." She pointed a finger at Jonas. "You told me that the box in the hotel safe contained wrapped notebooks. Why would Vera White keep her presents in a locked box in a hotel safe?"

"To keep them away from her husband?" Jonas gathered his things and brushed the heads of the dogs. "I don't know, but maybe Finn can enlighten us."

He looked at her. "We'll have to tread lightly, though. He's just out of the police's crossfire, and he won't want to get caught in ours."

Chapter Fourteen

As they approached the boathouse, they heard hammering coming from within. The wooden structure was painted deep red with white accents, and a year was carved into a lintel.

"1936," Delta read. "Wow, old stuff."

"Well maintained," Jonas said, slapping the side of the structure.

The hammering inside continued. There was a door through which they could enter onto wooden boarding where the boats lay moored. Some were rowboats, while others had outboard motors.

Finn was on his knees, hammering down a board that stood up a little.

"Hello, Finn!" Jonas cried over the banging sound.

Finn shot to his feet, the hammer in his hand posed like a weapon. He blinked at them. Then he lowered the hammer.

"Oh, Jonas. I hadn't heard you come in." He smiled wanly. "Nice day for a bit of boating, I suppose. Delta..." He nodded at her and wanted to resume working, it seemed.

Delta said, "We never got a chance to talk to each other really. I had no idea you were living in Tundish. Hazel did mention in the past that you love hiking and all, so I guess this place is ideal for it." She gestured to the water that rippled peacefully against the boats, carrying a few floating leaves.

As Finn didn't seem eager to chat about outdoor activities, Delta changed topics. "How was breakfast with Hazel?"

"Nice enough. But she shouldn't be so worried. The police never had anything against me." It sounded curt and dismissive, as if there hadn't been a murder but just a minor misunderstanding about a parking ticket.

"You should have told them about the bracelet right away," Jonas said. "They thought you were guilty or obstructing their investigation."

"I just didn't want Isabel to get into trouble. Rosalyn would have had a fit if Isabel had been dragged to the police station."

"Well, she has been arrested anyway. West was convinced you set it up together or were covering for each other. He treated her more roughly than he might have done if you had told the truth from the start."

"I didn't know that." Finn brushed back his hair with an agitated gesture. There was a smear of dirt on his cheek. "In hindsight, it's always easy to say what someone else should have done. Especially if you yourself are not involved in the case."

Jonas held out his hand with the scrap of paper in it. "Does this look familiar to you, Finn?"

Finn looked at it. For a moment, his expression of annoyance remained, as if the paper meant nothing to him, but then slowly the color drained from his face. "I don't... What... It's just a bit of paper."

"Yes. A bit of paper that was part of a larger piece wrapped around a present you bought at Wanted. For whom?"

Finn licked his lips. "I'm sure Hazel uses that wrapping paper a lot."

"Did you buy a notebook at Wanted?" Jonas pressed.

Delta noticed he had changed from *present* to *notebook*,

probably to put pressure on Finn, and added bluntly, "Did you give it to Vera White?"

Finn stared at her. "What are you two after? Getting me locked up again?" He dropped the hammer. It hit the boards with a thud.

The dogs moved back and growled.

Finn spun away from them and jumped into a boat. With a few quick movements, he cast off and pushed the boat away from the dock with an oar. Then he dipped both oars into the water and began to row. Delta had barely time to understand what was happening. She stood glued to the boards.

"Quickly," Jonas said to her, jabbing her with an elbow. "In that other boat, the one with the motor. It'll give us an edge."

"Right." She jumped in, Jonas followed with the dogs. He started the engine, and they went after Finn, who was rowing fast out onto the lake. The blustery wind grabbed Delta's hair and flung it back into her face. She brushed it away with one hand, holding onto the side of the boat with the other. Jonas was pushing the engine to full throttle.

"Finn!" Jonas called. "We only want to talk to you and understand what happened Friday night. Don't make this so hard on yourself."

"You're a cop, Jonas," Finn called back. "You always were, and you always will be. Get lost."

Delta asked, "Do you think he's guilty?" The wind drove tears into her eyes.

"I'm not sure." Jonas steered their boat beside Finn's rowboat. "Talk to us," he urged him again. "We just want to understand what happened."

Finn lifted one of the oars from the water and made a striking gesture in their direction. "Just stay away from me."

His eyes were wide and panicky. Delta wasn't sure what he might do if they kept pushing him.

As Finn's boat slowed, Spud tensed his muscles and jumped. He landed in Finn's boat and pressed himself to the angry young man.

Finn dropped the oars and hugged the dog, burying his face in his fur.

Delta watched as his shoulders began to shake, as if he was crying. Spud rubbed his head against Finn's and grunted.

Delta looked at Jonas. Her heart was thumping, and uncertain questions raced through her mind. Was she looking at a guilty man who knew the game was up? Would Hazel lose her brother?

Delta couldn't imagine how she would feel if Greg or Zach got accused of a crime as serious as murder. How devastating it would be to feel doubt as to whether they might be guilty.

Jonas cut the engine and let their boat bob beside Finn's. He leaned forward with his arms on his knees, his head turned away from Finn like he wanted to give him some space while still staying nearby. In silence, they waited for him to calm down.

The sun streaked across the water, conjuring up rainbows. Gold leaves whirled down from the brush along the shore and landed on the surface, gently rocking as the water moved.

In the distance, children laughed. A voice over a megaphone gave them instructions. It sounded like a game of hide and seek.

At last Finn looked up. "I made a total mess of everything," he said in a strangled tone. "Hazel did everything to help me out and... She even risked her shop for it. You probably have no idea what you got into, Delta. The financial..."

Jonas looked at Delta in alarm.

"I do know about the extra mortgage," Delta said as calmly and confidently as she could. "It doesn't matter. We'll make it work." Her friendship with Hazel was stronger than any problem that could be thrown into their path.

Finn looked up in bewilderment. "Hazel told you? But..."

"She had to, after the murder. She wouldn't have done so otherwise. But I won't tell anyone else. I promise."

Finn exhaled hard. "It'll get out now anyway. Rosalyn will make sure of that. She never liked me, and now this..."

He rubbed his eyes with his back of his hand. "That White woman ruined everything. She should never have come here."

"What does Vera White have to do with it?" Delta asked, her heart in her throat. One moment she hoped Finn had no real connection to the victim, the next she couldn't deny he had been seen with Vera White, arguing at the party. And Rosalyn had even accused him of having an affair with the woman. There had to have been some reason for her to assume this.

Finn sighed. He looked like a broken man as he sat there, his shoulders slumped, the big dog pressed close to him. His hands fumbled with Spud's ears as he began to speak slowly. "Vera knew about my gambling. Don't ask me how. I only ever borrowed money off a colleague. My debts weren't registered anywhere. But she knew. She told me she knew why I had left LA in such a rush. I shouldn't think I could hide out here, because she would tell everyone about me, starting with the Taylors. She said she was close to them and they would believe her right off the bat."

Jonas asked, "Did she ever mention the word 'gambling' or 'debts'?"

Finn stared at him. "What?"

"Did she mention your gambling, the debts? Or did she just say she knew why you had left LA in a rush and would reveal it to the Taylors?"

"I just said so," Finn responded, raking a hand through his hair. "She mentioned being close to the Taylors and them believing her, and I just panicked. As soon as Rosalyn found out, she'd have had me fired."

"So you never checked what Vera actually knew?"

"Man, I couldn't think! Ever since I came to Tundish, I had been afraid it would all come back to bite me in the butt. If people were talking and fell silent as I approached, I was sure they knew something." Finn's breathing was ragged. "It wasn't just the job at the Lodge I was worried about. But Isabel." His features contracted. "What if Rosalyn found out and told Isabel I was after the Taylor money, and Isabel believed her? I'd lose her just like I lost Tamara earlier."

Delta remembered Hazel had mentioned that a previous broken relationship had hurt Finn deeply, and it had taken him months to recover from the blow. He had been understandably afraid it would happen again.

"Vera wanted money to keep her mouth shut, and I decided right away it would be better to pay up. My instructions were to buy a notebook at Wanted and have it wrapped. Then I had to open the wrapping paper carefully and put money between the pages of the notebook. I had to put the wrapping paper back in place and pass the notebook to her. She'd put it in her luggage like it were a souvenir she'd bought along the way. To keep her husband out of it."

Jonas looked at Delta. "Clever. He wouldn't open up a package from a stationery shop."

"Right. I had to leave it for her at the birding hut. She said she didn't want me passing anything to her where we could be seen. Around the hotel there's always someone coming or going. People can look out of windows or... She had the whole idea worked out. I think she has done it before."

"This could have been her regular handoff place," Jonas said to Delta. "Remember she went to the hut several times, alone?"

Delta nodded. She said to Finn, "And after you left the notebook with money for her at the hut?"

"I never spoke to her again."

"That's a lie," Jonas said. "You talked to her at the party. The police showed us pictures of it. You talked to her, you pleaded with her."

"All right." Finn drew a shaky breath. "She asked me to dance, and then during the dance, she told me she needed more money. She said it couldn't be delayed. I had to buy another notebook and put money in it and leave it for her. I said I couldn't get any money on short notice. It wasn't payday and... I have no savings left."

He swallowed hard. "She didn't care, though. She said I should borrow money or even steal it from the hotel. That the Taylors were so rich they'd never miss it."

"And then?"

"I walked away, wondering what I was going to do. Then later that night when some people were already going home, I saw her go into the bar. I hesitated, as I wasn't sure it would make any difference to plead with her again, but in the end, I decided I had to tell her I couldn't raise the money. That I would turn her into the police if she kept harassing me."

"Firm words," Jonas said.

Finn looked at him. "You think I would have been too scared to tell her that. But I was desperate. And I'd had a few drinks. I thought it was now or never. I went into the bar and she...was on the floor. Stabbed, dead. There was blood and... I just didn't know what to do. I saw the bracelet in her hand, recognized it immediately, and I took it away to avoid Isabel getting... I thought she had asked Isabel for money as well and Isabel had given her the bracelet by way of payment."

Finn rubbed his eyes again. "It was stupid, I know. But I didn't kill her. I never did anything to hurt her."

Jonas frowned hard. "Did you see anyone going in or coming out before you followed her into the bar?"

Finn shook his head. "Isabel dragged me outside to say goodbye to a few people she knew. They were flying out of state for an anniversary, so they left early to have a few hours' sleep before they had to catch their plane. I barely remembered who they were because I was so nervous and just wanted to get back in and confront Vera. Tell her it had to be over. I don't know who went into the bar while I was out there."

Jonas groaned. "That isn't helping at all."

"I'm sorry. This is all I know." Finn sat slumped. "How can I face Hazel if she hears I was blackmailed, and I paid up and have nothing left? She believes I'm saving again and building my life."

"Better than for her to believe you're a killer." Jonas nodded at him. "Row around the lake a bit to get that pent-up energy out of your system. It's not nothing to have been locked up for days. Spud will keep you company. We'll be at the boathouse. Take your time."

He turned on the engine and steered their boat away, back to the shore and the boathouse.

Delta asked doubtfully, "Are you sure he's okay to be alone?"

"Let him unwind a bit. Spud will look after him." Jonas grinned. "He gave me a start when he jumped into that rowboat. Finn had just been waving that oar around. I wasn't sure what he was going to do."

"He'd never hit a dog." Delta sighed. "He must feel terrible. Blackmailed, cornered, then arrested and accused of murder."

Jonas said, "Vera White was a blackmailer. It shouldn't surprise us, since we already knew about that altercation with her sister-in-law."

"Yes," Delta said, "Vera must have been blackmailing Amanda as well. Amanda threatened to reveal the truth to her husband, Ralph, but Vera warned her that it would hurt her just as much. Because the truth was something Amanda couldn't afford to have her husband know."

Jonas nodded. "We know Vera was planning to divorce her husband. Such proceedings can take a long time before they are finalized. As soon as Herb would know his wife was planning to leave him, he wouldn't give her another dime, perhaps even turn her out into the street. So was this blackmail money meant to support her?"

"Maybe. Her motive might not have been solely monetary. She might just have enjoyed her power over people. Like those writers of poison pen letters?"

Jonas waved a hand. "I'm no profiler, so I don't know all the ins and outs of the psychology of criminals. I just ask myself: Did we come across any clues, apart from the altercation you overheard, that Amanda has something major to hide from her husband?"

"Concerning Fred Halliday maybe?" Delta suggested. "I

do think he's very familiar with her, like they are more than friends. What if Amanda lied that it was Vera's idea to come here? What if she suggested it herself, and after coming here, Vera realized that Amanda had wanted to meet up with Fred again, and she used it to taunt and frighten Amanda? Mrs. Cassidy told me that during their visit to the museum, the two ladies were watching each other like they were suspicious of each other and waiting for a move. It all fits."

Jonas sighed. "Yes, but unfortunately, blackmailers usually have more than one victim and more than one person who might want them dead. You said Ray Taylor also bought a notebook at Wanted. Was he being blackmailed too, and given the same instructions as Finn?"

"I assume that, if we asked him, he wouldn't confess. He knows Vera is no longer around to tell us the truth."

"No, and what if he was the one who made sure that she wasn't?" Jonas docked the boat and fastened it. "We have to ask West to check all stationery items in the victim's possession for money. There were notebooks in that box she had stashed in the safe. The sheriff probably hasn't looked closer at them because he was focusing on valuables and the envelope with the information about the divorce."

Jonas pulled out his phone and started to call. "Yes, this is Jonas Nord. Can I talk to the sheriff? I know he's busy, but it's important. Urgent too." He wiggled his eyebrows, and Delta had to laugh.

"Sheriff, good afternoon. I have a question. Do you still have that box that you took out of the hotel safe? The one with Vera White's personal belongings? Yes, could you maybe get it out and have a look at some notebooks in it? I am assuming there are notebooks in it."

"One with peacocks on the cover," Delta whispered.

"One with peacocks on it, for instance. But check all of them. What? You already checked them when you went through the box. And? Nothing special about them? I see. And did you pay attention to the covers? The inside of the front and the back page. Could something be hidden in the covers? Extra paper pasted… Yes, I'll hold."

Jonas looked at Delta. "He's curious enough now to go and have a look." He listened to the sounds on the other end of the line.

"Put it on speaker phone," Delta urged.

Jonas held out the phone between them. There were footfalls and muffled talking. Rustling. More talking. A thud.

Delta waited with bated breath.

Then she clearly heard a cry. "Look at this!"

Jonas clenched his fist and waved it at her. "Success," he mouthed.

West's gruff voice came over the line. "The covers all have an extra sheet pasted onto them, and underneath, something is hidden. Two hundred-dollar bills. In each cover. Each notebook is worth four hundred dollars. And how many are there in that box?"

Another voice said, "Ten. No, twelve."

"A real collector then." West sounded cynical. "How did you know, Nord?"

"I didn't know anything, Sheriff. I merely guessed. You see, Mrs. White was getting divorced, and her husband doesn't know a thing about that. She had to make sure she had some money to live off once he found out, don't you think? Because he doesn't seem like a man who would have given her another dime once he had known she was walking out on him. It would have taken time before a settlement was reached about her rights to his fortune."

"And why did you ask about the one with the peacocks?"

"I'm in the middle of nowhere, Sheriff. I think I'm losing you. Hello? Hello?" Jonas pushed the Disconnect button. He grimaced at Delta. "I don't want to tell him more right now. You should talk to Ray Taylor first, see if he'll confirm that Vera blackmailed him as well."

"We can't be 100 percent sure that Ray was involved. She might have bought a peacock notebook herself. She did buy notebooks from us during the workshop. She probably needed more room to stash her cash. Or another victim bought a peacock notebook for her. They are pretty popular."

"It's not conclusive evidence, no," Jonas agreed. "But the sheriff will run all notebooks and bills inside them for fingerprints. He might get a partial from Ray on the peacocks one, and then..." Jonas grimaced. "I almost wanted to say *we* got him. But considering I assured the sheriff I'm not muscling in on his investigation, I will just say he'll have to answer some questions from the police."

He lifted his binoculars and swept the lake. "Finn looks pretty calm now, rowing at a nice, steady pace. Spud is sitting in the front of the boat like he's on the lookout." His smile deepened.

Delta patted King, who was sitting beside her. "You did a good job too. You found the little bit of paper. You're a real tracker. Huh?"

King looked up at her and barked.

Delta's phone dinged. She pulled it out of her pocket and swiped to the new message.

Lethal Liz wrote: "My sis works at the dry cleaners, and she told me that on the morning after the murder, a woman came in to have a party dress cleaned. She gave her name as Rivers. My sis thought nothing of it until she saw a picture in the newspaper this morning of the victim and her family, who had been staying here. Then she recognized Mrs. Rivers in that photo. It's the victim's sister-in-law."

"Amanda White!" Delta exclaimed.

Jonas looked at her. "What's that?"

"Amanda White turned up at the dry cleaners on the morning after the murder to have her party dress cleaned. She gave a false name." Delta felt a wriggle of excitement in her stomach. "Why would she be in a rush to have her dress cleaned? And why not say who she was?"

"But the sheriff talked to her the night of, I assume?" Jonas frowned. "If there was something wrong with her dress, it being stained or something, he would have noticed and taken the dress to the station for analysis. He wouldn't have let her keep it so she could get it dry-cleaned to erase evidence."

"I guess not. Can you call him again and ask about questioning Amanda White on the night of the murder?"

Jonas rolled his eyes, but he did retrieve his phone and place the call. "Nord here… No, I don't need the sheriff if you can tell me. Was Mrs. Amanda White questioned on the night of the murder?… I know you don't have to tell me, but I just heard some news that could indicate she has been meddling with evidence. All I want to know is if she was questioned and if her clothes were looked at. Her party clothes… Oh. I see."

Jonas's tone had increased. Delta sensed they were on the brink of something vital. She clenched her free hand into a fist.

"It seems she delivered said party dress to the dry cleaners on Saturday morning, giving a false name. I don't know if the dress got cleaned or not. It probably was, as the lady working there didn't realize it was Mrs. White bringing it in until this morning. She recognized her because of some photo in the *Tundish Trader*... You will? Great. Thanks."

Jonas lowered the phone. "They never saw her party dress. She had already retired to her hotel room when the murder was discovered, and they questioned her there. She was wearing her dressing gown by then. They'll call the dry cleaners right away and ask for the dress. Even if it got cleaned, there might still be something on it. Blood is notoriously hard to clean off completely. In any case, it's better if they have it and then confront Amanda White so she will feel pressure to admit to something."

Chapter Fifteen

They came back to the Lodge together, Jonas with one dog, Finn with the other, and Delta tagging behind. As they crossed the parking lot, she pointed out the dark-blue station wagon with the moose on the back to Finn. "Do you know whose car that is?"

"Sure. It's Ray's."

"Ray's?" Delta and Jonas echoed in unison.

"Yes." Finn stared from the one to the other. "Why is that so odd?" He pointed at the moose. "That's the emblem of some club Ray used to play for. The Moose Musketeers or something like that."

Jonas looked at Delta. "Ray picking up Ralph White, away from the hotel. Seems strange."

Delta nodded. What had the two been up to together? What might they have been talking about? Ralph had earlier accused Ray of having had an affair with Vera. He had also mentioned money Vera had lent Ray and Ray hadn't wanted to pay back. Had Ralph maybe asked for that money?

Finn said goodbye to them and the dogs, then rounded the hotel to see if Isabel was in the garden or at the stables.

Delta and Jonas stood eyeing each other as if they weren't quite sure what to do next. Delta said, "I could go see if the police are done at Wanted, and we can open up again. It would be a nice distraction."

"Yes, I wanted to talk to you about that. Since the damage was done overnight…"

Jonas's next words were drowned out by a sports car

screeching into the parking lot. The driver stopped it and then let the engine growl. His passenger squealed with delight. She wore a thin scarf over her hair, which made her look like a fifties movie star. Her face was years younger in carefree laughter.

Jonas stepped up to the car to open the door for her. “Mrs. White.” He nodded at the driver. “Fred.”

Fred Halliday, sporting flashy reflecting sunglasses, raised a hand to Jonas and Delta. “Hello there. Nice day for a ride.”

He smiled at Amanda White, who had stepped out of the car and was smoothing her dress. “I’ll text you.”

Then he pushed the accelerator, and the car jumped forward with an eager growl. Halliday took a spin around the parking lot before turning into the road again.

Amanda stared after him with the doe eyes of a besotted teen. Delta couldn’t help asking, “Is your husband not around? He didn’t seem to like your friendship with Mr. Halliday much.”

Amanda looked at her. “Ralph is up in our hotel room on the phone for business. Herb is in no state of mind to decide about anything and, well, things have to continue somehow. The world didn’t stop just because Vera died.”

“I’m so sorry about your dress,” Delta said. “I remember seeing it Friday night, and it was quite special.” In truth, she had no idea what Amanda had worn, but she had to confront her about having handed in the gown at the dry cleaners. “But it got stained, right?”

She kept her eyes on the woman’s face, hoping to see a flash of guilt there.

“Yes, I bumped into someone, and their wine spilled on me.” Amanda seemed surprised by the turn the conversation was taking, but not suspicious or anxious. "I tried to wash it off in my room, but it just didn't work. I took it to the dry cleaners with the hope they could get it out."

"I see. Well, it would be a shame if such a great dress were ruined." Delta smiled at her. She could hardly mention she knew Amanda had given a false name at the dry cleaners. It might look like she was stalking her or something.

On to the next important topic then.

Delta held her gaze on Amanda, determined to read any emotion she might unconsciously betray in her features. "By the way, did you know Vera was getting a divorce from Herb?"

Amanda's eyes widened. "Why on earth would she? She had a great life with Herb. I can't see..."

She corrected herself with an effort. "I couldn't have seen her fending for herself. Having to go find herself a job or something." The undertone was mocking, almost spiteful.

"I don't think the late Mrs. White would have had to work if she had divorced her husband," Jonas said. "I heard that her lawyer had already confirmed to her that she would be entitled to half of her husband's fortune. With the successful dolphin-spotting business..."

Amanda stared at them as if this revelation took her completely by surprise. "Herb would have had to pay her a lot of money? Taking it from the business? But he couldn't have. The business would have..."

She fell silent. Her eyes strayed away and got a vacant look, as if she were suddenly seeing a whole new picture.

"Did you know anything about this, Mrs. White?" Jonas pressed.

"No. I knew nothing about it." Amanda seemed to force herself to pay attention to the conversation. Delta would have gladly paid to be privy to her thoughts right now.

"And your husband, Ralph?" Jonas continued. "Did he know? Did he suspect, maybe, that his brother's marriage was shaky and the business might suffer if it came to a divorce?"

"You mean..." Amanda turned very pale. "No, Ralph knew nothing about it. He would have mentioned it to me if he had. I'm sure."

But the way she wrung her hands betrayed that she wasn't quite so sure. It seemed to have occurred to her now that Ralph might have known and not been happy about it. That he might have...*removed* Vera from the scene to save the business?

Delta said, nodding at the ring with the diamonds and emeralds on Amanda's finger, "What a beautiful ring. I think I saw it before. Wasn't Vera wearing it earlier?"

"It's mine." Amanda wiped a strand of hair from her face. "I'd better get in," she said in a low, hurried tone. "Good day to you."

Jonas waited until she was out of earshot before speaking. "The idea that her husband could have known something about the impending divorce shook her to the core."

"Yes. She must know he would be upset if he had discovered such a thing. He seems like a man who likes to have things his way and who gets aggressive when it turns out differently. I can see him pick up an ice pick and stab the sister-in-law who threatened his business empire."

"Yes, but he didn't deliver his suit to the dry cleaners because there was a stain on it. She did." Jonas frowned. "Can they have been in on it together? You did hear the ladies fighting in the garden."

"Yes, and Amanda struck the blow. That proves she has a temper too. I bet if someone really spilled wine on her dress, it happened when she rushed inside after Vera to apologize. She was, of course, worried Vera would make good on her threat to betray some secret about her. To reveal a truth that would hurt her as well."

Delta tapped her fingers against each other, considering the other odd thing. "She claims the diamond ring she's wearing is hers. If so, then why was Vera wearing it earlier?"

"Don't women borrow each other's clothes and jewelry?"

"Not when they don't like each other."

Jonas waved a hand. "The police will talk to her about the dress. They might get further with her than we did. Now I want to talk to you about Wanted. I'm not sure the brick through the window was a one-time occurrence. I'd like to keep an eye out tonight. How about me, Spud, and King staying at the shop?"

"You'd want to do that?"

"Sure. I can put an inflatable mattress and a sleeping bag somewhere where they can't see me from the outside."

"The old cells!" Delta enthused.

Jonas grimaced. "A night in a cell?"

"It's a fabulous plan. Maybe you can catch the culprit red-handed. If he returns so quickly, of course." Delta frowned. "But do you think it's too soon after the previous incident? Would someone return the next night?" She could already envision Jonas wrecking his back on an air mattress while nothing happened.

"I don't care. I want to do something. I'm spending the night in the shop."

"Good. I'll stay with you during the evening. We can talk about the case and see if we can come to some sort of a solution. We gathered a lot of evidence already; we just need to make sense of all we know. Fit the pieces into a meaningful whole."

Jonas seemed reluctant to accept her offer, but Delta said, "I insist on it. I'll bring something to eat and drink."

She grinned. "It will be just like an old-fashioned sleepover."

Chapter Sixteen

Delta ruefully recalled that sense of excitement when she entered the empty stationery shop from the back. The darkness with nothing but the streetlight coming in from the outside through the glass pane in the door made it kind of eerie. It was so quiet too. The boarded-up window gave the shop an abandoned, "ready for demolition" sort of feel. Not the setting for a cozy sleepover.

"Jonas?" she whispered.

A shadow slipped toward her, and she suppressed a cry when something pressed itself against her. Then she sank to her knees and hugged Spud. "Hello there." His warm fur and comforting presence made her heartbeat quiet a bit. King stood a few feet away, waiting for his greeting. She rubbed his head and scratched him behind his ears. It was comforting to have two large dogs there.

Jonas's solid shape appeared in the entrance into the cell. "Got anything to eat? I could do with a break."

"A break? What have you been doing?"

Delta came over to the cell. Inside, the only light was the blue shine from Jonas's tablet screen. He gestured at it. "I've been emailing a PI friend of mine, giving him some information he can use to look into the persons involved here. I want to know a bit more about Amanda White. What she did before she married, etc."

"That must be decades ago."

"He's thorough." Jonas sat cross-legged on his mattress.

Delta came to sit beside him and opened the bag she

was carrying. "Hazel insisted on preparing a complete picnic for us. She felt rather guilty for diving into her warm bed while we would be out here waiting for a culprit to turn up." She pulled out a thermos. "Coffee." A packet wrapped in aluminum foil. "Turkey sandwiches." Then a bowl. "Salad to go with them. Hazel insisted we needed something healthy." She grinned as she added, "I put in the chips and double chocolate cookies. Healthy, fine, but a sleepover needs snacks, right?"

"Right," Jonas said as he took a cookie and bit into it, crumbs flying everywhere.

Delta leaned back against the wall. The quiet tickled across her tight nerve ends. "I don't even hear traffic in the street."

"This is a small town. People sit in front of the TV or are already in bed. The only cars that do pass through town at night are tourists coming back from dinner or the casino."

"Can you gamble around here?" Delta asked, remembering Finn's addiction. Had he started again? Had Vera been blackmailing him with that knowledge, and had he lied to them to keep it from Hazel?

"The casino is twenty miles up the road." Jonas gestured with his hand. "I've never been inside, so I can't tell you much about it."

"Do you think Finn is still gambling? You work with him."

"He didn't strike me as having some hidden addiction. But I don't see him for hours on end, you know. We meet up every now and then, do a tour together. He could be hiding it."

Delta sighed. "Hazel took an extra mortgage on the shop to help Finn. I don't want her to get into trouble because she wanted to support her brother."

"Most of all, you don't want her to be disappointed in her brother." Jonas leaned his head against the wall. "Are you close with your brothers?"

"I told you Greg is traveling the world as a motivational speaker. I hardly ever see him. He doesn't even do Christmas at home. It's too bad, because I want to see Olaf grow up. With little kids, it goes so fast. They change from one week to another."

"And your other brother?"

Delta had been dreading that question. "I haven't spoken to Zach in years."

Jonas picked up the thermos and screwed off the cap. He poured two cups. That he didn't pounce right away and ask why made Delta feel a bit better.

Jonas handed her the cup of coffee. "Family can be a tough thing," he observed.

"I guess it was self-protection," Delta said. She stared into the coffee, trying to put into words what she had concluded about the family situation over the years. "Zach never liked Greg being the great athlete and my parents traveling the world with him. He also wanted attention from them, but he didn't get it. Not like Greg. You know, they were on the road with Greg, and they had put me up with Gran…and Zach just had to fend for himself. He was in college and…I guess we all supposed he would be fine. He got a degree in finance and started working at a bank. He met this girl and they decided to get married. The wedding took place on a day when Greg had to compete for a title. I guess that…it was Zach's way of testing if Mom and Dad would come to his wedding or if Greg's sport meant more. Like it always had."

Delta's throat went tight. She clenched the coffee cup,

feeling the heat sear into her fingers. "Mom wanted to go to the wedding. Dad said that Zach had done it on purpose and he could have chosen another date. They argued about it for weeks. In the end…Dad stayed with Greg to support him in the competition. Mom came over for the wedding. Dad blamed her for it, but she went against him, for Zach's sake. Zach was disappointed anyway, because he had wanted Dad to come. It was always about Dad, you know."

She took a deep breath, feeling the old frustration wash over her. "I was angry at Zach for turning Mom and Dad against each other like that. For forcing them into making choices that would only hurt people's feelings. I didn't say anything at the wedding, because I didn't want to ruin it for him or for his bride, but…afterward he called me and tried to turn me against Dad as well. Or at least it felt that way. I told him I didn't want him to call me if he was going to be like that. And that was it. He never called me again."

Delta looked at Jonas's profile. "Do you think I did the wrong thing?"

"What did you do? You told him you didn't want to be caught in the middle. When he realized you weren't going to choose his side, he didn't want to be in touch anymore. That was his decision, not yours."

"I know. But still…I don't know how much Mom and Dad's choices for Greg's career hurt Zach. We just never talked about it as a family. We could have sat down, and he could have told us his side of it, and…"

"Maybe that wouldn't have solved anything." Jonas sipped his coffee. "My father never liked me wanting to be a police officer. He tried to set me up in the businesses of friends. I did try that world for a summer, but it wasn't for me. While I was with the police, it was hard to meet Dad at birthday parties and over Christmas. He'd never ask how I was doing, to show he didn't approve of my choice."

"And when you quit the force?" Delta glanced at him. "Did things change then?"

Jonas hesitated before saying, "He doesn't know I quit the force. I know he won't ask about my work, so I don't have to lie about it. And I just can't bring myself to fess up to him that it didn't work out. Like somehow it would be admitting he was right all along. But he wasn't. Because I will never work in his friends' businesses. You know?"

"I think I understand." Delta wanted to know why Jonas had left the police, but she didn't think asking directly was the best way to go about it. "You were right. Family is a tough thing."

They sat in silence, sipping coffee and staring ahead into the darkness.

Outside, a car engine hummed by, then died down in the distance. Overhead, the ceiling creaked. Spud moved about in his place, grunting before he went back to sleep. King lay with his legs stretched out, just a shadow in the darkness. The ding of an incoming email sounded loudly, and Delta jumped. Jonas reached for the tablet. "My PI friend," he reported. "About Amanda White."

He read in silence for a few minutes, then whistled softly. "Seems like she picked up substantial debts a few years ago. Buying luxury stuff like shoes, designer bags, home decor. All on credit cards away from her husband's scrutiny. She was on the edge of having process servers turn up at her door when her debts were paid off over a short span of time."

"Did her husband find out and step in before it became public?" Delta ventured.

"No. Seems she took care of it herself. But it's unclear

where the money came from. And now this is interesting. The payment of the debts happened shortly before her birthday. Before the party where she introduced Vera to her brother-in-law Herb."

Delta sat up. "You think...Vera found out about Amanda's problems and paid off the debts for her in exchange for an introduction to Herb?"

"Finn told us Vera had found out about his gambling debts, right? But what she said to Finn was only that she knew why he had left LA in such a rush and would tell on him. She suggested she knew a lot more than she might have. So Vera could also have found out about Amanda White's credit cards being overdrawn, maybe because she was a customer at the same boutique and overheard when Amanda's card was refused or something like that. Then she followed her and suggested a solution: the introduction to Herb in exchange for clearance of the debts." Jonas nodded in satisfaction. "That could also explain why Amanda said to Vera that if Vera didn't stop flirting with Ralph, she'd tell the truth. About the introduction at the time."

"And then Vera retorted that the truth would hurt Amanda as well, because it would mean confessing to her excessive shopping and the debts, which had led her to agree to Vera's scheme." Delta nodded. "That could all fit."

"Question is," Jonas said, "whether this can constitute a motive for murder. Amanda was worried Vera would talk. Her husband would be livid, not just about the money wasted but also about her using his brother. He would blame her for having brought Vera into their lives—Vera, who was about to get a divorce and walk away with half of Herb's fortune. Endangering the future of the business Ralph and Herb had built with a lot of hard work and sacrifice."

"Yes, but did Ralph know about Vera's divorce plans? Did Amanda know about them?"

"If they knew, it would have made it all worse. Imagine being Amanda." Jonas held Delta's gaze. "You take a woman into your family who turned out to be flirty, manipulative, showy, drinking too much, embarrassing you. Then you find out she's also going to walk away with a fortune, leaving your family in financial trouble. And, with the truth about the introduction out, exposing you as the cause of it all. You'd do anything to prevent that from happening. By killing Vera, Amanda would have made sure that Vera wouldn't get a dime and the blackmail that brought her into their lives would never become known."

"Clever," Delta said. "I hope the police can still do something with her dress."

"Yes." Jonas stared ahead with a frown. "But can we really assume Amanda knew about the impending divorce? It seems like Vera was careful to keep it quiet. She had the paperwork sent to the local post office here in Tundish and picked it up herself. She hid it in her box in the hotel safe. She even hid the notebooks with the blackmail money in that same box, to ensure nobody found out she was hoarding money to support herself during divorce proceedings. How can Amanda have found out about it?"

"We don't know, and maybe it doesn't matter. Maybe the fight I overheard in the garden triggered it all. Maybe Amanda was so worried that Vera would tell the truth about the past that she killed her for that alone. Maybe they kept fighting in the bar and Amanda grabbed the ice pick and stabbed her on impulse, in a flash of anger. It may not have been well thought out or logical."

"Of course not. I've worked on cases where someone

did something extreme merely because a lot of small incidents had been stacking up, and they couldn't take the pressure anymore. Amanda and Vera never got along, so maybe the tension between them on the night of the party was just the final straw." Jonas held up the thermos. "More coffee?"

"Definitely. I have to stay awake."

"No, you don't. You can leave the watch to me." Jonas poured the steaming coffee into Delta's cup. "Assuming Amanda killed Vera leaves a few points unclear. Why did Ralph get into Ray's car in town? Why did Ray lie about knowing Vera earlier? If he's not involved in her murder, he could have been upfront about having met her before she came to the Lodge."

"There's something I've been wondering... Did Ray break up Rosalyn and her fiancé?" Delta mused. "If so, why? Does it prove he has a mean streak? That his kindness is just an act to delude us all?" She closed her eyes a moment. "Maybe I should ask Ray about it and see how he responds. And what about Fred Halliday? He seems so close with Amanda. If Amanda is the killer, might she have killed for Fred's sake? To keep their...relationship a secret?"

"Well, they're not exactly secretive about seeing each other. Or enjoying each other's company."

"Right. That doesn't make sense. But it could make sense to assume Fred killed for Amanda. He claims to have been boating during the party, but at some point, he came back to the hotel. He said it was when the police were already there, but what if he's lying and it was earlier? What if he found out about the fight between Amanda and Vera, maybe because he ran into Amanda, being all upset? What if Fred confronted Vera in the bar and told her to leave Amanda alone? But she wouldn't. I heard her responses in the garden. She could be really cold and callous when she wanted to."

"And to defend the honor of the lady he loves, Halliday picked up the ice pick and killed her? I can't see him being so gallant. He is charming to all the ladies, but I believe he mostly loves himself."

"Hmm." Having just seen Halliday with a female hotel guest at the antique fair, Delta could hardly deny he seemed like a ladies' man. She opened her eyes again and picked up her phone. "I'm going to have a look at the digital newspaper our Mr. LeDuc Jr. put together for the day." She looked for the site and scanned the headlines. "His leaf-peeping photo competition continues to deliver stunning pics. This one..." She held out the phone to Jonas to show him a forest lane where the yellow trees formed a huge gold arch across the path. A little boy was kicking up leaves. "Are you participating?"

"I'm on the fence about it. Maybe it's more a thing for the tourists. I mean, the grand prize is a balloon ride. I've taken those in other places, so I'd rather have someone else win it."

"How altruistic." Delta clicked through to another page. "Oh, listen to this. Local hotel takeover? Serious rumors have surfaced that the Lodge Hotel is up for a takeover. An offer has been made, for an unknown amount of money. The attorney who presented the deal to the Taylor family is said to work for an undisclosed party in—"

Jonas waved a hand. "Bad reporting. He doesn't know the amount of money or the party..."

"In Miami!" Delta finished her sentence anyway. "Remember the Whites are from Miami?"

Jonas stared at her. "But the Whites are into dolphin-spotting. Why would they want to take over a hotel in Montana? There are no dolphins in the lake."

"No, but the lake offers other boating options. And our boating man is Fred Halliday, who happens to be an old friend of Amanda White. Maybe he pointed out the business opportunity to her and she passed it on to Ralph and Herb? They might have traveled here to check out the premises in person and then make their offer through the lawyer mentioned in this piece."

Jonas shook his head. "The hotel has been in the hands of the Taylor family ever since it was built. Why would they sell it?"

"A takeover doesn't always mean big changes. The new owner might want to keep things as they were. Suppose Rosalyn could stay on as manager and everyone could keep their jobs. The only thing that would change in that scenario would be the ownership, the name on the papers. And the financial risk would transfer to someone else. Would a takeover like that be such a bad deal?"

Jonas shrugged. "I don't see the Taylors working for someone else."

Delta narrowed her eyes. "Ralph claimed that Ray borrowed money from Vera White. What if she wanted her money back but he couldn't give it to her, and he told her that he had a share in a hotel coming, and her husband and his brother might buy into this hotel?"

"Which is not his to negotiate about," Jonas objected.

"We don't know what Mr. Taylor's will says. If he splits the hotel equally between his three children, Ray may argue he will own one third of the hotel. What if he promised Vera to put pressure on his father and the other family members to agree to the takeover? Rosalyn doesn't like Ray, but his father seems to listen to him, and Isabel adores him. That could explain why Rosalyn didn't want him in the family portrait. She's livid because he's splitting the family over this hotel takeover." Delta pursed her lips. "I think that first thing in the morning we should find out if there is any truth in the rumors about a takeover and the undisclosed party from Miami possibly being the White brothers."

Delta awoke with a shock, immediately aware that she wasn't in her bed. Her neck was twisted, and her forehead seemed to touch something hard. She opened her eyes, but it was too dark to make out anything. Feeling around her, she realized her head must have slipped off the air mattress she had sagged onto as she had fallen asleep. A sound from the shop jerked her to full alertness. Was someone there?

She felt beside her for Jonas. He was gone.

Her heart pounded hard as she pushed herself up. Had the perpetrator who had broken their window returned? Armed with a new threat?

She had nothing to defend herself with, so she picked up the empty coffee thermos. Clutching it, she tiptoed to the doorway from the cell into the shop.

In the light that came in from the street she saw Jonas standing in the shop, hiding behind the wooden boards that closed up the broken window.

"What's wrong?" she whispered.

"Go back in there," he hissed to her.

She retreated. Her heartbeat sped up even more as she waited for something to happen. Was last night's assailant outside, intending to throw another brick, this time through the pane in the door? Would Jonas be quick enough to go out after him or her and catch the culprit?

The silence seemed to stretch on endlessly. Even the slightest tick in the wooden floorboards made Delta jump.

Then Jonas appeared in the doorway. "False alarm. Someone was in the street, stopping at the door. But it was just a man with his dog. I caught sight of them as they crossed the street."

"A man with his dog?" Delta checked her watch. It was nearly 2:30. "Odd time to be walking your dog."

"Some people watch TV until well into the night. Especially if they're elderly and don't have to work anymore." Jonas rolled back his shoulders. "I guess you can go back to sleep."

Delta hid her face in her hands. "I hadn't meant to fall asleep in the first place. I'm stiff as a board."

"I told you to go home to the cottage."

"Well, I'm here now, and I'm not leaving in the middle of the night." Delta yawned. "I think a turkey sandwich would be great."

"Midnight snacker, huh?" Jonas asked with a half grin. "Want one too?"

They divided the sandwiches between them. The turkey meat was soft and tasty; the sauce Hazel had whipped up, smooth and rich.

Delta hmmed. "She should ask Mine Forever's owner to put this on the menu. It would attract fans."

"Since we're wide awake," Jonas said, reaching for his tablet, "I might as well show you a little photo gallery." He pulled up a series of photographs.

Delta said, "People in party dress. Are those...? But I thought your memory card was with the police."

"Sure. But one of the deputies returned it to me last night. They copied off the contents, so there was no reason for them to hold onto the memory card. Now let's see if we can find something meaningful in here. It's a ton of shots, some out of focus or overexposed."

"I'm not judging a photo contest but looking for clues." Delta chewed the last bite of her sandwich and studied the photos closely. Most involved people talking, dancing, accepting drinks from passing waiters. A few captured Vera White's demonstration dance with Ralph. Even in these stills, it was clear the couple had been light on their feet. Glamorous.

Delta went back and decided she should look at specific people. Ray for instance. He was in a couple of shots. She looked at his face, his hands, his clothes, looking for anything amiss. Nothing special struck her.

Isabel, then? Nothing either. Just that the bracelet she had worn earlier, in the family portrait, was gone later that night. It fit with Finn having found it in the dead woman's hand. But how had it gotten there?

Finn… Yes, she also had to look at him with an open mind. Assess if he had been behaving oddly. But there were no pictures of him talking to Vera White, other than the one the sheriff had pointed out to them, and nothing else he was doing seemed out of character or unusual.

Rosalyn…

Jonas yawned and drew his knees up to his chest.

"You can go to sleep if you want to," Delta said. "I can wake you if I hear something."

"I wouldn't be much of a guard if I fell asleep."

"Here." Delta showed him a picture of Rosalyn talking to an elderly couple. "Do you think that's a bracelet on her arm?"

Jonas looked. "Hard to tell. She's half turned away. Could be a flash of something gold there. But it could also be reflection of something else."

"Yes. I wonder... She wasn't wearing any bracelets earlier that night. I got a good look at her when she welcomed us and got into the family portrait. She was wearing elbow-length gloves but no bracelets. Here, wait. There we have her again. Look! She *is* wearing a bracelet."

Jonas pulled the tablet from Delta's hands and swiped through the pictures. "You're right. And it's the same one Isabel was wearing earlier. Isabel passed it to Rosalyn for some reason."

"So if Rosalyn had it and then later Vera White..." Jonas tapped the tablet on his upper leg. "What does that mean? She never said she had it."

"No, and the police didn't find her fingerprints on it because she was wearing gloves. She wouldn't have left prints on the murder weapon either."

Jonas held her gaze. "You think Rosalyn might have killed Vera White?"

"Why not? She didn't tell the police she had handled the bracelet. She acted like she was so concerned when Isabel was arrested, but she said nothing about her having had the bracelet later on the party night. And consider this. What if she found out that Ray had informed the White brothers that they might take over the hotel and his loan from Vera was the cause of all of this? Rosalyn can be very emotional when it comes to the hotel."

"And Vera pulled the bracelet from her arm during a struggle or something?" Jonas frowned hard. "Wouldn't Rosalyn have noticed that and taken it back, knowing it could implicate Isabel?"

"Maybe she stabbed Vera on impulse and then ran off right away, afraid someone would come in and see her."

"It's a possibility, of course. West should see if there

is any indication the weapon was handled with gloves on. Some gloves leave fibers on a surface."

Delta leaned back and closed her eyes. "I'm going to ask Rosalyn about her fiancé as soon as I can. I have a feeling it's important somehow. She and Ray, the feud between them."

Jonas said, "Just as long as you don't get yourself into trouble."

Delta heard him speak in the distance as if he were fading away. She wanted to say something else, but her head sagged to the side, and she drifted off into sleep.

Chapter Seventeen

"I can't recommend anyone sleeping on an air mattress," Delta messaged to the Paper Posse the next morning. She pushed her back against the car seat to stretch her stiff muscles. Beside her, Jonas seemed to be fresh and eager to start the day. "Well, at least not if you're not lying down on it in a proper fashion. I'm exhausted. But the show must go on. Who has got something to give?"

Rattlesnake Rita chimed in first, reporting that a volunteer at the museum had told her she had seen the dead woman's best friend, Amanda White, with a man in a flashy sports car. "If she thinks those two were friends," Rita wrote, "she never paid any kind of attention. But the sports car might be important."

"We know who it belongs to," Delta replied, "and we tracked the owner of your moose car as well. But what it all means..."

Calamity Jane wrote, "The *Tundish Trader* had a fascinating headline this morning: *Dead woman's stationery jackpot.* Apparently, the sheriff found cash money inside the woman's notebooks."

"How did LeDuc find out about that?" Delta exclaimed.

Jonas, who was driving, threw her a quick look. "What editor found out about what?"

"The *Tundish Trader* has a headline suggesting they know about the cash found in the notebooks. Someone at the sheriff's station must have leaked it to them."

"I guess it caused some excitement and it got out." Jonas looked disapproving but resigned. "You can't prevent that in a small town. People walk in and out of the police station to report a missing chicken or a stolen wallet, especially in this busy tourist season, and then they overhear the deputies talking."

"I wonder what Herb White will think about that. Maybe we can ask him at the hotel." Delta checked her watch. "He should still be at breakfast."

At the Lodge, they found Herb White in the breakfast room with his brother, Ralph, beleaguered by three reporters who all tried to hold their microphones to his face. The logos on their shirts revealed they were with various local TV or radio stations. The revelations about a "stationery jackpot" seemed to have convinced them there was a story there to fill a slot in their news programs.

"I didn't know anything about it," they could hear Herb say, holding up his hands in a gesture to ward them off. "I had no idea my wife had money of her own. I don't know where it comes from or what she wanted with it. It must all be a misunderstanding."

Jonas hitched a brow and looked at Delta. "Cash purposely hidden in notebooks a misunderstanding?"

Ralph White barked to the reporters, "Leave us alone. We're trying to have a peaceful breakfast. We're not going to say anymore. Just go away now."

He gestured to a waiter who rushed over with a silver coffeepot, apparently intending to refill his cup. But Ralph held a hand over his cup, snapping, "Can you send these people away? They're harassing us."

The waiter seemed reluctant to intervene, but Rosalyn breezed in and immediately headed for the reporters. "Please leave," she said in a crisp tone. "You're not guests, you have no right to be here."

"How about a statement on the hotel's takeover position?" one of them asked. They immediately shoved their microphones forward and waited eagerly, firing off questions in quick succession. "Who is the unknown party who made you the offer? How much money is involved? Are you seriously considering it? What would it mean for the hotel? Will there be dismissals? Will the name stay the same?"

Rosalyn repeated "No comment" a couple of times before adding an exasperated "Now leave, before I call the police."

As she reached into her jacket pocket for her cell phone, the reporters retreated into the lobby.

Rosalyn smoothed back her hair, which was sleek and parted in the middle today. She looked tense.

Delta went over to her. "Could I talk to you for a moment? Not here, but in private?"

Rosalyn seemed to want to say no, but then her eyes landed on Jonas and she waved them along into the lobby.

At the reception desk, the reporters were badgering the clerk about the hotel takeover. One of them asked, "Do you know how much money is involved?"

"I really don't…" the clerk fumbled.

Rosalyn snapped, "Get out of here now! Or I *will* call the police."

The reporters looked at each other and walked out of the door, halting just two steps away from it to talk to Fred Halliday, who was sauntering up with an oar in his hand.

Rosalyn groaned but seemed to conclude that she couldn't prevent him from talking to the reporters if he wanted. She waved Delta and Jonas along into her office.

As soon as the door was shut, Delta said, "Is there any truth to these takeover rumors? I understood the hotel has been in the hands of the Taylor family for many generations. I can imagine it's a heritage you wouldn't want to turn over."

Jonas added, "Did the takeover offer come from the White brothers? If their plans for the Lodge are as tacky as their slogans to promote their dolphin-spotting business, I shudder to think of what the Lodge will become."

Rosalyn eyed him coldly. "Why would you care about the Lodge? Or are you worried they might fire you and hire on new staff, against lower pay?"

Before Jonas could respond, Rosalyn focused on Delta and spat, "You said earlier you came here to look into the murder to clear Finn. Finn is free now, so your job is done." It sounded like she wasn't happy about him being free.

Rosalyn's head-on approach put Delta in fighting mode as well. She said sweetly, "Isabel is still considered a suspect because of her fingerprints on the bracelet. I'm surprised you didn't make a statement to clear her. I thought you genuinely cared for her."

"Of course I do." Rosalyn looked unbalanced for a moment, trying to work out what Delta was referring to. "And what statement do you mean?"

"That it was you who last had the bracelet before Vera White ended up with it in the bar. We saw it in photos from the party."

Jonas added, "West has those photos as well. He will notice and understand what it means."

Delta doubted that the sheriff was going through all the photos in as much detail as they had, but she kept her mouth shut.

"What do you mean?" Rosalyn asked Jonas. Her voice

was icy; her eyes, calculating. Her hands resting on the desk lay very still, as if her whole being was focused on the conversation.

Delta wondered if they were sitting across from a murderer who was dead set on escaping justice.

She said, "You handled the bracelet before it came to Vera. Did she pull it off your arm in a struggle? You must have had some reason not to tell the police. It would have cleared Isabel."

"Not necessarily." Rosalyn stared up at the ceiling for a moment.

Delta wanted to know what she meant by those cryptic words, but Jonas said, "I have to bring it to the sheriff's attention. You were wearing gloves that night, so you didn't leave fingerprints on the bracelet."

Rosalyn's eyes shot sparks at Jonas. Delta was sure she would just keep her mouth shut. Then Rosalyn seemed to come to a decision. "All right, so I did handle the bracelet. Isabel had told me before that the clasp wasn't working well anymore. During the party, I saw it lying on the floor. It had come loose and fallen from her arm. I picked it up and put it on my own arm. I took a bit of flexible wire from a flower arrangement on one of the standing tables to secure the clasp so it wouldn't come open again. Isabel has always been rather careless with her things. I wanted to tell her off about having lost it. At an appropriate moment, of course."

"And then?" Delta asked.

"Vera White"—Rosalyn hesitated—"approached me. She wanted money to keep silent about her affair with Ray and money she had supposedly lent him. I don't much care about Ray's reputation, but I do care about my family. A married woman conducting an affair, staying at our hotel, money involved. I didn't want her to talk about it or maybe even turn to the press with it. The tabloids have always liked to write about Ray. I had no money at hand, and therefore, I gave her the bracelet. I figured that since Isabel had lost it in the first place, nobody would be able to determine later what had happened to it. Vera took it and left. I haven't seen her since. I certainly don't know who stabbed her."

Jonas laughed softly. "A likely story."

"It's all Ray's fault. If he had never played around with her and used his charm to get money out of her, money he couldn't repay..."

"Are you sure he did?" Delta asked. "He denies it. Both the affair and the loan."

"Ray is..." Rosalyn fell silent. She stared at the desk with a bitter expression.

Remembering Rosalyn's happy expression in the family photos when her fiancé had still been there, Delta felt for her, but still she was determined to get to the bottom of the breach and Ray's possible part in it. She asked, "Did Ray cause the breach with your fiancé? He wrote to you from France to end the relationship, and Ray was in France at the time."

Rosalyn looked at her, startled, it seemed, at the mention of this personal detail.

"The *Trader* wrote about someone missing from the family photos," Delta explained. "And I found out online that Ray was in France at the same time as your ex. It seemed like an odd coincidence."

Rosalyn flinched when the *Trader*'s report was mentioned, but she controlled herself again quickly. Only the way she clenched her hands together betrayed the hidden hurt over what had happened. "Yes. If you have to know, Ray gave him money to stop seeing me. At the time, Ray's career was booming, and he was afraid Daddy would want him back here for the hotel in case I got married, got pregnant, and wanted to leave the business. So he made sure I never got around to marrying."

Rosalyn banged the desk with her fist. "And now that his career has ended and he's got no place to go, he's back here wanting the hotel. First, he ruined my engagement, so he wouldn't need to come home, and now he's back to throw me out of the hotel that cost me everything I cared for. Bastard. *Bastard.*" Her voice cracked on the latter word, and she clenched her jaw as if fighting tears.

Delta held her breath. If this was true, Ray Taylor was a terribly selfish and callous man. Someone who only cared for his own success, safety...

Someone who might be willing to kill?

Rosalyn took a deep breath, leaning her hands on the desk again as if to steady them. "Now you know everything."

"Do we?" Jonas said. "Has someone really offered to buy the hotel?"

"I'm not sure. Father knows more, I guess, but he's not telling me." Rosalyn's expression contorted. "Why would he? I'm only the manager. It's not like I have a right to know."

"She's pretty bitter," Jonas observed as they stood outside the hotel.

Delta released her breath slowly. Inside, there had been so much tension that she hadn't noticed how stiff she was holding herself, not allowing her body to relax for a single moment. She pulled back her shoulders and stretched. "I guess she has every reason to be. Ray used her to take care of the hotel when he didn't want to, and now that his career is over, he's ready to step in and leave Rosalyn empty-handed."

Jonas frowned at her. "That's her story. We haven't heard his. We don't know if any of what she told us is true."

Delta tilted her head. "You're suddenly supporting Ray Taylor?"

Jonas scoffed. "I'm not supporting him. I'm just saying we don't know what really happened when Rosalyn's fiancé broke it off with her. Maybe she just couldn't accept it was over and she invented this story of Ray having come between them to make it easier on herself."

"An outward cause for the breach instead of having to ask herself what had gone wrong between the two of them?"

"Exactly."

A jazzy tune filled the air, and Jonas dug into his pocket, extracting his phone. "Sorry, have to take this call. Hello?"

He turned his back on her and walked a few paces away, holding the phone to his ear. "And you're sure about that? OK. That's very helpful. Thanks."

Delta was at his side the moment he turned back. "Helpful? In the case?"

"My PI friend. It turns out Herb White knew about the impending divorce. He'd been to the bank to ask if he could get a loan to ensure his business stayed on its feet if he had to pay off his wife."

"So he did know she was going to leave him." Delta pursed her lips. "And he realized it would mean parting with a lot of money."

"Money he couldn't afford to lose." Jonas pointed his phone at her to underline his conclusion. "The bank turned him down. So if the divorce had gone through and Herb had had to pay up..."

"He might have lost the business."

"In any case, he would have been in trouble, looking foolish to his brother Ralph, business relations, etc. He had every reason to prevent the divorce."

"But with murder?" Delta asked softly.

Jonas held her gaze. "Well, now he's the poor widower everyone feels sorry for. And he doesn't have to pay Vera a dime."

Delta nodded slowly. "The murder happened in the bar. Vera was walking around with that gold bracelet in her hand. She was also pretty drunk. When she came into our workshop, she was already acting rather giggly and unstable on her legs. Later in the night, she must really have been...maybe talkative? Telling Herb she was getting ready to walk away?"

"Or he simply asked what she was doing with the bracelet, and something she said or how she acted put him onto the blackmail. He picked up the ice pick and stabbed her, thinking the police would suspect someone else of having killed her. There were enough people around to provide plenty of potential suspects."

Jonas tapped the phone in the palm of his free hand. "It could fit, but we do have a problem."

"How to prove it," Delta said at once.

"Herb White is a clever man. He knows the police don't suspect him. All he has to do is sit tight and not make a mistake, and he will get away with it."

"Then we have to force him into making a mistake," Delta said.

Jonas looked her over. "How do you mean?"

"We have to make sure he learns that there is something that could give him away. Evidence that might point in his direction. And that we are looking for it to clear Finn and Hazel. Then he will get desperate, try to ensure that we don't find what we're looking for, and we can catch him red-handed."

Jonas looked doubtful. "How can we let him learn something?"

Delta looked around her. "What room is he in? What does he do around the hotel? Is there a place he often goes? Somewhere we can be sure to find him?"

Jonas shrugged. "I heard that he's a secret smoker. The hotel has a strict no-smoking policy so he has to do it outside. Halliday mentioned to me that there were cigarette butts lying on the wooden plateau overlooking the lake." He gestured toward the place where Delta had overheard Vera and Amanda fighting.

"That's perfect." Delta clapped her hands together. "Sound carries far when you're outside. The plateau is higher, and there's a path leading down to the lake running away from it. We can stand there and discuss the evidence while Herb is up there smoking."

"And then?" Jonas asked. His eyes betrayed that he still wasn't convinced it could work.

"Herb also knows his wife went to the birding hut alone. By now there is talk about her and possible affairs. So we can say we are sure she hid something at the birding hut. He will think it has to do with the divorce and will come to look for it."

Before Jonas could say it was a lousy plan, Delta continued, "He is bound to come out to smoke before dinner. Then we can do our little act. He'll go out to the birding hut at once to search before nightfall. We'll catch him, and it'll be over."

Jonas considered her proposition in silence. "And what if he doesn't come?"

"Then maybe we're wrong about him, and he didn't kill his wife. We'll have to continue looking for another killer."

Jonas played with his phone. "I don't like it."

"I never said I liked it either. I just think it's a way to try and see if Herb White is our man. Why would he have lied to the police that he had no idea that his wife was looking into divorcing him?"

"Because it would have given him motive for murder."

"Yes, but would he have thought that far ahead if he was truly innocent?"

"He's a proud man. Arrogant, full of himself. He'd never admit his wife was about to walk out on him. That doesn't mean he's a murderer."

"Maybe not, but we can try to find out. What do we have to lose?"

Jonas put his phone away. "OK. Your way. We'll see if he pops out to smoke before dinner, and then we'll let him overhear our conversation. But I doubt he's going to act on it. Why would he? His fingerprints aren't on the murder weapon. The police can't prove he touched it. Or that he was even in the bar."

"I know. Oh, look, there's Ray." Delta pointed to the tall, ex-footballer appearing with a few teens by his side. He had mentioned earlier that he was taking groups of them boating. They were laughing and talking, then the teens said goodbye. Delta went over to Ray. "Hello there. Had a good time? You look like you're really great with teens. Maybe you can do something with them, for a new career?"

Ray tilted his head, studying her from under his baseball cap. "Why would you be thinking about what I should do for a new career?"

Delta shrugged. "My older brother was a professional

athlete. I know how hard it can be to start over when all of the sports commitments are gone. You need a new challenge, and doing something you love is the best start."

Ray nodded. "I see. What did your brother do?"

Delta told him a bit about Greg's achievements, even showing him some photos online of medal ceremonies. Ray seemed to relax.

Lowering her phone, Delta said, "You see there is life after the sports career. I could put you in touch with Greg if you want to."

"Nah, I don't see myself turning into a speaker. But something with kids, that would be nice."

"I'm sure you can look into ways to do that." Delta took a deep breath. "If you get out of Rosalyn's hair, you might also improve your relationship with her. You mentioned to me repeatedly that you used to be great friends and she supported you. Maybe she can support you again?"

She waited a moment and then added, "Of course, you'd have to clear up the bit about...what happened in France."

"France?" Ray echoed.

"Yes. You met up with her fiancé there, didn't you? When you were in training camp and he was on a business trip?"

"How do you know that?" Ray's expression, which had been relaxed discussing Greg's sports career, turned tense and guarded. He fidgeted with his cuff link.

"You were there when he was there. France is of course not exactly a tiny country, but isn't it logical you would have met? The man was planning on marrying your sister. At the time."

Ray's features were tight. "It's a good thing it never happened. He wasn't what Rosalyn believed him to be."

"Is that why you helped things along?"

"Excuse me?"

"Rosalyn thinks you gave him money so he'd stop seeing her. She's upset about it. Understandably. But if you can prove to her he was no good and..." Delta doubted Rosalyn would be open to hearing this, but she wanted to see how Ray responded.

Ray sighed and studied the ground. "I can't tell her what happened. She'd be humiliated."

"She already suspects you. It can't get any worse."

"Oh, but it can." Ray looked up at her. "Yes, I gave him money because he claimed he needed it for the wedding. He didn't want to admit to Rosalyn that he couldn't afford all the frills she wanted. I believed him—Rosalyn was kind of a bridezilla, you know—so I gave him some money. Then he broke it off with her and vanished."

"Ouch!" Delta flinched under the implications of the story. "Was he ever really interested in Rosalyn?"

"No. Looking back on it, I'm sure he came after her only because he intended to get money out of the Taylor family at some point. Having access to me, abroad, provided him with the perfect opportunity. He looked me up, not vice versa."

"But he had money of his own." Delta was confused. "Terry at Mine Forever mentioned that he breezed through town in a Jaguar, no less."

"Rented car. All done to impress us and work his way into our confidence. Once he vanished, I had a PI look into him. Nothing he told us was real."

Ray leaned over to her and continued urgently, "But I can't tell Rosalyn that. She was so upset when it ended. I don't want her to realize he never loved her."

Delta stared at him. "You kept your mouth shut because you wanted to protect her feelings? But she hates you for what happened! She thinks you bought off her fiancé. She stopped supporting you because of that old incident. You lost all the money you gave the fellow for the wedding, and you also lost your sister's love."

Ray shrugged. "I didn't know Rosalyn believed that until you told me Isabel had said Rosalyn hated me for something from the past."

"You have to talk to her. You have to tell her the truth."

"Why would she even believe me?"

"Ray." Delta put her hand on his arm. "The man in question left your lives years ago. He got his money, which is what he wanted. But you still have each other. You have to clear things up, also for the sake of your father and Isabel. I'm sure deep down inside you all want to be a family again. United, not divided."

Ray rubbed his forehead. "This whole thing is such a mess. With the murder and all, the takeover rumors... I don't want my father to sell the hotel to strangers."

"You don't?" Delta tried to sound super surprised to lead up to her next question. A little lie might help to get him into talking. "Oh, but...after LeDuc Jr. exposed the takeover plans, the town is abuzz that you wanted the takeover and even led the Whites to make an offer."

Ray shook his head. "I met with Ralph White to talk about the takeover plans. He wanted to get me on his side so I could put pressure on my father to accept. But I refused to cooperate. Imagine him offering me a role in the daily operation of the hotel by way of a bribe!" Ray scoffed. "The Whites can't count on me to help them acquire the Lodge. But what if Dad thinks he has to sell because we, his kids, can't stick together and make it work?"

"Then you have to talk to him, too, and tell him you will

do anything to make it work. Not talking leads to so many problems." Delta thought of Zach and how he had walked away because he had felt like his family had never acknowledged him. She had to think about a way to make amends, open up a conversation.

She smiled at Ray. "Think about it. It could be worth it. Now I have to get going."

As she turned away, her full focus returned to the plan she had made with Jonas. A plan to lure Herb White into a trap. It relied on him acting on what he overheard, and it might not work at all, but they had to try.

Delta's heart beat fast as she realized how precarious Finn's position still was and how Hazel still sat in the shadow of suspicion. How could her best friend have a decent life in a small town like Tundish if people kept whispering that her brother might have killed someone?

They had to clear up the case and prove someone else did it, beyond a doubt.

"I told you he wouldn't come." Jonas shifted his weight in the narrow space beside Delta. They had hidden themselves behind a stack of logs near the birding hut. Peeking over or around it, they could keep an eye out for anyone coming to the hut, but their view was half-obstructed by brush. Right behind their backs was brush as well, and the thin twigs pricked painfully between Delta's shoulder blades.

Spud, who had come with Jonas as their secret weapon, lay on the ground, relaxed.

Jonas nodded at the dog. "Even Spud knows it's a no-go."

Delta elbowed him to make him shut up. After they had

followed Herb into the garden before dinner started at the hotel and had seen him flick out his pack of cigarettes and his lighter, she had felt incredibly motivated to make this work. While Herb ambled to the wooden plateau, Jonas had led her by way of another path down to the lake and along the bank so they could reach the path to go up again, as innocently as if they weren't aware of anyone standing over their heads.

Jonas had tapped her arm and gestured for her to sniff the air, and as she had also smelled the sharp sting of cigarette smoke, she had felt excitement rush through her veins. They were actually going to pull it off. They had to.

Their discussion had been brief and charged as it would have been had they really been exchanging new, vital information in the case. Jonas had said he'd look in the hut later that night, since he first had to pick up some guests who were arriving at the train station.

"Halliday would have done it," he had said in an annoyed tone, "but he's having dinner with the Whites, *again*. I think he fancies Amanda."

That would have struck Herb as the truth, probably, and as a reason why Jonas would have to play chauffeur for the hotel.

As they had walked away, Delta had thought anyone could hear her heart drum in the silence, just as it was doing now. It didn't matter that Jonas said Herb wasn't coming. She willed him to come. She needed this to work.

A twig snapped in the forest. In the silence, it sounded as loud as a gunshot.

Spud raised his head, his ears turning forward.

Jonas put a hand on his head to keep him quiet. The dog didn't make a peep but kept looking in the direction of the sound.

Jonas carefully stretched his neck to peek around the stacked logs. "Someone just went inside," he said. "I couldn't see who it was."

Delta's breath caught. What if Herb White was innocent? What if he had mentioned as dinner began what he had overheard while he had been smoking? Maybe scoffing at those "armchair detectives" who were poking into his wife's murder, messing it all up with their amateur actions? And what if someone else at that table had taken the hint? Who was waiting in there for them?

Could it be Ralph? The brother-in-law who had become a little too cozy with his dancing partner and had then realized that Vera wasn't just quick on her feet, but also rather poisonous in what she might do to his marriage? Had he become tired of the callous way in which she treated people? Had they argued in the bar, and had Ralph stabbed Vera?

Or was the figure who had just entered the hut Fred Halliday, the secret lover of Amanda White who had stabbed Vera to keep their affair a secret? But Fred and Amanda showed themselves together around the hotel, without caring who saw them or thought something of it. That made no sense at all.

Delta's mouth went dry. Could it be Amanda, who had taken her dress to the dry cleaners right after the party? Had there been blood on the dress? Was she her sister-in-law's killer?

Jonas rose to his feet. "I'm going to see what he's doing."

"He or she," Delta whispered. "I'm coming too."

Jonas motioned for her to stay, but she followed him on tiptoe, careful to avoid stepping on anything that could create a loud noise in the quiet forest.

A few birds sang in the distance and a mouse rustled away,

but otherwise it was still, as if even the forest knew something was up and held its breath, waiting for the showdown.

Inside the birding hut, tapping resounded, muffled dragging.

Delta stopped beside Jonas and glanced at him. His expression betrayed concentration, an attempt to visualize what was happening inside.

Spud, pressed close to Jonas's side, held his head up, muzzle moving to sniff the air, inhaling the intruder's scent.

A muttered curse rang out. The voice was low, probably male.

Delta wished they could just go in there, but Jonas had said in advance the room inside the birding hut was too small for a confrontation, and they'd have to wait outside. Delta had no idea how whoever was in there would respond to being discovered, but she did know she'd have felt a lot better if Jonas had still been in active service and carrying a gun.

Red streaked the skies above as the sun began to set, and some geese flew over, the dark silhouettes outlined against the skies in that distinctive V shape.

Then, all of a sudden, a figure emerged from the hut. The man stopped and stared at them, his hands halfway up as though about to grab at something.

It was Herb White. A fleece jacket was slung over his suit, a baseball cap drawn deep over his eyes. He watched them a moment, then he began to laugh. "Oh boy. You really think you're cops, don't you?" He slapped his knee. "You tell a story, and now I came up here, and you're looking at me like it somehow makes me guilty. Well, I'll tell you what. I lost something here. A gold lighter. Worth a pretty penny. So when I heard you talking about the hut, I figured it might be here and I'd better find it before you did."

"And did you?" Jonas asked, his voice deceptively calm.

"Yep." Herb dug into his pocket and held up a lighter. "All's well that ends well, huh?"

"Not quite," Jonas said, still leaning back on his heels as if relaxed and enjoying a little chat during an evening walk. "You see, we know that you knew. About your wife planning to divorce you. About the money she'd demand to settle the divorce. About the trouble you'd be in with the business."

Herb White stood motionless, his eyes flickering over them as he waited for more.

Jonas said, "You love your business. You built it with your own hands, your hard work. You were away for long days on end while your wife just spent your money. It would hardly be fair if you had to share with her. But she had gone to a good lawyer and...well, maybe it's unfair to say now, but once upon a time it was true: you were in love with her and you were blinded as to her real motives for coming into your life. You wanted her to have money. You'd never divorce her anyway. So you actually agreed to some settlements..."

"You have no idea what kind of bitch that woman was." Herb White's voice was low and threatening. "She smiled at me and wrapped me around her little finger. I was a wreck after my wife's death. I never went anywhere, I never did anything. I just worked. Then I met her. She came over, she talked to me. She even got me to dance with her. I felt her warmth and I...was alive again. After years of being dead, I was alive again."

Delta's heart clenched for the heartfelt emotion in the man's features as he spoke. As if just saying this out loud wrenched his gut.

Herb continued, "She listened to me talk about my wife. She didn't say I should be over it by now. She was so kind and understanding. Until she had me right where she wanted me. I was married to her. She had access to my money."

He wrung his hands into fists. "I loved her," he hissed. "I wouldn't have denied her anything. But still she complained. She pouted, she sulked. It was never enough, what I did for her. If I took her away for the weekend to Orlando, she had wanted to go to Venice. If I gave her a silver necklace, it should have been gold. She told me I had enough money in the bank but I was stingy. I was cheap."

His features contorted. "She was the one who was cheap! Flinging herself at every man, even my own brother. I couldn't bear to look at it. But I wasn't going to divorce her either. Give her half of what I had worked for? Never." He bit down hard.

"Over my dead body, is the appropriate thing to say in such cases," Jonas supplied. "But it turned out to be her dead body, not yours."

"You have no idea what it's like to feel people look at you. See the pity in their eyes when they see your wife flirting with other men. That young little wife while you're older, graying, carrying too many pounds. No wonder she's looking elsewhere. No wonder? No wonder?! She married *me*!"

He was screaming now, the forest echoing with his anger. "She married *me,* and she had to live with that. In exchange for access to the beloved money. The thing she married me for. Not for me. Never for me."

Delta stood motionless, wondering how they'd ever get this frantic man into the hands of the police. He seemed ready to lash out at them.

Herb said, "I couldn't take it anymore. The people watching, whispering. The looks on their faces, half-sorry, half-smirking. Especially later in the night when Vera was drunk. I followed her into the bar. I wanted to stop her from drinking even more. I wanted to tell her enough was enough and… She just laughed at me. She held out something gold to me, waving it in my face. She said she could get from others what she had never gotten from me. I saw her through a red haze. I picked up something. It was cold in my grasp. It was sharp, and it sparkled in the light."

Herb sucked in a breath. "I had to stop her from laughing at me. Laughing at the foolish little man I had been, dying for her warmth and her tenderness while all she had ever wanted was my money."

He stared at the ground. "It was so easy to kill her. One little stab, and she slipped to the floor. I didn't even try to revive her. I wasn't sorry either. Just cold inside like that thing in my hand. I cleaned it and put it back in the ice bucket. She was like ice. Her heart, her soul. If she even had one."

Herb stood and stared into emptiness, his face suddenly devoid of emotion, as if he had become a shell of a man now that the anger had rushed out of him in that stream of words. He stood and breathed the forest air while the red of the setting sun increased, painting the sky in blood.

Then his eyes came back to life. He stared at them a moment, a trapped animal staring at his hunter. He turned and ran, fast for an elderly man, who carried, by his own admittance, too many pounds. He was gone in a flash, around a corner of the path.

Jonas let Spud go. "Take him down," he ordered.

Delta raised a hand to her mouth. "Is he going to bite him? Hurt him?"

Jonas shook his head. "No. But he does know what to do when someone wants to get away."

They heard the dog barking and followed him quickly.

Delta bit her lip as she ran beside Jonas through the bend in the path.

Herb White lay facedown in the dirt, his legs kicking, but without conviction. Spud stood over him, his front paws on his shoulders. He barked triumphantly.

Jonas came up quickly and took the dog's collar, pulled him back, then extracted a rope from his pocket and tied Herb's wrists together.

"You have no right to do this," the man hissed. "You are no cop."

"Ever heard of a citizen's arrest?" Delta asked, even though she had no idea if it was applicable to this situation.

Herb groaned. "You should have arrested that bitch and put her behind bars for what she did."

"She was a blackmailer," Jonas said. "If you had managed to prove that, by having some victims cooperate, she might indeed have gone behind bars. Or, to avoid that, she might have agreed to leave you, without taking half of your money with her. You could have negotiated to get her out of your life. You need not have killed her." He dragged Herb to his feet.

Herb stared at him. His clothes were dirty, his hair stood up. His eyes searched Jonas's expression. "You're not serious," he croaked.

"Yes, I am. You could have solved it without violence."

Herb hung his head, working his jaw as though barely keeping himself from bursting into tears.

Jonas gave his arm a little tug. "Come along now. It's all over."

Spud rubbed his head against Delta's leg and looked into her eyes. His warm brown gaze seemed to say, "Yes, it's over. Are you happy now?"

Delta squatted and gave the dog a hug. "You did great." She hid her face in his warm fur. "Thanks, buddy."

Chapter Eighteen

"Is there room for one more in here?"

Jonas's voice made Delta turn away from the noisy crowd in Wanted.

He stood at the door with Spud by his side, giving her a lopsided grin. To be honest, Delta hadn't expected him at their official "joined owners" party. Jonas just wasn't the sort of guy who enjoyed social gatherings.

But there he was, looking around uncomfortably and waving off an eager member of the Paper Posse who tried to offer him pink lemonade.

Delta said, "Sorry about the shop being so crowded."

A loud cheer went up from the back where kids could put their hand in a barrel full of newspaper shreds and pick out a small, wrapped gift. A young girl was grinning from ear to ear as she held up a zebra eraser. Hazel and Delta had decided not to go for the cheaper gifts, like a balloon or marbles, but put in items they were actually selling and would have appeal to kids, like the animal-shaped erasers and washi tape with bears or cars on it.

Admittedly, it was more expensive to do it that way, but they had agreed it was also better advertising for the shop, and they needed as much town support as they could possibly get after being involved in the murder case.

The *Tundish Trader* had featured Herb White's arrest in his wife's murder on the front page for days, quoting "sources who had direct access to the investigation" describing Herb's motive (he had seen his wife kissing the tennis instructor at the hotel), the murder method (he had lured her into the bar where he had been waiting with the ice pick to stab her in the back), and the arrest (the sheriff had pursued him in a police car, eventually forcing him off the road).

None of it had been accurate, but nobody had cared, as the mere fact that the husband was the killer was shocking enough in itself. It had been the talk of the town for days, with people being angry at Sheriff West for first accusing locals when it turned out an outsider had done it.

Ralph White and his wife had taken a hurried leave, and Jonas had told Delta that Amanda's dress had turned up nothing but the traces of wine stains after all. Fred Halliday didn't seem dejected that his former high school friend had left again but was his charming self to the ladies at the hotel, taking them boating or for a spin in his car, no matter how much their husbands objected.

Most locals seemed happy to get back to normal and to act like they had never suspected Finn, Isabel, or Hazel, even if they had been spreading incriminating rumors just days before.

And because they didn't want to make matters worse, the formerly accused parties pretended they had no idea who had said anything negative about them and embraced their reacceptance into the town fold without question.

The Paper Posse had met at Mine Forever for a celebratory meal of all-you-can-eat pancakes, and Hazel had insisted on buying Spud a present as a reward for capturing the killer. After consulting Jonas, they had agreed on a decoy that Spud could fetch from the water, since he loved to swim.

Jonas said to Delta, "I won't stay long, but I just wanted to look in." He rolled back his shoulders as if they were stiff.

"Late night?" Delta asked. "I thought you were going out with some die-hard bird watchers?"

Jonas winced. "Don't get me started about that." He nodded across the crowd. "Glad to see Finn is here."

Delta nodded. After the killer had been arrested, Finn had confided that he wasn't sure if he would stay in Tundish.

Delta had known Hazel would hate for her brother to leave town but had also secretly figured it might be better, as Finn would never get a chance to grow up if Hazel kept mothering him.

However, Isabel had insisted on Finn staying. Her love for him seemed to have deepened now that he had lied to the police to protect her, and they were together more often than before. Delta feared that the dreaded Christmas engagement Hazel was none too fond of would follow anyway.

For herself, she wasn't sure what she was thinking about Ray. Whether she wanted him to stay around or see him leave to do something other than annoy Rosalyn at the Lodge. A ship could not have two captains at the helm.

Mrs. Cassidy appeared by her side. "Hello, Mr. Nord. Aren't you trying our pink lemonade? It's not as sweet as it looks."

She laughed at his grimace. "But you must try some of the snacks. Jane did her best to make them special. Notebook cookies, pencil bacon-and-cheese strips. Over there."

"That does sound rather tempting." Jonas winked at Delta and made his way through the crowd to the snacks table.

"I think we did a rather good job," Mrs. Cassidy said to Delta. "I don't mean the party, although it's nice enough. I mean the murder case. It made me wonder. Maybe there isn't an outlaw in my forebears after all, but a Pinkerton agent or a sheriff?"

"Don't let Sheriff West hear you say that. He's still angry we got involved. And I vowed to myself I will never do it again."

"Not even if someone you care for got caught in the middle? Or if it involved the shop?"

Delta made a gesture. "Don't suggest that. I think one murder in my life has been quite enough. I'm glad the sheriff thinks he has the evidence he needs to get Herb White convicted. It was clever of him to wipe away his fingerprints. It makes me wonder if he was quite so upset during the murder as he claimed to us that he was."

"It's odd," Mrs. Cassidy mused, "how some people can be emotional on the one hand and cold and calculating on the other. Both things serve their purpose, I suppose. I never liked him from the moment he put his slogan on the church bulletin board. It was a rather bad slogan too."

Delta laughed. Hazel toasted her with a glass of pink lemonade from across the room. Delta raised her own glass and toasted her back. This was her shop, her things to sell, her workshop idea on the blackboard outside inviting people to come to the Lodge the next Friday. This was her new life, which Gran had made possible for her.

She pulled her phone from her pocket and took a selfie, toasting Gran, with all the people milling about in the shop in the background. She sent it right away with a message reading, "Grand opening today, if you can call it an opening when a shop has been in business for a year already. But I'm here now, and today it really begins for me. I'm starting to feel my way into all aspects of it and can't wait to see what's up next. Thanks so much for making this possible for me. Wish you were here. Love, D."

More people tried to work their way in, a few errant dry

leaves rustling in with them. The height of the leaf-peeping season would soon be over, and the town would gear up to offer other fall festivities, such as the Tundish Harvest Craft Fair, where Delta and Hazel would man their booth full of stationery stuff, offering people the chance to hand in a design for their own notebook. Delta couldn't wait to see the winning design proudly presented as a limited edition in their shop and online.

They had also put together new workshops that would be hosted at the Lodge. Now that Herb White was in prison and money from the Whites' communal assets flowed away toward his defense, the takeover had fallen through, and the hotel would remain the exclusive property of the Taylors. Delta looked forward to seeing it gear up for Christmas, with trees appearing and fake snow and Rosalyn thinking up some kind of grand Christmas party for the guests.

Now that she knew Ray had never tried to break up her engagement, but he had also been a victim of her fiancé's conniving to lay a hand on part of the Taylor fortune, their relationship might improve, and there would be a moment where a photo could be taken of all of them together again. Wary at first perhaps, tentatively feeling out a way back to the feelings of old when they had stood together, supporting each other, no matter what.

Delta thought of Zach and whether she might send him a Christmas card just to see how he responded.

If he responded at all.

Mrs. Cassidy breezed by to refill her glass. Delta toasted her and then the entire room. "To the future."

Which might hold more possibilities than she had ever imagined.

Acknowledgments and Author's Note

I'm grateful to all agents, editors, and authors who share online about the writing and publishing process. A special thanks to my amazing agent, Jill Marsal; my wonderful editors, Anna Michels and MJ Johnston; Adrienne Krogh and Anne Wertheim for the great cover; and the entire dedicated Sourcebooks team, especially Ashlyn Keil for her hard work on the author newsletter.

This series combines two of my loves: stationery and the great outdoors. I had a fabulous time building the fictional little town of Tundish, which was inspired by real-life towns in Montana's Bitterroot Valley; developing the characters who make up the community; and introducing my first big lead dog in a cozy series: Spud. Usually writing smaller dogs, I felt like the setting—with the western elements, gold-mining history, and outdoor activities—needed a dog who could bring an active role to the investigation, and retired K9 officer Spud and his handler, Jonas Nord, were born. I still couldn't resist putting in a small dog as well: Mrs. Cassidy's diva, Nugget. Dogs just bring a book to life for me, and I love writing their very different personalities as much as I love writing my human characters.

For those who are inspired by Mrs. Cassidy's fascination with outlaws, have a look online for the intriguing histories of individual outlaws and gangs, especially the female gang members who were, as Mrs. Cassidy puts it, "seamstress by day, bank robber by night." That they willingly posed for photos while they were wanted described their attitude to a tee. I'm delighted that the Paper Posse's Wild West names can keep a little bit of their stories alive.

And thank you, reader, for your visit to Tundish and to Wanted. I hope you will be back for Delta's next adventure in her brand-new hometown, "the town with a heart of gold."

About the Author

Always knee-deep in notebooks and pens, multi-published cozy mystery author Vivian Conroy decided to write about any paper crafter's dream: a stationery shop called Wanted. Her other loves, such as sweet treats, history, and hiking, equipped the series's world with a bakery, gold-mining museum, and outdoor activities. Never too far from a keyboard, Vivian loves to connect with readers via Twitter @VivWrites.